WILD WALES

By the Author

McCall

London

Innis Harbor

Last First Kiss

Wild Wales

Laying of Hands

Return to McCall

Visit us at www.boldstrokesbooks.com

WILD WALES

by
Patricia Evans

2024

WILD WALES

ISBN 13: 978-1-63679-771-7

THIS TRADE PAPERBACK ORIGINAL IS PUBLISHED BY
BOLD STROKES BOOKS, INC.
P.O. BOX 249
VALLEY FALLS, NY 12185

FIRST EDITION: SEPTEMBER 2024

CREDITS
EDITOR: STACIA SEAMAN
PRODUCTION DESIGN: STACIA SEAMAN
COVER DESIGN BY TAMMY SEIDICK

WILD WALES

CHAPTER ONE

A isling parked her convertible under the stars and started up the steep stone staircase leading to Dalwart Abbey, a fifteenth-century Scottish monastery perched at the tip of the cliffs jutting out over the Atlantic Ocean. The moon hovered like liquid silver over the sea as she climbed, and as she got to the top and replaced her stilettos, two dark owls swooped through the mist hovering over the grounds, stirring it with their wings. It was close to midnight, but Aisling was still working. The Wentworth wedding the next day was by far the most important event of her career. A copper wave of hair slipped suddenly out of the French twist at the back of her head, and Aisling pulled a hairpin from her inner jacket pocket and pinned it back into place as she walked.

The Wentworths were richer than the Queen, or perhaps Aisling was just recalling a recent quote from the London society pages, but the total bill for the event was already well into six figures, not including her services as the wedding planner. No expense had been spared for the only daughter of Hamish Surrey, the owner of the *London Daily Times*. It was the wedding that would elevate her to partner status in the event planning firm she'd been working with for a decade, Slate & Crystal Productions. Their clientele was elite, the waiting list famously long, and she was poised at the edge of a very lucrative offer as partner in the firm if this wedding went off without a hitch. Of course it would be flawless—she was Aisling Moss. A recent client had described her in an industry magazine as equally capable of running a wedding or the country, and it wasn't far from the truth.

She walked through the double doors to the central lofted expanse of the monastery, surrounded by crumbling stone walls and golden lights strung from pillar to post in shimmering layers of opulence. Aisling glanced at her watch. The wedding flowers were being delivered in six hours and twenty-seven minutes, which would warm and soften the space, but even without them the look so far was perfect, marred only by the few scruffy workmen on ladders replacing bulbs.

Aisling stood in the center of the three-story monastery, the roof long gone and replaced by a million glittering stars and endless black silk sky. The four central walls had crumbled at the top centuries ago after the roof disappeared, but there were still twenty-four meters of towering stone stretching into the night sky. Cold November air swept in off the sea, ruffling Aisling's hair and rocking the strings of lights like an invisible hand.

She turned and scanned the lights overhead, strung from the entrance to the far end of the building. It had taken most of the day, but finally there didn't seem to be a single missing bulb in the hundreds of glowing orbs layered between the sky and the stone under her feet.

"How long until everything's done, lads?"

The foreman turned to face Aisling from the top of his ladder and scanned the room, dropping a screwdriver back into his shirt pocket. "The last of the spent bulbs have been replaced and are working now, ma'am, and I'll be here in the morning to ensure they stay that way."

"It looks beautiful, Eugene," Aisling said, turning to him with a warm smile. "Thank you again for all your hard work."

Aisling had observed early on that a common misstep made by top-tier wedding planners was to leave the details to the "day laborers," as they often referred to them, and then treat them as such. Aisling figured out early in her career that the smallest details were often the most important, as were the people in charge of them, and had always been careful to treat every employee with respect, in every situation.

"Everything looks perfect, gentlemen."

Aisling nodded to the crew as they packed up the ladders and equipment around her. Within minutes they were gone, and the silence settled heavy and reverent in the way it does only in a place of worship. Her footsteps on the stone floors echoed as she stepped outside the rear door to ensure the light above it had been replaced as well. She flipped the main power lever to the off position as she stepped back inside, pulling the heavy wood door shut behind her. The lights overhead darkened instantly, and she was left with only the moon, framed like a painting by the open walls reaching up to touch the handful of stars scattered across the sky.

"Aisling?"

Aisling flipped the flashlight app on her phone and shone it into the moonlit space. It was Caroline Wentworth, barefoot, clad only in pink satin pajama pants and a T-shirt emblazoned with "Bride" in tiny crystals. She walked the length of the aisle, a champagne bottle dangling precariously from her fingertips, until suddenly her face crumpled into her hands and her shoulders shook with silent sobs. Aisling gently took the bottle from Caroline and guided her to one of the bright white wooden chairs that had been delivered that day and arranged into perfect rows on either side of the aisle. Aisling had pulled a tape measure from her pocket after they'd finished setting them up and measured the angles of the corners herself, ensuring the left side of the aisle was a perfect mirror image of the right.

"What's the matter, Caroline?" Aisling said with a discreet glance at her watch. "You should have been asleep hours ago. You have a big day ahead of you tomorrow."

Caroline just shook her head and swiped at her flushed cheek with the heel of her hand. When she spoke, her voice was barely there, as if she knew what she was about to say shouldn't be spoken aloud.

"I shouldn't be crying about this." She sniffed, eyes fixed on her pale bare feet against the cold stone floor. "I know it's too late."

Aisling pulled a pressed linen handkerchief from the inside pocket of her suit jacket. "Too late for what?"

Caroline stared at her hands, where she was twisting the handkerchief into the diameter of a wire, as Aisling's stomach dropped. Over the last decade, she'd handled almost every issue imaginable for her brides, from late grooms to splashes of cognac on bespoke silk dresses. She knew instinctively when a problem was serious. This was serious.

"Whatever it is," Aisling said, "I promise it seems bigger now than it will in the morning."

She watched Caroline closely, hoping she would take her advice and smile, then dry her tears and promise to go straight to bed. No such luck—not that Aisling really thought there would be.

"I have to tell you something." Caroline hesitated, looking up at her and biting her lip before she went on. "I have to tell someone or I'll go crazy."

Aisling braced herself, her face a calculated balance of calm and concern. Caroline hesitated again, then looked up at the sky as another tear fell from her cheek to the unused handkerchief still twisted in her hands. Caroline was the kind of pretty that money could buy. She was a bit too thin, which Aisling knew was overweight by the moneyed set's standards, and her features were attractive, but nothing quite kept them from fading quietly into the background. She tucked a lock of wheat-colored hair behind her ear and looked at Aisling.

"I read in a magazine once..." Caroline searched Aisling's eyes. "That you're a lesbian."

One eyebrow shot up for just an instant before Aisling caught herself. It wasn't easy to shock her; before tonight she'd thought it impossible. She didn't know what she'd expected Caroline to say, but *that* was certainly not it.

"I am gay," Aisling said, nodding, her voice so soothing the words seemed to drift into the air like faint curls of smoke. "But what does that have to do with your beautiful wedding?"

Caroline pulled her bare feet off the chilly stone floor and tucked them underneath her on the chair. She looked up at Aisling for a long moment, and when she finally spoke, her voice was a whisper.

"Everything."

It was just one word. But it had the power to change everything.

"I mean, I don't know if I'm...you know, gay," Caroline continued, the words coming thick and fast, as if the door holding them back had been flung open. "But I know something doesn't feel right. The crazy part is, I'm the only one who sees it. Everyone else keeps assuming it's nerves or cold feet or whatever they're calling it, but I've always felt this way."

Aisling took a breath, then thought longingly of the flask in her glove compartment as she asked another question she didn't want to know the answer to.

"You've always felt what way?"

"Like I'm some stupid actor in someone else's play."

They both looked up as an owl the color of cooled ash swooped overhead, then perched on the highest point of the wall beside them. She stretched out her wings against the black night sky, the breeze ruffling the feathers, then settled and swiveled her head toward Caroline as if she were listening.

"But if I marry Harry tomorrow, I'm signing up to be on that same bloody stage for the rest of my life." She looked up at Aisling, her eyes glittering with intensity. "And I'm not sure I'm willing to do that."

Aisling thought for a moment before she answered. Over the years, she'd seen hundreds of nervous brides mistake wedding jitters for true misgivings, only to see them vanish like seaside mist as soon as the sun rose on their wedding day.

"You might not believe me, but I think you'll feel completely different tomorrow. I've seen it happen a thousand times." Aisling took her hand. It was cold, and surprisingly delicate. "You've been running around like a banshee for weeks. You're exhausted."

Caroline nodded, wiping a tear from her cheek with the back of her other hand.

"When did you know?"

"Know what?" Aisling said. "That I was gay?"

Caroline nodded. The late November air had grown cool around them, and the sound of the icy waves hitting the rocks below made it seem even colder. Aisling took off her suit jacket and draped it around Caroline's shoulders.

"I guess I didn't know for a long time. I was in relationships with guys when I was your age—"

"And how old are you now?"

"I'm thirty-three."

Aisling winced at the words. She'd always assumed she'd be married and settled by now, but instead she'd worked her ass off to become the most sought-after wedding planner in the UK, which left her with about two hours per calendar year for dating.

"I guess I just kissed a girl one day and it felt like a puzzle piece slid into place." Aisling's voice was soft with the memory. "And the rest is history."

Caroline slid her arms through the sleeves of Aisling's jacket, which looked surprisingly hip with the crystal letters of Caroline's T-shirt underneath it. She wasn't wearing a bra, and the soft curve of her breasts and taut nipples added an edge to the look that was impossible not to stare at.

Aisling looked away briefly and refocused. It was time to steer the conversation in another direction, clearly.

"You fell in love with Harry for a reason," Aisling said, looking back and squeezing her hand for emphasis. "You've been together for almost two years. That means something."

Caroline looked up at her. "Do you think it's just jitters?"

Aisling paused, wishing Caroline had asked her any question but that one. She took a breath and smiled, choosing her words carefully.

"Every bride has nerves the night before the big day. All you need to do is put this nonsense to the back of your mind and get a good night's rest." Aisling realized suddenly that she was still holding Caroline's hand and subtly let go as she continued. "This will all seem like a dream tomorrow morning when you wake up and realize it's your wedding day, the happiest day of your life."

Caroline bit her lip, searching Aisling's eyes. "Do you really mean that?"

Do I mean it? What if she really is gay and the poor girl is reaching out for advice?

Aisling squared her shoulders and reminded herself that this wasn't her decision to make. Only Caroline could decide what was right for her, just like only Aisling could create the life she wanted for herself. And she knew what she wanted: the corner office in the corporate headquarters with the floor-to-ceiling windows and the ridiculously inflated salary.

"Yes," Aisling said. "I do think it's just nerves."

Caroline ran her hands through her hair and looked up at the sky. It was a long moment before she looked back at Aisling and held her eyes.

"If that's true," Caroline's words were slow and deliberate, "then kiss me."

There was a long pause while Aisling tried to make Caroline's words fit another meaning. Any other meaning.

"Pardon?"

"Kiss me." Caroline turned toward Aisling and the jacket fell open again, her sheer T-shirt clinging to her nipples.

Jesus Christ, Aisling thought when she realized that she was actually looking. *Get a grip.*

"You just told me that you think it's just jitters, that I'm not gay,"

Caroline said, her eyes dropping to Aisling's mouth. "So I should feel that when I kiss you."

"That's definitely not a good idea." Aisling shook her head slowly as she locked eyes with Caroline, who clearly wasn't budging. "Not to mention completely unprofessional."

"Fuck professional." Caroline stopped herself and took a deep breath. "You told me you didn't know if you were gay or not until you kissed a girl. Why should it be any different for me?"

Aisling sat back in her seat and rubbed her temples. This was a bad decision, the one coming together like a dark storm in the back of her mind. It was unprofessional. It was rash, immature, and completely out of character. And it was happening.

Aisling turned to face Caroline and slid a hand lightly around the back of her neck. She met her eyes and held them, bringing her slowly closer until she could feel the heat of her skin. She paused, then brushed Caroline's lips with her tongue, tracing the shape of them, her touch as light as air. She felt her hold her breath as Aisling pulled her into the kiss, tongue stroking Caroline's lightly until she felt her start to kiss her back. When Aisling finally pulled away, she touched her forehead against Caroline's and kissed her again before she thought to stop herself.

After, Caroline stood, swigged the rest of her champagne, then set the bottle back down on the chair. She walked back up the empty aisle, glancing back over her shoulder at Aisling before she disappeared through the main doors and into the night.

The next morning, Aisling was on her third espresso before she pulled up to the venue, thankfully just before the caravan of refrigerated trucks delivering 12,000 curated roses in soft shades of pale pink and dove gray, as well as the calla lilies they'd had flown in from South Africa. The sun had barely risen over the edge of the sea, but the press was already setting up cameras at every conceivable angle, carefully avoiding the boundary markers Aisling had set up for them. She'd called on the way and had one of her assistants deliver the message that any photographer that stepped even one foot over them would be escorted off the premises immediately.

Caroline was a Wentworth, one of the oldest and most powerful families in London, which meant there would be a handful of token celebrities attending the wedding. And where there were celebrities, there was always press jostling for the perfect shot to sell to the *Daily Mail* for their gossip pages. It was a necessary evil. High-profile accounts came with their own logistical challenges, but more press meant a higher commission and nationwide exposure for the company.

Aisling paused for a final look in the rearview mirror before she stepped out of the car. Her naturally wild copper hair had been tamed into a prim, tight bun at the back of her head, and she'd chosen her favorite herringbone suit with a pencil skirt that hugged every curve and subtly laced down the back, ending perfectly at her knee and accented by a silk blouse and tailored jacket. She'd learned a long time ago to stop trying to hide her lush, perfectly rounded ass; her waist was tiny and only drew more attention to it, so she'd finally just embraced it and found a good tailor.

She reached into her bag and dotted a bit more concealer under her eyes, smoothing it in with the tip of her ring finger. The smattering of light bronze freckles across her face had been completely hidden by foundation, and the only visible hint of her natural complexion was the golden-brown specks in her pale green eyes. Her lips had always been more sensual than professional, but there wasn't much she could do about that, except to tone them down with understated Chanel lipstick.

The sky was crystal blue as she walked up the uneven stone steps to the monastery, and the wind that swept up from the sea carried a cold salt scent that Aisling had always loved. Autumn in Scotland was vast and regal with endless blue skies and icy sea sprays, warmed at the edges by groves of birch trees, the leaves crisp and so vivid they looked on fire.

She was based in London now with Slate & Crystal, but she missed the north and frequently lobbied for the accounts that would take her to northern England and Scotland. Aisling had grown up in Newcastle, just south of the Scottish coast, and toning down her distinctive accent was a constant struggle. Because of the proximity, the language and lilt of the Newcastle and Scottish accents were similar, and in the posh world of professional wedding planning, both were seen as crass and unprofessional. Over the years she'd learned to sand the edges of her accent until she blended in seamlessly with the London elite, which was no easy task. Even now, when she was rushed or exhausted, her carefully guarded posh facade slipped quickly if she wasn't careful.

The morning flew by in a rush of details, and before she knew it the guests were seated, the string quartet sat poised and ready at the front of the monastery, and only three minutes remained until the bride was scheduled to walk down the aisle. When Aisling saw Caroline round the corner of the vestibule on her father's arm, she spoke quietly into the wire attached to her earpiece, cuing the string quartet to start the first familiar bars of Mendelssohn's "Wedding March." She greeted Mr. Wentworth warmly as they approached and touched Caroline softly at the small of her back as they faced the tall Gothic doors leading into the monastery.

"Caroline, you look lovely," she whispered. "Are we ready for this?"

As Caroline nodded, a tear fell onto her cheek, and Aisling dabbed it silently, then nodded at the attendants on either side of the doors to open them together on her cue. A bright swirl of flashbulbs and shutter clicks commenced, mingled with the requisite gasps of awe from the guests. As they started down the aisle, Aisling cued the doors shut and stepped back, pressing her back against the cool wall of the vestibule. She had forty-one seconds before they reached the altar at the end of the aisle, and she needed every one of them before she slipped into the monastery and took her place just out of sight to the right of the guests.

As she silently stepped in, the vicar was just beginning his opening remarks, and Aisling scanned the room for potential issues. A guest near the front had risen a few inches off his seat to get a clear shot of the bride and groom, enormous camera in hand, and the light from the chandeliers was glinting off his bald, oily head. She tapped her earpiece, nodded toward him, and watched one of her assistants quickly neutralize the situation. A minute later two women in the back-right quadrant were speaking behind their hands, eyes darting around at the other guests, and Aisling watched intently until one of them let out a muffled laugh. At that point, she stepped discreetly into their line of sight and locked eyes with the pair of them. They dropped their hands and regained their manners in a matter of seconds, and soon after, Aisling heard the vicar start the vows.

Following British tradition, the groom was first, and she smiled as she listened to Harry repeat the vicar's words to Caroline. His voice was clear and confident enough to fill the room, which she knew would translate well onto video. He placed the ring on Caroline's finger, and the vicar turned, smiling, to recite the vows for Caroline to repeat to her groom. He said the first two lines and paused, waiting to hear her voice recite them back.

"Wait."

The single word echoed off the stone walls like a gunshot and instantly silenced the room. The only sound remaining was the incessant clicking of the camera shutters, and time seemed to slow as Aisling watched two hundred people lean forward in their seats like a single wave falling onto shore.

Caroline looked terrified as she glanced back at her parents in the front row, then closed her eyes and squared her shoulders. She looked back at Harry and dropped her hands from his.

"I'm so sorry," she said, her voice as thin and fragile as spun glass. "I thought I could do this, but I can't."

"Do you have something you need to say, dear?" The vicar looked at her with kind eyes and closed the prayer book, holding it in front of him.

Harry stepped back, glancing back at his groomsmen in shock.

"Yes..." Caroline's voice trailed off and she looked back at the vicar, who nodded encouragement.

The air was thick and silent, and Aisling felt her world shift slowly under her feet. She leaned back against the cold stone wall behind her. For once, there was nothing to do but wait.

"I can't marry you," Caroline said to Harry, tears flowing down her face as she turned toward her family. "When Aisling kissed me last night, I—"

Harry stepped back up to Caroline. "Who the hell is Aisling?"

Caroline paused, then scanned the crowd and nodded to Aisling in the back. "Aisling Moss, our wedding planner. I realized I was gay last night when she kissed me."

Caroline's mother raced to the altar and led her daughter through the side exit as flashbulbs and shouting exploded from every angle. The world she'd felt shift under her feet suddenly fell away completely as the room started to spin.

❖

Two days later, Aisling saw the letter that had been slipped through her mail slot. She recognized the stationery as she picked it up slowly and sank down onto the cold marble floor of her apartment.

It was from Slate & Crystal's lead attorney, writing to inform her of her immediate termination due to the pending lawsuit against the company being filed by the Wentworth family. She scanned the rest, picking up the key phrases *gross misconduct* and *ten days to vacate the corporate apartment* before she crumpled the letter in her fist and lay down on the icy marble floor. She'd been there two hours before she opened her eyes and noticed the second envelope.

She reached over and picked it up, the floor still pressed cold against her back. The return address was Cwylldbridge, Wales. She ripped it open and scanned the letter, letting it drop to the floor beside her when the meaning of the words began to settle like a stone over her heart.

"Fuck."

She heard herself say the word out loud, as if someone were there to listen.

CHAPTER TWO

Finn Morgan worked her spatula across the grill in the café kitchen, the metallic scrape slicing through the heavy quiet that hovered in the air after the staff had gone home. A glance at the grease-clouded clock told her it was after midnight, but cleaning the grill was the last thing she had to finish before she left for the night. She'd worked back-to-back shifts, and she had to be back at 6:00 a.m. to start it all over again tomorrow.

She stopped when she heard the back door to the café open, the hinges creaking as footsteps replaced the silence.

Fuck, Finn thought, dropping the charcoal block she'd just picked up and leaning onto the grill. *Five more minutes and I would have missed her.*

She'd been fucking Megan Harrison for three months now, which had started off as a distraction, but now it was becoming clear that Megan wanted more than orgasms. She wanted Finn. Which was inconvenient since she was her boss's wife.

"Finn?"

"Jesus Christ," Finn muttered under her breath, then plastered a neutral look on her face as Megan teetered around the corner of the stockroom and into the kitchen. She was wearing skinny jeans and sky-high heels, her signature outfit, with a strapless white top that Finn could see her nipples through. It wasn't that she disliked her, she just wasn't interested in anything more than watching Megan's clothes hit the floor.

"Hey, sexy," Megan said as she walked up to Finn and stood too close. "Got any energy left?"

"I was just about to head out the door, actually," Finn said, finishing the last section of the grill with the brick and washing the black dust from her hands in the prep sink. She turned to Megan and raised an eyebrow. "It's past midnight. Isn't Brett wondering where you are?"

"He's at the other restaurant." She rolled her eyes. "Where he always is."

The owner of the café and Megan's husband, Brett, had opened some hipster pizzeria in Brooklyn last month and Finn hadn't seen him at the café for weeks, not that she was complaining. Finn lifted her stained apron over her head and tossed it in the laundry bin, running both hands through her hair. Megan's eyes dropped to the tight definition of Finn's arms.

"Why do you like this place, anyway?" she said, kicking a dropped sponge under the prep table with the toe of her stiletto. "I could probably get Brett to hire you at the pizza place. He's looking for a manager."

"Nah," Finn said, too quickly. "I'm good."

"Well," Megan said, stepping up to Finn and tracing her arm with her fingertip, "what do you want?"

Finn weighed her options. She could stay and fuck Megan, or she could try to explain to her that she was too wiped out, then end up fucking Megan anyway. She picked her up by the waist and sat her on the edge of the prep table.

"I want you to lose those jeans."

Megan bit her lip as she removed her heels and slid her jeans and red lace thong down her legs. Finn stepped up between her thighs, reaching behind her to unzip her top and toss it to the end of the table. Brett had bought her a new set of tits last year for her birthday, and Finn loved the way her hands looked wrapped around them.

"Do you have your strap-on?"

"Yep," Finn said, brushing Megan's nipples lightly with the back of her hand. "It's in the walk-in."

Megan looked confused and glanced toward the main restaurant refrigerator.

"I'm kidding. Of course I don't have it here," Finn said, laughing. "Why would I bring it to work?"

Megan smiled. "I guess we've never actually done it here, have we?"

They usually met at one of Megan's empty houses. She was a real estate agent, and something about fucking in other people's houses turned her on. The first time they'd hooked up, Finn drove to the address she'd texted her and walked in to find Megan standing naked in the living room wearing only a pair of glossy black stilettos. Her Instagram-worthy blond hair fell in waves over one shoulder, her tan legs were endless, and her nipples were already hard. Megan had walked over and dropped to her knees, then unbuttoned Finn's jeans and taken every inch of her strapped-on cock into her mouth. Finn still remembered her red, glossy lips and wet tongue sliding up and down the length of it. Needless to say, she'd brought it every time after that.

"But…" Megan hesitated, her fingers playing with the button on Finn's jeans. "I don't know if I can come without it."

Finn wrapped Megan's legs around her hips.

"Trust me," Finn said, her fingers sliding deep inside Megan as she spoke. "You won't even remember I have one when I'm done with you."

It was two thirty in the morning when Finn finally walked into her apartment and dropped her bag on the couch. Well, technically, it was the apartment of her best friend Tamara, who'd let her move in when the shit hit the fan with Finn's girlfriend a year ago. There was a note on the table.

Go through your mail already. If you don't, I'm going to fill out those Visa applications you're always getting and go shopping.

Shit. That was the last thing she felt like doing. Well, maybe not the last thing. Listening to Megan ask her again when they were going on a "real date" was the last thing.

Finn pulled a Corona out of the fridge and popped the top, watching it as it pinged off the tile floor and rolled under the oven. She needed to figure out how to slow the Megan thing down before she got her ass caught by the boss. The obvious solution was to quit her job, but that just seemed like too much trouble. She made decent money there, rarely had to talk to anyone, and she didn't hate it. But she didn't love it, either.

Before she worked at the café, she and her ex, Casey, had been co-owners of one of the top wedding catering companies in Brooklyn. They were always booked months in advance, and it was the one thing Finn had ever done that she truly loved. Every day was different, and working with her girlfriend had been challenging, but worth it. Until the day Finn proposed and Casey's answer was hopping on the next flight to Mexico. The ring was still sitting in the stupid velvet box on Finn's windowsill, shrouded in dust, a reminder that love was a fairy tale she didn't care to buy into again.

She walked over to the pile of mail and rifled through it, dropping all the junk mail into the trash. The last envelope was marked Par Avion and had several odd-looking stamps on it. She ripped into it and unfolded the typed letter inked on thick, professional stationery. Finn flipped the envelope over and checked the return address. Cwylldbridge, Wales.

Dear Ms. Morgan,

This letter is to inform you that your paternal grandmother, Rose Morgan, died peacefully of natural causes on 18 November 2019. Please accept my deepest condolences for your loss.

As your grandmother's solicitor and the executor of her estate, I wish to inform you that your presence is requested at a reading of her will on 2 December 2019 at 4:00 pm at my office in Cwylldbridge. Any questions regarding travel or accommodation can be directed to my assistant at the number listed below.

Please understand that per instructions from Ms. Morgan, if you are unable to attend the reading, any claim you may have had to her property holdings or estate will be considered null and void.

Sincerely yours,

Padraig Clydd

Finn sank to the floor, holding the letter to her heart, until dawn warmed the floor with unwelcome sunlight. She finally stood to grab her gym bag slouched in the corner of the living room and started taping her hands and wrists. She wound the tape around and around, ripping it off with her teeth and swiping at her tears with the back of her hand as she threw her boxing gloves into the bag. She turned her cell phone off and slammed the door behind her as she walked down the steps of the brownstone to the sidewalk, crisp, weightless leaves swirling in the breeze around her feet.

❖

Late that afternoon, she unlocked the door to the apartment again and turned on her phone as she unwound the tape from her hands. She winced as it pulled the dried blood from her knuckles, leaving raw patches of wet skin. She flexed her fingers and gritted her teeth against the searing air hitting the open wounds, making her slightly nauseous as she leaned on the entry table. She listened to her phone ping as seventeen text messages flashed across the screen, all from either the café or Megan.

She picked it up, sent both the same two-word text, then went to her room to start the hot water for her shower. She passed her windowsill as she walked into the bathroom and paused, turning the ring box over in her hand as the dust stirred and hung in the sheer, fading sunlight. She set it back where it had been for a year, then opened her laptop.

Right, she thought as she clicked through the Delta Airlines website. *I'm buying a two-thousand-dollar ticket to some town in Wales I can't even pronounce. What could possibly go wrong?*

CHAPTER THREE

"Well," Aisling muttered to herself as she wedged her carry-on bag into the overhead compartment above her seat, "this is about as much fun as a bag of dicks."

Being able to revert to her own Newcastle accent was the only perk of the entire wedding disaster. Until now, she hadn't even allowed herself to think in that accent, much less pull out her favorite phrases and well-worn curse words, but her days of pretending to sound posh were well behind her now, whether or not that was a good thing.

She'd stopped at her parents' house on the way to the airport, a semi-detached brick Victorian on the edge of the city. She knew her mum would be at work, but she found her dad pruning ivy in the back garden and made them both a cup of tea. Catching him up on the drama, including her rather appalling lack of future plans, took less than ten minutes. Her dad was a man of few words; he listened well, and if he didn't have anything to say, he didn't. It was one of the things she liked best about him.

She sank down into her seat with her laptop bag, scooting it as far as possible under the seat directly in front of her. The miniature seats were yet another reminder that, for the first time in a decade, she no longer had her corporate credit card from Slate & Crystal. Not that she'd needed another reminder. The waif-thin blonde they'd hired to replace her had arrived at her flat that morning with a team of movers and watched with disdain as Aisling struggled to wedge the last of her boxes out the door. A sudden gust of air blew her hair across her face as the door to her flat swung shut behind her, scraping the skin from the back of her ankle.

The flight from London to Wales was short, thank the merciful Lord, and at least she'd managed to get a window seat. Aisling had finally placed everything where she needed it when she saw him coming down the aisle: a large balding man in a sweat-soaked tropical shirt, tufts of chest hair damp and stuck to his skin at the open neck. Impatient passengers queued behind him in the aisle as he leisurely looked down every row and ambled toward her. Aisling sighed as she watched beads of sweat roll down his scarlet face as he approached. Of course he was in her row. He sank down in the seat beside her, the damp flesh of his arm draped over the seat rest between them as he attached his seat belt and pulled it together with a grunt.

Aisling turned back to her iPad. The incident at the Wentworth wedding was approaching legend status as word got around the industry, and rival companies that would have knocked themselves out trying to recruit her before weren't even returning her calls now. The one time she'd actually managed to speak to someone on the phone, he didn't mince words. He told her within the first thirty seconds of the conversation that her career was over and that she needed to move on.

"Most things blow over," he'd said as Aisling listened to the faint clink of ice cubes in a glass. "But this is not one of them."

She was still holding the phone to her face as the line went dead, and the reality of her situation settled over her like a cold fog.

"How ya doin' over there, little lady?"

Her seatmate looked over at her with an expectant smile and popped a breath mint into his mouth. His accent was vaguely Australian, but what caught Aisling's eye was his boarding pass in the seat back pocket in front of him. It showed he should have been sitting on the aisle, leaving a seat between them.

"I think you may be in the wrong seat." Aisling nodded toward the boarding pass and raised an eyebrow.

He took it out of the seat back pocket and crumpled it up, kicking it under the seat in front of him.

"I think you have a cracking set of tits that suggest otherwise," he said, his eyes scraping across her breasts. "Although I think I'd need to see more of them to know for sure."

Aisling shook her head and stared out the window. She thought about requesting a different seat, but even if she succeeded, the chances of edging past her seatmate to the aisle without being molested seemed slim to none, and a quick glance around told her the only empty seat was the one directly across from the toilets. The plane had started to pick up speed down the runway as she pulled the solicitor's letter from the outside pocket of her bag. The force of the plane leaving the ground pressed her back against her seat, and she closed her eyes, sifting through the memories of the last time she'd been in Wales.

Aisling had turned twelve that year and her family had rented a beachside cottage off the coast of Cardiff. She'd been to Wales before; her father was raised there and they visited his mother in Cwylldbridge every summer, but there was something different about that vacation. Or maybe there'd just been something different about her. She was an only child and her mother had always kept close tabs on her in the city, but that trip she'd managed to convince her she was old enough to explore the coast on her own.

She'd disappeared for hours every afternoon to wander down the beach, standing barefoot on the wet rocks, arms stretched out to either side. Waves the color of storms crashed all around her, and she breathed the icy salt spray into her lungs until it burned, and even then she was reluctant to let it go. There was something wild and windswept about Wales that summer, as if the ghosts of heroines past were whispering to her at every turn.

The evening before they'd returned to Newcastle, her mother had sent her to the village market for a pint of milk. She'd gotten there just before they closed and hurried to the counter with the milk, three pound coins tinkling in her pocket as she walked out the door. On her way back to the cottage, her footsteps slowed and she looked behind her at the crumbling thirteenth-century castle in the grassy field between the village and the edge of the sea. She stopped on the path, the gravel grating under her black Converse, considering her options. When she'd left the cottage a few moments before, her mother was on her second gin and tonic, laughing with her father on the back deck, which might buy Aisling a few minutes before she started to wonder where she'd gone, so she stepped off the road and wandered into the field.

Aisling noticed as she got closer that the roof of the castle had long since disappeared, and the remaining massive stone walls seemed to glow as she approached, the sun setting behind them in slowly shifting layers of gold and violet. She closed her eyes as she walked, her fingers interlaced and resting on top of her head. She'd always loved this time of evening, the violet hour where everything white seemed to glow lavender in the dusk and the warm air was the same temperature of her skin. It swept soft past her cheeks, and the only sounds were the wind moving through the tops of the trees lining the field and the far-off call of seagulls over the water. Long grasses swayed from side to side in the evening breeze, and as she climbed the stairs at the castle entrance and stepped through the empty arched doorway, a flock of birds took off into the sky from their perch at the top of the walls, stirring the air around her.

She felt time stop and hold its breath around her as she walked inside. She turned in slow, silent circles, taking in the quickly darkening sky framed like a watercolor painting by the open roof. A massive empty hearth sat at one end of the great room, blackened and empty, crisscrossed with silvery spiderwebs. A staircase was opposite that at the other end of the room, winding upward in a tight spiral, leading into a tall, slender turret that faced the sea. She went toward the staircase first, trailing her fingertips along the far wall of the room, the stones gritty and still under her fingertips.

The tight curves of the staircase were nearly pitch-dark, the last of the light trapped outside by the endless spiraling stone walls. Aisling started up the stairs slowly, her hands in front of her face to break up the shimmering spiderwebs that stretched from one side of the narrow stone staircase to the other. She climbed until she was dizzy, passing long, slender window openings cut into the stone at every turn. The wind blew stronger and colder through them as she climbed, and when she finally got to the top, the narrow Gothic doorway opened suddenly into only sky.

When she looked down, the scuffed toes of her sneakers hung over the edge of the last stair. Cold wind rushed beneath them like river water, and underneath there was only the ground, several stories below. There was no roof left to step out onto, so Aisling held on to the doorframe and leaned out into the navy blue night sky, the wind blowing her hair around her face. She closed her eyes, breathing in the still, cold scent of night sweeping in from the sea.

Soft shades of copper sunset were quickly fading into night by the time Aisling came down the stairs. As she reached the bottom, she heard something, like a whoosh of air being drawn up around her, and she slowed as she turned the corner of the staircase into the main open area of the castle. Her footsteps stopped with a soft scrape and she stared, lowering the pint of milk she was still carrying slowly to her feet.

A fire popped and flared in the hearth, crackling with gold sparks that rose into the dusk. Aisling walked quickly to the entrance to see who'd been there, the scrape of raw stone under her shoes the only sound. But there was no one there, just the dark expanse of the field she'd walked through and the silvery tops of the grasses still swaying in the silent coastal breeze.

She stood there, frozen under the doorway for a long moment, eyes fixed on the distant glow of the streetlights lining the main street of the village. She knew the sensible thing was to run out the door, but something drew her to the fire that crackled and popped in the fireplace. She walked toward it, listening for anything else around her, but there was nothing. She finally sat down on the wide rock hearth, which had been swept clean, a small handmade broom propped beside it. Night fell around her as she sat beside the fire, head tipped back and arms wrapped around her knees, watching the silver wash of stars gathering in the black velvet sky, hovering above the woodsmoke that curled up the walls and disappeared into the darkness.

It was surreal, like being fully present in both the past and the present in one moment. A reverent silence hung in the air as if a story were unfolding onstage with herself as the only actor, and the fire and broom the only props. She leaned back against the wall of the hearth beside the flames, arms extended and resting on her knees, and closed her eyes as the sounds started to drift in. At first it was distant, muffled sounds of laughter and the clank of metal and pottery. When she relaxed her concentration, it grew closer until it enveloped her.

When it had grown as real as the present, she tensed without thinking against the strangeness of it all, her mind scrambling for an explanation. The sounds faded sharply away in proportion to her fear. It was then that she sensed she needed to relax into what was happening, to allow it to wash over her, and it soon was all around her again, as near as her breath.

A few moments later, when she finally opened her eyes, the sounds fell into silence instantly, leaving a distinct echo that hung in the air around her. Translucent orbs of golden light danced in the space between the ragged tops of the castle walls and the inky velvet sky, as if they were considering whether it was safe to come closer, studying her like the dark shadow of a beast in a forest. She watched them, her eyes soft as they dropped slowly closer, some spinning and darting from side to side, the others sinking closer with a palpable wariness.

Their light was brighter as they drew closer, yet softer at the same time, if it was possible for those two things to coexist. Scenes, like memories she'd never had, shimmered at the center of each if she relaxed her gaze, only to disappear instantly if she tried to focus on them. She sensed a trust from both sides at some point and stood slowly, expecting the orbs of light to retreat. They did, but when she wordlessly asked them to return, they swirled into the air around her like gold dust, studying her, dipping closer, only to shoot up into the sky and spin around each other. She turned slowly, arms outstretched, and they followed, stirring light into the cool, dark air.

After a few moments the orbs gathered above her head and into a broken line along the top of the fireplace mantel, illuminating it with undulating light. Aisling leaned in, the stone scraping her fingertips as she trailed them over the slab of rock mantel. Heat rose from the fire beneath and warmed her palm as she traced the pattern carved into the surface. It was a repeating pattern of three, made of two small triangles on either side of an etching that resembled a bare tree in winter. She knew it like she knew her own heartbeat.

"Ma'am?"

Aisling jumped, startled out of the memory.

"Would you like something to drink?"

Aisling shook her head, then changed her mind at the last second.

"Actually, could I have a tomato juice, please?"

The flight attendant handed her a blue foil bag of pretzels, then poured her tomato juice from a small can and handed it to her with a napkin. Her seat companion glanced over at the glass or her breasts, it wasn't clear which.

"You should've ordered a vodka with that," he said, leaning back in his seat and spreading his thighs as far as possible in either direction. "Might loosen ya ass up just a bit."

Aisling clicked her tray table back into place and stood, slipping her bag onto her shoulder as she tipped the plastic glass of tomato juice into his lap with one finger.

"You should really get some stain remover on that, love."

She edged by him as he sputtered, tomato juice rolling off his lap into his shoes. That empty seat she'd spied by the toilets was suddenly looking pretty damn good.

That night, after she'd finally managed to drag her bags up the stairs to her tiny, overly floral room at the Cwylldbridge B&B, Aisling sank down on the bed, staring at the frosted glass light fixture on the ceiling. She'd been trying to think about anything but London since she'd left, but she was too tired to fight it and let herself long for the gorgeous marble tub in her flat. Sinking down in billowy bubbles to her chin right now seemed the only thing that might put the pieces of her world back together. But another glance at the dead flies trapped in the dusty light fixture reminded her that wasn't going to happen.

What *was* going to happen was a paper boat of takeaway curry chips from the chippy round the corner followed by a cramped shower in the shared bathroom down the hall. Slate & Crystal Productions might have blown her career to dust, but they'd also underestimated her. She was good at what she did, the best in fact. She'd built a career for herself once and she'd do it again. As soon as the meeting with the solicitor was over the next day, she'd be back on the next plane to London to pick up the pieces and do it all over again.

❖

Finn swung her canvas duffel bag up into the overhead compartment and settled back into the aisle seat at the back of the plane. The only flight that would get her to Wales in time for the meeting the next day left JFK airport in the middle of the night, and she almost didn't make it through the TSA screening in time to get to the gate. She hadn't packed much; a quick Google search told her Wales was cold and damp more often than not, so she'd tossed in a few pairs of jeans, a handful of T-shirts, and two gym hoodies. She'd grabbed her old army jacket just before she'd closed the door of her apartment, shrugging it on as she patted the inside pocket for her sunglasses. She'd never been to Wales, but the sun had to come out occasionally, right?

As the plane prepared for takeoff, she caught the attention of a flight attendant walking up the aisle. She was young, with full lips, pale blond hair, and a name tag that said *Ashley* in gold letters.

"Hey," Finn said, taking off her sunglasses and running a hand through her hair. "Is there any chance I can get a shot of whiskey before we take off?"

Ashley started to shake her head automatically, then paused and glanced quickly back down the aisle toward the front of the plane.

"I'm actually working first class, but I wouldn't be able to get that for you anyway. We don't serve drinks in coach before takeoff." She stopped, her eyes lingering a second too long on Finn's hands. "I can't, I'm sorry."

Finn nodded, then held her eyes as she lowered her voice and leaned closer. "I hate to fly. I'd consider it a personal favor."

Ashley smiled, her eyes dropping to Finn's mouth. "Look, I can't get you a drink back here, but we've got a spare seat in first class if you want to sit up there." She nodded toward the front of the plane, then turned back to Finn. "Then I can give you anything you want."

Two minutes later Finn was in the soft leather seats at the front of the plane, ice cubes clinking softly as she swirled the smooth, amber whiskey in a cut glass tumbler.

It was morning when she finally landed in Cardiff and caught the western bus to Cwylldbridge. She'd been to Wales only once with her dad, to visit her grandmother Rose when she was a child, but she barely remembered it. She leaned her head against the cool glass of the bus window as it left the city and rumbled through the countryside. The city buildings stopped suddenly as if a page had been turned, and everything around them seemed to turn to a deep, wet shade of green. Endless stone fences divided the fields into uneven squares, and just beyond that the ocean was a restless shade of steel, defiantly tossing white spray in the air as the waves hit rocks on the shoreline. Finn cracked the window beside her and icy air rushed in, carrying the scent of woodsmoke and salt.

The road followed the sea around curves and cliffs that made the forty-minute ride to Cwylldbridge seem endless, but finally Finn saw the village in the distance. As they got closer, the road narrowed enough to completely disappear under the bus, and the faint line down the center faded away. It was still paved, but that was the only thing that linked it to the twenty-first century. Sheep dotted the hills on either side, their backsides all marked with an odd swipe of blue or pink paint.

Finn rubbed her temples and closed her eyes against the headache forming like a storm behind her eyes. She hadn't slept much on the plane; she'd never been able to relax when she wasn't working, and what she needed to do was get back to Brooklyn as fast as possible and get another damn job. Preferably one where she wasn't fucking the boss's wife.

As the bus turned the next corner, single-family homes with wildflower gardens gave way to tall row houses with chipped slate tiles, bright doors painted in glossy slicks of lavender and sunny yellow. Every building seemed to follow a gentle downward slope, and as the bus rolled into the city center, the far edge of the town seemed to drop off into the sea, where rows of white sailboats were anchored, sails clanging against the masts in the wind. A broad stone walkway with cut-in stairs led down to the boat landing, and the whitecaps beyond dotted the vivid blue water that disappeared into the low blanket of dense fog not far off the coast.

Finn slung her bag across her back and glanced at her watch. The meeting at the solicitor's office was in one hour, which hopefully gave her enough time to find it and a place to stay for the next couple of days. She stepped off the bus at the seawall and walked back up the hill, looking for a hotel, or hostel, or whatever the hell they called it here. The air was sharper than she'd expected. The wind blowing up from the water smelled of ice shards, and the scent of fresh seafood and salt in the air reminded her she hadn't eaten since yesterday.

The headache started to pound behind her eyes, and she ducked into a corner shop on the main street that reminded her of a Brooklyn bodega. It was tiny, the size of her kitchen at home, and every available surface was stacked with sleeves of cookies, bags of dried pasta, boxes of tea bags—apparently, everything but ibuprofen.

A teenager with a blank name tag and a bright pink cell phone stood behind the register.

"Excuse me," Finn said, scanning the wall behind her as she spoke for anything that might knock out her headache. "Do you carry aspirin or something here?"

The girl looked up at Finn with no expression. She was thin, with long, coltish limbs and thick black eyeliner. She reached behind her without looking and plunked a red paper box on the counter, eyes flicking back to her phone.

"What's this?"

She looked up briefly, then back down, thumbs flying across the keyboard of her phone. "It's paracetamol."

Finn picked up the box and flipped it over in her hand. "Will it work on a headache?"

The girl looked up with one eyebrow raised. "Aye."

Finn reached over to the open cooler beside the counter and grabbed something that resembled Gatorade and laid her debit card down beside it. The girl nodded to the sign on the register. *Cash only.*

"Shit," Finn said. "I haven't gotten cash yet. Where's the nearest ATM?"

"All the way up the hill, outside the bank." She studied Finn for a moment, then pulled her purse off the floor from behind the counter. "You're not from around here, are ya?"

"I'm from Brooklyn." Finn picked up her debit card and slipped it back into her wallet. "I'm just here for a couple of days to wrap up some family stuff."

She looked Finn up and down, pausing at her blue and white Dodgers sweatshirt. "You have family in Cwylldbridge?"

"Wait, say that again?" Finn leaned on the counter as she slipped the wallet back into the back pocket of her jeans. "How do you pronounce it?"

"The C is silent, I guess, so it sounds a little like 'wild bridge.' And there's a castle at the edge of the village and some people get them confused, but the castle is called Dun Laoghaire castle."

Finn shook her head. "One more time?"

"Dun Laoghaire. Like, 'I'm done with being leery.' Done Leery."

Finn thanked her and glanced at her watch as the girl dug in her purse. Her hand finally emerged with an identical box of paracetamol and she popped two of the tablets out of the blister package.

"Just take these," she said. "By the time you got up to the cash point and back down the hill we'd be closed. You look like you need them."

The girl reached under the counter and handed her a half-full bottle of Lucozade. Finn suddenly realized she was giving her her own bottle of whatever the hell that was to take the pills with, so she accepted them both with a smile and knocked the pills back.

"Thanks," she said, noticing for the first time the girl might be pregnant. "What's your name?"

"Alwen."

"Well, thanks for saving my ass, Alwen," Finn said, handing her the bottle back. "I owe you one."

Alwen smiled for the first time as Finn walked out and rounded the corner.

❖

Aisling shifted in her seat and straightened the collar of the green tweed suit jacket she'd paired with a crisp white shirt and dark skinny jeans. The cognac leather folder engraved with her initials perfectly matched her knee-high leather boots, but she set it aside when she noticed one of her boots was laced up a bit tighter than the other, which undoubtedly made them look slightly uneven from the back. She retied them twice until the lacings lined up perfectly.

She'd just finished and picked her folder back up when she saw someone burst through the door and pause at the small receptionist desk, where the secretary checked her name and nodded her through to the waiting area. She wore pale blue Levi's and a sports hoodie, with trainers that had seen better days. Her skin was darker than Aisling's by a few shades, although to be fair nearly everyone's was. Aisling watched as she sank into her chair and swung a worn duffel bag onto the seat beside her. Her shoulders were broad, and Aisling could see the definition in her thighs through her jeans. When she met Aisling's eyes, it was a long second before she looked away. For a ruffian with duct tape on her bag, she was startlingly attractive.

Aisling picked up her phone and scrolled through tomorrow's flights between Cardiff and London again, hoping a seat had opened up on one of the earlier departures. Since the day that letter had dropped through her mail slot and she found that her grandmother Joan had passed, she'd tried to think of anything but her, but being stuck in the hometown she'd visited her in as a child made that more difficult than she'd expected.

She'd had nothing to do after breakfast earlier in the day, so she took a walk around the village, carefully avoiding the path to the side of the church that led to her grandmother's cottage. The church itself looked exactly the same, down to the seagulls circling above her head and sudden church bells echoing over the rooftops signaling noon mass. Dun Laoghaire Castle loomed in the background, just beyond the village square in the open field. She was dropping her espresso cup in the trash at the edge of the square when she saw it, and for the first time she let herself remember.

Some memories are like books—if you take them off the shelf and handle them every day, they eventually grow worn, the edges fray, and the ink fades gradually as if it were never there. But this memory had been untouched for two decades. She closed her eyes slowly where she stood on the sidewalk, a shop awning fluttering overhead and the wind pressing her coat tightly around her.

The memory of that night in the castle rushed around her, swift and vivid. She still felt the rough stone of the hearth under her fingers as she gripped the edge with her hands and the unexpected sounds of clinking glasses when she closed her eyes. Voices and laughter had surrounded her gradually as if they'd spilled through a crack in the wall of time, and the fire had warmed her back as the golden orbs dipped and swirled through the inky darkness in front of her.

"All right, dear?"

The voice seemed to come from far away, but as she opened her eyes she saw an older gentleman standing on the sidewalk in front of her, his green wool cap barely containing a thick shock of white hair.

"I'm sorry," Aisling said, shaking the memory from her head. "What did you say?"

"I was just asking if you were all right, dear. You seemed away with the faeries just then."

"Thank you," Aisling said, pulling her coat tighter around her. "I'm fine. Just remembering something."

By lunch she was dying for a drink, but thought the better of it and bought a ham and pickle baguette at the newsagents for lunch and ate it at the seawall, her feet dangling over the water below. She ran her fingers over the naturally occurring crystals embedded in the seawall. They were plentiful in Wales, clear as water and beautiful. Aisling had loved to collect them on the shore when she was little, rinsing them in the foamy seawater and watching them glint in the sun.

It was the sudden silence of Wales that bothered her the most. It stretched time, the last thing she needed. For the last ten years she'd lived in London with its blur of bright lights and constant sound, which had swiftly erased the memory of anything else. There was always something to do, something to buy, something else she had to have. But in the village, there was nothing but silence and seagulls, still and deafening at the same time. She couldn't hear her own thoughts—at least the constant stream of thoughts she used to have, but perhaps they were never really hers at all. Maybe the perpetual hurry and noise of London had crept in over the years and she'd started to forget what her own thoughts, her own breath, sounded like.

Her mum and dad had received the news of Joan's death the same day she had, but apparently they hadn't been asked to attend the reading of the will. When she'd stopped for a cuppa with her dad the day she left, she'd asked him about it, and it felt like he was holding something back, but he usually was. He'd swiftly turned the conversation back to the appalling lack of chocolate biscuits in the house, and she'd let him do it. If he didn't want to talk about it, he wouldn't. And truth be told, after having just asked her parents if she could move back in with them until she found a flat of her own, she was too exhausted by the day to care.

"Ms. Aisling Moss?"

Aisling looked up to see Mr. Clydd, the solicitor who had sent her the letter, holding his office door open for her.

"I'm ready for you now."

Aisling gathered her overcoat and scarf and had just reached the door when she saw him nod at the ruffian out of the corner of her eye.

"And I'm assuming you're Finn Morgan? I'm ready for you as well."

She nodded, standing and tossing that bag over her shoulder, and passed Aisling on her way into the office.

"This won't take long, Ms. Moss," Mr. Clydd said as he waved her inside, the scent of cherry pipe tobacco following him as he stepped behind his giant mahogany desk. "Just have a seat."

"I must have gotten the appointment time wrong," Aisling said, sinking into one of the two chairs across from his desk and pulling up his email on her phone. "But your secretary had me on the books when I arrived." She looked up. "I'm here for the reading of my grandmother's will?"

"Wait." The woman the solicitor had referred to as Finn looked at her, then down at her watch. "I'm here for the same thing."

"Right you are," Mr. Clydd said, shuffling papers on his desk until he found a long manilla envelope. "You're both here for the same reason." He held up the envelope. "Because it's the same will."

CHAPTER FOUR

"Pardon?" Aisling said to the solicitor, with another glance at Finn. "I don't even know her. That's impossible."

"Well, this just got a lot more interesting." Finn smiled and pushed up the sleeves of her sweatshirt. "Let's hear it."

She leaned back in her chair and raked a hand through her hair as if she had all the time in the world, which swept the last of Aisling's patience into the wind. Her only priority was to be on the first flight to London tomorrow to start looking for a flat, so the less time she spent in Wales, the better. She could only live with her parents for so long without going completely mad.

"Ladies, this gets a bit complex, so bear with me." Mr. Clydd opened the folder and slid a stack of papers out, arranging them into a neat pile on his desk. "Ms. Morgan, your grandmother's name is Rose Morgan, is that correct?"

Finn nodded. He looked over at Aisling.

"And your grandmother's name was Joan Moss?"

"That's right." Aisling felt a slow dread building in the center of her chest. "She was my grandmother on my dad's side."

Mr. Clydd cleared his throat. "Ladies, forgive my frankness here, but as you know, Rose and Joan were both very private people. Before we can tackle the task at hand, there are a few details you may be lacking regarding their private lives."

"She never talked much about her own life." Aisling closed her eyes as she spoke, a deep wrinkle forming between her brows. "But why does that matter now?"

"Well, I think you'll find that in this situation," Mr. Clydd said, "it matters very much."

"Now I wished I'd asked more about what was going on in her life." Finn glanced at Aisling, then back to Mr. Clydd. "So fill us in. What do we not know?"

Mr. Clydd leaned back in his chair. "Were either of you aware that your grandmothers had female life partners?"

Finn and Aisling both shook their heads slowly, and it was a moment before Finn spoke. "I guess that does make sense, though. I know she lost her husband while she was still young..."

"Same here," Aisling said slowly. "And Joan never remarried, as far as I know." She paused, letting the information settle in her mind. "I can't believe I didn't know that about my own grandmother." She looked up at Mr. Clydd, her words thoughtful. "But I do remember meeting a close friend of hers once. I believe I was twelve at the time, and we were on holiday in Wales."

"I had no idea," Finn said. "I've only been to Wales once, and I was too young then to remember anything."

Mr. Clydd sat back in his chair and tapped his pen on the surface of his desk. Aisling waited for him to say something, which he did not. She let a moment pass, then opened her mouth to speak.

"Holy shit." Finn cut in before Aisling got out the first word, looking blankly at the desk as if a ghost had just appeared and taken a seat on Mr. Clydd's leather desk blotter.

"What?"

"Our grandmothers were together." Finn smiled and looked over at Mr. Clydd, who winked at her and nodded.

Aisling shook her head. "What are you talking about?"

He leaned forward in his chair and peered across his desk at them.

"Aisling, your grandmother and Finn's grandmother were, for all intents and purposes, married for more than sixty years." He paused, slowly turning a framed photo on his desk around to face them. "This is a picture of them, and my partner Thomas, in 1957. The four of us were friends for a very long time, which is why they entrusted me with this responsibility."

Aisling leaned forward in her chair to peer at the photo, then sank back, shock coloring her face. "How long were they together?"

"Sixty-three years. They met shortly after the war. Both lost their husbands in the Cardiff bombing."

"That's right, I remember my dad said my grandfather died in the war." Finn's voice was soft, as if her father was a memory she hadn't recalled in a while.

"My father is an only child, but..." Aisling shook her head and her voice trailed off. "So each of them had one son?"

"Yes," Mr. Clydd said, reaching into his desk and pulling out a well-worn packet of pipe tobacco. He opened the top slowly and sniffed the contents. "And because they got together after the war and never officially remarried, those boys were the only children they had."

Aisling's fingertips traced the edge of the leather folder on her lap. "My father doesn't have any biological siblings, but he used to talk about a lad he was close to in his youth whom he called his 'brother.' They had a falling-out ages ago, long before I was born, so I never met him. But when he got word that he'd passed away, I remember my dad being utterly devastated."

Her words hovered in the air, as if looking for ways to piece themselves together.

Mr. Clydd packed the tobacco carefully into the bowl of the pipe and shook a match out of the box on his desk.

"I'd offer to not smoke this if you two had any objections." He struck the match and watched it flare to life. "But honestly that wouldn't be sincere, so I'll save us all the time."

He passed the flame over the bowl to char it, puffing a few times until the tobacco lit and swelled, then tamped it down lightly with a silver tamper and lit it again. The dark, velvet scent of vanilla emerged, warmed by the smoke that floated it into the air. He looked at his pipe admiringly and leaned back in his chair.

"So does this mean she and I are..." Aisling looked over at Finn as if approaching a roadside accident. "Related?"

"Not at all," Mr. Clydd said, lowering his pipe. "You're in the somewhat odd situation of having family in common, but there's no blood relation whatsoever."

Finn and Aisling were quiet as darkness started to fall against the office windows. The streetlights suddenly clicked on from below and illuminated a fine silver mist in the air.

"So what does all this mean?" Finn said. "And why tell us this now, after all this time?"

"I understand you were both close to your respective grandmothers?"

Finn nodded. "We talked a lot when I was growing up, and even more as I got older." Finn glanced out the window and steadied her voice. "She was the one thing in my life that was always the same. I guess I never thought about her having a life of her own."

Aisling felt herself choke up. She hadn't yet let herself cry about her Nana Joan, and now was certainly not the time. She took a deep breath and looked up at Mr. Clydd.

"Yes," she said, her voice suddenly too loud in the still room. "We were close. But I don't understand why she'd hide this major part of her life from me. Especially after I came out to her as a teenager."

Finn looked over at Aisling. "I think it's fair to say they grew up in a much different time, and this is a small town. Maybe they just never felt comfortable enough to talk about it."

Aisling nodded, smoothing her palm over her leg as she crossed one over the other. "I guess that makes sense. It's always safer not to rock the boat, especially back then. I just wish she would have shared that with me. Trusted me." She paused, suddenly overwhelmed by her own selfishness as Finn's words echoed darkly: *A life of her own.* Aisling's mind reeled with all the missed opportunities and lost conversations she could never recover as her eyes started to burn with tears.

There was a long silence then, until Mr. Clydd cleared his throat and met their gaze.

"You should know they both died peacefully of natural causes." His face softened with the words. "Rose passed two weeks ago today, of pneumonia, and Joan slipped away two days later in her sleep."

"Was there a funeral?" Finn swiped at a tear with the heel of her hand and looked out the window as she composed herself. "Why did no one tell us when it happened?"

"I'm sure it won't surprise you to know that both were adamant there be no fuss when they passed, as much as we would have loved to make one."

Aisling smiled to herself. Nana Joan was no-nonsense to say the least, and Aisling knew that according to her, funerals were nonsense.

"They were very careful to work out exactly what they wanted and how they wanted it carried out, whether they passed together or years apart." He paused, then glanced toward the window. "But I knew when Rose passed, Joan was ready to go."

Mr. Clydd looked down at his tweed vest and adjusted the pocket square more than once, then cleared his throat and looked up, tears still shimmering in his eyes.

"So it's my job to make sure their wishes are carried out to the letter," he said. "But I'll need your help."

"What can we do?" Finn sat up straighter in her chair. Aisling watched her as she started to speak again and decided against it.

"As you know," Mr. Clydd said. "Rose taught school for her entire career here in Cwylldbridge, and Joan owned a tailoring shop in town. Joan left the proceeds from her shop to a struggling family here in the village, and Rose made a sizable donation to St. Mary's primary school, which they were very thankful for."

He paused to relight his pipe, but when he shook the matchbox, it was empty. Finn handed him a brass lighter from her back pocket. He relit the bowl, drawing in air in puffs until the embers lit and glowed, then leaned across the desk and handed the lighter back to her.

"Your parents will receive a set sum, of course, but Joan and Rose invested most heavily…" He paused, lowering his pipe. "In the two of you."

Finn and Aisling turned to look at each other.

"What do you mean, 'invested'?" Finn asked, turning back to Mr. Clydd.

"Before they died, they bought a property here in Cwylldbridge that's been empty and on the market for six years, since the previous owner moved to Las Vegas."

"Vegas?" Finn smiled, one eyebrow arched. "That's quite a switch from Wales."

"Aye. But it seems to suit her."

"So why did they buy it?" Aisling said. "Was it an investment property?"

"That's exactly what it is. But not in the traditional sense." Mr. Clydd set down his pipe and pulled out real estate summaries for each of them and handed them over the desk. "They want you two to restore it." He paused and cleared his throat. "For the village they loved."

There was a single picture at the top of the sheet of paper of a timber-framed, whitewashed pub with rounded doorways and empty flower boxes. A dented estate agent's sign leaned precariously against the door, and one slate shingle dangled from the edge of the roof, looking as if it might drop and shatter on the sidewalk below at any second.

"Gwenllian's Sword?" Finn peered closer at the heavy wooden sign in the picture. "What does that even mean?"

"It's the name of the pub. Until six years ago, it was the center of Cwylldbridge, and had been since it was built in 1758. Joan and Rose bought it recently and wanted to restore it themselves, but obviously time grew too short, so they've entrusted you two with the task." Mr. Clydd paused, evaluating the blank stares across from him. "There's more than enough money set aside to make any improvements you see fit, and you'll both be paid a monthly stipend. In addition, operating expenses will be covered in full for the first year by way of a trust that I will oversee."

"So not just restore it," Finn said with a glance at Aisling. "They want us to stay here and open it for business?"

Mr. Clydd nodded, evening the edges of the stack of papers in front of him into a perfect square. He paused, then tapped the stack with his thumb as he spoke.

"At the end of the first year, the pub property and Joan and Rose's cottage is yours, and you can then decide together to keep them or sell them both and split the proceeds."

"An entire year?" Aisling shook her head, handing the paper back over the desk. She closed her eyes against the headache that seemed to be pushing its way out from behind her eyes. "I'm sure I could hire someone to do the job if that's what it takes, but I need to be back in London no later than tomorrow."

Mr. Clydd pushed his chair away from his desk and stood. "Ladies, your grandmothers were very clear in what they wanted, so I'll speak frankly here, and then you can decide together what you want to do."

He walked to the window, watching as the mist turned to rain and slicked the sidewalks below.

"When the pub closed six years ago, the village slowly drifted apart. We saw each other less and less, and no one is connected like we used to be. Connected to the village or, quite frankly, to each other." He turned and settled back into his chair, setting his pipe back down in its holder on his desk. "It was so important to Rose and Joan to see the pub restored, and now they're asking you to do it for them, which means you'd need to move here for a year."

Finn stared at the photo. "And where would we live?"

"Their home, if you'd like. You probably remember it, it's the stone cottage with the orange and pink rose bushes directly behind the church. It was always beautifully kept, so it's ready to move into."

"I remember it," Aisling said, rubbing her temples with the tips of her fingers.

Mr. Clydd pulled a gold pocket watch from his vest and opened it. "Why don't you two have a think about it tonight and let me know tomorrow?"

Aisling and Finn looked at each other as he clicked the pocket watch shut, then pulled a set of keys out of his drawer and pushed them across the desk.

"Here are the keys to the pub. It's the only set, so don't lose them. There's the main serving area downstairs, and upstairs you'll find a small flat, although it would have to be repainted and small repairs completed to be livable. I believe that project was in progress not long ago, so you'll find some tools and supplies there." He dropped the pocket watch back in the pocket of his vest. "Go have a look around and a chat. Ring me tomorrow and let me know what you've decided."

Aisling nodded in the direction of the pub as they stepped out of the building and walked down the brick sidewalk toward the town square, bright yellow ginkgo leaves blowing across the path under their feet as Finn fell into step beside her. Deep evening shadows had fallen thick across the small park in the center of the square, lined with gnarled oaks and peeling park benches. Three-story row houses lined each side of the square, with streetlights that illuminated their glossy doors and brass mail slots.

Aisling had remembered the building instantly when she saw the real estate flyer: two tall stories of whitewashed brick, with a wide timber-framed door and flower boxes under each window that dripped color onto the sidewalks—or at least it had looked like that to Aisling when she was a child and the flower petals had fluttered across her path with the breeze. It took up the entire east corner of the square, facing the park, and now seemed to loom taller as they approached.

As they walked to the door, the swinging wooden sign creaked in the wind above them. Aisling pulled the long skeleton keys from her pocket, and they clattered to the sidewalk before she even got them into the lock.

Finn picked them up and handed them back to her. "I'm Finn Morgan, by the way," she said. "I guess I should introduce myself if we're going to be working together."

Aisling looked her up and down. Her patience with this entire concept was fading. Fast. She closed her eyes and took a measured breath before she looked up and answered.

"Aisling."

She turned back to the door, and managed to turn the key and push the door open into the cold darkness. Finn followed her inside and ran her hand over the walls on either side of the door while Aisling flipped on the flashlight app on her phone and followed the beam over to a rounded booth with a table in front of it, upholstered in dusty red velvet. She reached under a glass lamp and pulled the chain, gold light spilling over the seating area.

"Some of these old pubs don't have overhead lighting," she said, clicking on another lamp near the windowsill and glancing up at the plaster ceiling. "And I'm guessing this one doesn't either considering the number of lamps scattered all over."

Finn dropped her duffel bag near the door, and together they turned on every lamp they could find, including two on each end of the bar. The pub seating area was centered in a wide half-moon shape around a massive mahogany bar. Carved wooden posts on each end of the bar led to intricate stained glass above and an old mirror that served as the backdrop, the edges like silver lace where the mercury had peeled over the years. Finn peered behind dusty bottles one by one until she found a row of light switches. Light bulbs fluttered to life behind the stained glass panels, the colors suddenly shimmering and vibrant, casting a sheer wash of color across the bar's surface.

"Wow," Aisling said, gazing up at the faceted glass panels. "Those are beautiful."

"It looks like a painting." Finn stepped back to get a better look at two nude women with long hair tossed around by the wind against the backdrop of an angry sea. "Are those mermaids?"

"They're sirens."

Finn arched an eyebrow and leaned against the bar, waiting.

Aisling managed to suppress the desire to roll her eyes and gave her the short version.

"Sirens are mythical creatures, especially in Welsh mythology, that took the form of beautiful naked women and sang near the shore to entice nearby sailors closer." She traced one of the panes with her fingertip and glanced back at Finn. "Until their ships wrecked on the rocks and they died."

"That sounds familiar." Finn smiled. "I think I may have dated a few of those."

Distracted, Aisling walked slowly toward the end of the bar closest to the door, running her hand over the rounded edge until she stopped suddenly and screamed, swiping at her head with her hands.

Finn hopped over the bar, but Aisling spun around in the opposite direction and wiped her face furiously on her sleeve.

"What's wrong?"

"I just walked into a massive spiderweb," she said, shaking out her hair and getting more panicked with every breath. "I detest spiders, and now they're in my hair."

The pitch of her voice spiked upward as she frantically spun and swiped at her head. Finn stayed back until Aisling's breathing grew hoarse and shallow, then morphed into a sob.

"Aisling," Finn said, stepping up to her and gripping her shoulders lightly. "Look at me. There are no spiders."

"You don't know that!" She suddenly shook her head maniacally with such force she threw herself off balance. "There could be hundreds of them crawling all over me right now."

Finn caught her right before she tipped over and centered her back on her feet. She dipped her head until Aisling looked at her and held her eyes.

"Look, I know this is scary, okay?" Her voice was a curious combination of strong and soothing. "But let's get a look at what we're dealing with here."

Finn lifted her by her waist to sit on the bar, which shocked Aisling into silence for a few seconds before she swiped again at her face with her sleeve and shook it with the same level of panic.

"Hold still," Finn said, her voice as soft as Aisling's was shrill. She turned Aisling's face gently to the left and leaned closer. "I'm looking at your hair under the lights and I don't see a single spider."

"They're there, I feel them."

Aisling's breathing grew more labored. She gripped her chest, tears flowing down her face.

"Aisling," Finn said, shifting her focus from the spider search back to Aisling. "I promise, if I saw anything I'd tell you, but there's nothing there."

"I can't breathe." Aisling started to choke on her tears and squeezed her eyes shut. "I can't breathe."

Aisling felt Finn step closer and lift the hand she'd tightened into a fist. Finn uncurled Aisling's fingers and placed her hand flat onto the center of her own chest.

"I know you feel like you can't breathe," Finn said, her voice low and calm. "But you can. I want you to inhale and exhale when I do, okay?"

Aisling shook her head, her other hand now clutching at her chest. Finn took a deep, slow breath and let it out.

"Did you feel that under your palm?"

Aisling nodded, every muscle in her body clenched tight.

"Great, so let's do it together this time."

Aisling nodded slightly and took a shaky breath when she felt Finn's chest rise under her hand. Finn waited a beat, then exhaled, placing her hand over Aisling's.

"That was great. Just keep doing that with me."

Aisling shut her eyes tighter, still and frozen, tears dropping onto the front of her shirt.

"Open your eyes for me," Finn said softly. "I've got you."

Aisling just shook her head and kept her eyes shut tight, but she followed Finn's every breath until her hand relaxed slightly against Finn's chest.

"Take your time. Don't rush it."

Aisling took two more breaths, slower this time, then opened her eyes and pulled her hand slowly back.

"Thank you." She looked down at the bar, avoiding Finn's eyes. "I'm so embarrassed. I don't know what's wrong with me."

"Nothing," Finn said, squeezing her knee and stepping back around the bar. She handed Aisling a white cloth handkerchief from her pocket, embroidered with the initials *F.M.* "There's nothing wrong with you. It happens to the best of us."

"Right." Aisling smiled as Finn took two rocks glasses off the shelf. "You don't exactly look like there's a lot out there that scares you."

"I'm going to take that as a compliment." Finn shot her a smile over her shoulder and pulled a dusty bottle of Jack Daniel's from the row under the mirror. "But that's definitely not true. I used to be a semipro boxer, but I'd get panic attacks sometimes if I had to talk to a reporter or do an interview. I hated it."

She poured the whiskey slowly into both glasses and handed Aisling hers.

Aisling swiped at the last of the mascara under her eyes with a weak smile and clinked her glass to Finn's. "Did you take meds for it?"

"It might have helped me if I had, but no, I just learned to breathe."

"Do you still box?"

Finn swirled the whiskey in her glass. "Only with my punching bag."

They fell silent for a moment. With the spider crisis passed, the memory of what they'd heard in the solicitor's office crowded the room again. Aisling finished the rest of her whiskey in one swallow and set it back on the bar with a *thunk*.

"What the hell are we going to do with this place?"

Finn smiled, refilled her glass, and put the bottle back on the shelf. "We're going to fix it back up, apparently."

Aisling watched as Finn ran her hand over the glossy mahogany surface of the bar. The color was on the brown side of dark cherry, although it seemed deeper than that, multilayered, as if every year that passed had left its own translucent layer of color on the surface. "Although I'm still not sure why Rose and Joan thought we were the two for the job."

Aisling looked at her for a moment, choosing her words carefully. "So, you're just going to drop your life in the States, move to some tiny village in Wales you know nothing about, and restore a random abandoned pub?"

Finn swirled the drink gently and handed Aisling her glass. "Looks like it."

Aisling sipped, then put it back down on the bar and closed her eyes, rubbing her temples with her fingertips. "I can't believe I'm even considering this."

"Do we really have a choice?" Finn finished her whiskey and set her glass in the small ceramic sink at the end of the bar. "I mean, we loved them, right? They trusted us, so we've got to do this."

Aisling looked up at the ceiling for a moment, then decided quickly against it when she saw the intricate layers of spiderwebs spanning every corner.

"Oh, for fuck's sake."

"What?"

"How can I not do it when you put it like that?" Aisling finished the rest of her drink and handed the glass to Finn. "And it's not like my career is actually at its peak at the moment, anyway."

"What do you do?"

"I was a wedding planner." Aisling smiled and slid off the bar back down to the floor. "But it seems I've fucked that up for myself permanently."

Finn smiled, hit the lights, and hopped back over the bar. "Well, if we're going to do this, maybe we should go check out the cottage. I'm dying for a shower."

Aisling nodded, picking her coat up from the end of the bar where she'd left it and sliding it over her shoulders. "Only if we can stop at the chippy and pick up a takeaway."

Finn switched off the last lamp and opened the door for Aisling. Cold wind rushed around the corner and blew wild copper waves of hair around Aisling's face, but she wound it into a quick twist and secured it with the pen from her leather folder. Finn smiled, then took the key from Aisling and locked up the pub.

"I have no idea what you just said, but if it has anything to do with food, I'm in."

CHAPTER FIVE

After they'd locked up the pub, they stopped at Aisling's B&B to pick up her bags, and from there it was only a five-minute walk to the cottage, which was just off the square and past the church along a narrow path. Breath followed them like fog in the icy air. The full moon glowed above the treetops, and the only sounds were gravel crunching underfoot and ocean waves crashing onto the rocks down the hill from the cottage. Aisling closed her eyes and breathed in the scent of the ocean misting her face with salt that lingered on her lips.

Finn stopped suddenly on the path and looked at Aisling.

"What?"

Finn glanced back toward the square. "I just remembered he didn't give us keys for the cottage, only the pub."

"Don't worry, it won't be locked," Aisling said as they started down the path again. "I don't think she ever locked it. There may not even be a key."

"You're kidding," Finn said, then paused and glanced in her direction. "Right?"

Aisling slowed, nodding toward a small stone cottage to their right. The moon sank low over the traditional thatch roof, casting a pewter glow over the bare rose bushes and tangled vines that covered the mossy rock fence in front. A small metal plate affixed to the fence read *Rose Cottage*.

"It's smaller than I remember," Aisling said, her feet frozen to the gravel path.

"Yep. It's tiny. And dark." Finn opened the rusted iron gate for

Aisling with a creak. "And I'm pretty sure these vines are waiting to reach out and squeeze the life out of us, so I'll slip in first while you distract them."

Aisling laughed despite herself and stepped carefully through the gate and onto a stone path. It led to the antique wooden door with an arched top and inset Gothic window framed in hammered iron.

Finn turned the door handle and pushed it open, sliding her hand down the inside wall as she stepped through.

Aisling watched her with one raised eyebrow. "You just can't help yourself, can you?"

Finn shook her head as she searched the wall on the other side of the door. "What is it with Wales and the fear of adequate lighting?"

Aisling smiled and placed the pizza box she was carrying onto the small entry table, then switched on the lamp beside one of the two leather chairs near the fireplace. It was warmer in the cottage somehow than it had been in the pub, as if someone had just been there. The white hearth with a scarred pine mantel was the central point of the room, framed by a small couch with a linen slipcover on one side and the two leather chairs on the other. Each of the chairs was detailed with brass tacks and a wool plaid pillow. The room was simple but cozy, with warm throws and a faded rug between the chairs and the sofa. Two mission-style floor lamps with plates of amber and green glass, one on each side of the hearth, cast the area with light.

"I need to shower before I do anything else," Finn said, picking up her duffel and peering down the hall. "Which I'm assuming is this direction?"

"You'll find the bathroom down the hall on the left." She smiled and paused to look Finn up and down. "Good luck with that."

Aisling turned back to the living room and leaned against the wall. It was cozier, more masculine than she expected, but the ivory couch pillows stitched with rose vines and pink milk glass vases lined up on the mantel softened the look. It still smelled the same, like woodsmoke and vanilla sugar cookies, which she wasn't ready for, and sudden tears burned the back of her eyes.

"Aisling?"

Aisling turned to look at Finn leaning against the doorframe of the bathroom, her bag still in the same place on her shoulder.

"There is no shower." Finn raked a hand through her hair. "There is a tiny claw-foot bathtub the size of a Tic Tac…" She paused. "But there is no shower."

Aisling smiled. For some reason she was enjoying teasing the American.

"How tall are you?"

Finn arched an eyebrow. "I'm five ten."

Aisling considered that for a moment. "That should work, then. Just fold yourself exactly in half and you'll fit perfectly."

Finn rolled her eyes and disappeared back around the corner.

By the time Finn had gotten dressed and returned to the kitchen, Aisling was deleting the fourth text she'd written and erased, telling her parents that she'd be delayed getting back to London. By a year.

"What's burning?" Finn said, looking around the cozy kitchen with a '50s Formica table in the breakfast nook.

Aisling looked up from her phone, then hurriedly put it down and opened the oven, reaching for the pizza box she'd put inside to warm.

"Don't touch that," Finn said in a rush, pulling her back and grabbing the box out of the oven with a tea towel. "It's way too hot."

She dropped the smoldering box on the top of the oven and waved the smoke away from the cardboard that was starting to blacken and curl at the corners.

Finn gingerly lifted the lid and peered inside. "Well, I don't know how you did it, but the pizza itself is perfect. Not too hot."

"Thank God. I can't handle going to bed hungry on top of everything else today."

Aisling moved the pizza box to the table and returned with plates and silverware.

"What are you going to do with those?" Finn said, eyeing the forks and knives. "Put those back on the counter and I'll show you how we eat pizza in Brooklyn."

"How do you eat it?"

"With our hands," Finn said as she handed her a slice. "Like normal people."

Aisling picked the pizza up by the crust, and the entire slice immediately drooped toward the table.

"That's the saddest thing I've ever seen." Finn laughed and picked up her slice. "It's called the Flying V. Just hold your index finger in the center of the outer crust and sort of bend the two sides inward with your fingers. Not all the way, though, you're not trying to fold it in half, just stabilize it."

"Ah, I see." Aisling got the feel for it after a few seconds and took her first bite. "Actually, that's fairly smart. It gives it structure."

"Yeah, nothing's sadder than a floppy slice."

Aisling posed with the pizza next to her face with her best Instagram smile. "So do I look like a New Yorker now?"

Finn laughed, barely managing to keep her mouth closed around the bite she'd just put in it. "Um. No. You do not."

They ate in silence until Aisling thought to ask Finn what she did for a living now that she wasn't boxing.

"Nothing, really." She paused. "I mean, I work, but it's a shit job in a diner. I just wanted something I didn't have to think about."

Aisling finished her slice and Finn handed her another, which she surprisingly bent into the correct shape on the first try. "So why did you want something you don't have to think about?"

"I used to own a catering company with my ex, but when that went south, I just didn't have the energy to do it all again."

"I understand," Aisling said. "My career went tits up too, not long ago, actually."

Finn smiled and closed the lid on the empty pizza box. "What happened?"

"You don't want to know." Aisling shook her head and gathered their plates, setting them carefully in the sink before she turned back around and leaned against it. "But Jesus, the ever-present backlash from it seems a bit over the top. I mean, it's not like I killed someone."

She spoke slowly, more to herself than to Finn. Her voice trailed off, but she snapped back to reality after a few seconds and looked at Finn across the kitchen. "I kissed the wrong person, I guess."

Finn waited for her to go on, but she didn't. "How do you lose an entire career from one kiss?"

Aisling smiled, letting the silence speak for her.

"Oh shit," Finn said. "You didn't kiss the groom, did you?"

She laughed and pulled the pen out of her hair. "Um...not the groom."

"Then it can't be that bad. What's the big deal?"

Aisling ran her fingers through her hair and loosened the waves until they fell over her shoulders.

"It was the bride."

"Wow." Finn shook her head, smiling, and folded what was left of the charred cardboard box into the trash. "I did not see that one coming."

"I thought not. Most people don't."

Finn smiled and stepped into the living room, then leaned back in as soon as she passed the doorframe.

"This fire is beautiful. Did you do that while I was folding myself into the bathtub?"

Aisling didn't answer, just walked slowly into the living room, where a cheerful fire crackled and warmed the air. When they'd walked into the house an hour ago, it had been empty and dark, but now the entire room looked gilded, as if the firelight had melted into gold over every surface. Once again, the hearth had been swept clean and even the dented copper bucket next to the fireplace had been filled with freshly cut wood. Aisling stared into the flames, then slowly raised her eyes over Finn's head and up to the ceiling.

"What are you looking at?" Finn said, following her gaze to the cracked plaster ceiling arched above her head, secured at the apex with an unfinished wooden beam.

"Nothing," Aisling replied, her eyes scanning the room, half expecting to see the golden orbs of light she'd seen in the castle. But there was nothing. "Just a memory, I guess."

Aisling sank onto the couch and tucked her feet underneath her, her eyes suddenly softer than they'd been before.

"So," Finn said finally. "This is a unique problem, seeing as I met you about two hours ago, but I'm willing to bet there's just one bedroom down that hall, right?"

Aisling nodded, her gaze focused on the fire. Then suddenly what Finn was saying dawned on her and she looked up. "I didn't think about that."

"Don't worry, I'll sleep on the couch."

Aisling dropped her eyes to Finn's arms, her eyes fixed on the half sleeve of visible tattoos on both. "You're not an axe murderer or anything, are you?"

Finn laughed and threw another split long on the fire, sending a spray of red sparks up the chimney. "No, not anymore. They confiscated my axe at the airport."

Finn had changed into jeans and a white T-shirt, and Aisling watched the muscles in her arms flex into defined cuts as she stacked some of the logs on the hearth. The strong lines of her shoulders and abs were visible even under her shirt, and Aisling realized too late that she was staring.

"Aisling?" Finn smiled and held her eyes just long enough. "I asked if you knew where they kept their extra blankets."

She nodded, walked down the hall, and pulled a white duvet and two pillows out of the linen closet. She handed them to Finn as she came back in.

"Make sure you stay in that bedroom." Finn's eyes sparkled in the firelight as she took them from her. "I've heard what happened to that poor innocent bride."

Aisling rolled her eyes and walked back down the hall, clicking the light off as she went. "Don't worry, Boxer Boi. You're not remotely my type."

CHAPTER SIX

The next morning, a thin layer of ice glazed the village as they walked out of the house and pulled the door shut behind them. The sun glinted off the icy vines twisted around the fence, and the gate creaked noisily as Finn opened it. She stepped out onto the path and walked to her right a few meters, gravel crunching under her feet. She stopped, her gaze fixed on the choppy surface of the sea at the bottom of a steep downward path that was more of a cliff than a slope. The edge was only about ten yards from the cottage, but she hadn't noticed it through the darkness of the night before.

"Wow." Finn looked down. "Is that the ocean?"

"It is." Aisling glanced up, then smoothed her hair before she slid on her green cashmere beanie. "Don't you have one or two of those in the States?"

"Not really." It was a few seconds before Finn spoke again, and when she did her voice sounded far away, as if it were floating toward the vast expanse of sea. "Not like that, anyway."

The odd glimpse of the sea was sometimes visible from along the outside edges of the village, but because they were so close to the beach below, expansive views of whitecaps and cresting whales made the cliff look like the land had broken off and fallen into the water. Chalk-white cliffs framed both sides of the deep blue water leading to the open sea, and the waves breaking on the rocky shore below clung to the beach as if reluctant to leave, swirling into translucent tidepools among the rocks.

Finn turned back and caught up with Aisling on the path toward the church. The bells for morning mass clanged in the belfry as they passed, and people wrapped up in wool coats and hats streamed in, their breath following like fog as they stepped into the church and out of the crisp morning air.

"Hey," Finn said. "I went out for a run this morning before you woke up and I saw that castle in the field on the edge of town. Does someone actually live in that thing?"

"No, it's been abandoned for as long as I've been alive." Aisling looked in the direction of the castle. "I've only been there once. I've never forgotten it."

"Why, what happened?"

Aisling shook her head and nodded toward the square as they turned the corner. "Call me a chicken, but I'm a little afraid to see what the pub looks like in the daylight."

Finn nodded, squinting through the morning sunlight. "At least when we get in there and take a look, we'll know what we're dealing with. We can just take it from there."

"Have you ever been in a pub in the UK?"

"Yep," Finn said with a wink in her direction. "If you count last night."

"Holy Mary Mother of God," Aisling muttered. "I'm starting to think this may be karma for a lifetime of sins."

"I call bullshit." Finn smiled over at her as she pulled on the gloves she produced from the pocket of her black puffer jacket. "You don't look like you've ever been in trouble in your life."

Aisling looked at her and arched an eyebrow.

Finn realized what she meant and laughed. "All right, point taken. Aside from the one wayward bride and the crushing collapse of your glittering career."

"That's better." Aisling shot her a smile. "If I had to go down for it, I should at least get credit."

The pub looked more and more like an abandoned movie set as they got closer, and they stopped together across the street to take in the state of it. Structurally, it looked sound, aside from the one slipped slate shingle and the precariously placed sign that dangled by a rusted chain from a post near the door. It looked like what it was: abandoned, as if the energy of the people inside that had held it together all those years had suddenly disappeared, and the building had exhaled as it watched them go and never drew another breath.

Finn let out a deep breath that froze instantly and lingered in front of them. "It could be beautiful."

"It was once." Aisling's words were swept away as a cluster of schoolgirls in green plaid school uniforms passed them on the sidewalk, chattering as they juggled school bags over heavy coats. "Although I still don't understand why it was so important to them that we reopen it. Someone would have bought it eventually, even a foreigner." Aisling looked back to the pub. "I know for a fine fact that Americans love this shit."

The sun slipped out from behind a stack of clouds the color of charred steel and warmed the air, lighting up the still-icy branches and frozen red-gold tree leaves along the edges of the square.

"It's now or never, I guess." Finn nodded toward the pub. "Ready?"

Aisling didn't answer, but Finn smiled at her anyway, taking her sunglasses from her jacket pocket and sliding them onto her face.

"Let me phrase that in a different way. We can walk across the street or I can put you over my shoulder. Your choice."

"Right." Aisling shook her head as a dented red Renault passed between them and the pub. "Nice thought, but you wouldn't dare."

Finn swept Aisling up into her arms before the last word was out of her mouth and shifted her body over her shoulder as she started to cross the street.

"Finn!" Aisling kicked and twisted, but the only thing that changed was her hair, which instantly fell from its bun and flew around her face like a copper tornado. "Put me down! What the hell are you doing?"

Finn crossed the street to the sidewalk in front of the pub's main doors, noting that an elderly gentleman in a white apron had stepped out of his shop on the other side of the square to watch.

Finn held her with one arm and glanced at her watch. "People are starting to notice, so you might want to say 'please.'"

Aisling stopped kicking, her voice dangerously close to shrill. "What?"

"It's the least you can do after you made me carry you across the street like that."

Aisling's cheeks flamed red.

"Finn Morgan, put me down immediately."

Finn waved at the laughing gentleman, who had now called someone else out to look.

"Are you seriously going to make me say 'please'?"

Finn tried not to laugh and didn't quite make it. "Yes, ma'am."

"Fine. *Please* put me the fuck down." The effort required to keep her voice down made her words sound more like a hiss.

"That's better," Finn said, smiling as she lowered Aisling to the ground.

Aisling straightened her coat and punched Finn's arm as hard as she could, which yielded not even a flinch. Finn grinned as Aisling turned toward the laughter from across the square, confirming that someone had just watched the entire humiliating episode.

Finn held the door open with a wink. "After you, Ms. Moss."

Aisling leaned close and whispered as she stepped into the pub, "Fuck off, Ms. Morgan."

"If you two are through acting like hoodlums," a stern voice boomed through the darkness from the direction of the bar, "there is business to be discussed."

They stopped short just inside the door, and Finn reached over to click on the nearest lamp. A stocky older woman, gray hair in a painfully tight bun at the nape of her neck, was sitting at the bar, accompanied by what looked like a stack of logbooks and the contents of a large filing cabinet.

Aisling shook her head and asked the obvious question.

"I'm Ms. Helen Greystone," she said, managing to look them both up and down with one sweep of her deep brown eyes, nearly hidden behind gold half spectacles perched halfway down her nose. She waited after she said it, as if the mere mention of her name would clear up any lingering questions. "Obviously you haven't heard, but I'm the business consultant in charge of this little…experiment."

"We hadn't heard, but it's great to meet you," Finn said, offering her hand as Aisling pulled two barstools slightly out from the bar and sat primly on the far stool, eyeing Greystone, who stared pointedly at Finn's outstretched hand until it was dropped.

Finn settled onto the stool beside Aisling, and all three stared at each other in the dense silence.

Finally, Greystone cleared her throat. "Do either of you have any experience at all in running a pub?"

"Well," Aisling squared her shoulders, "I'm one of the top three wedding planners in London, so I think I may be able to figure it out."

Greystone looked from Aisling to Finn.

"And you? What qualifies you for taking on this challenge?"

Finn met her eyes and smiled. "Absolutely nothing. But I'll outwork anyone else in the room and I'm a quick study."

A hint of a smile warmed the older woman's face before she thought better of it, and she shrugged off her wool overcoat and handed it to Finn with a nod at the row of hooks near the door. "Well, that's a start."

Finn took her coat and hung it carefully on the hook closest to the door. Greystone turned to Aisling. "I'll have a brandy, then, to take the chill out of the air, and we'll get started."

Aisling got up slowly with a pointed glance in Finn's direction, choosing a glass hanging in the rack above the bar. She rinsed it in the sink, which sputtered and spurted as if being woken up from hibernation before settling into something resembling a steady stream. She dried the glass carefully and chose a bottle of brandy from the row of dusty bottles behind the bar.

"It seems I've been chosen, may the saints preserve us"—she glanced skyward and crossed herself, then settled her gaze back on Finn and Aisling as Aisling pushed the glass of brandy across the bar—"to get you both up to speed on day-to-day operational tasks."

She pulled a typewritten sheet of paper from a folder and placed it on the bar.

"This is a list of suppliers, for everything from food to linen services, that you'll need to get the initial stock in place. From there you can decide what you want to offer as far as food, and I've made an appointment for a brewery representative to pay you a visit to get you up to speed on the licensing requirements for alcohol here."

"Food?" Aisling said with a glance beyond the bar to the left, where double wooden doors with set-in windows hinted at a possible kitchen area. "I didn't realize we'd be serving food."

"Well, of course." Greystone tossed back her brandy in one swallow and pushed her glass to the edge of the bar. "Where else do you think the punters will be eating when they're drunk and the respectable restaurants are shut for the night?"

Finn smiled. "Punters?"

Aisling shot Finn a glance and settled her gaze back on Greystone. "That's Welsh for 'customers.'"

"Right." Greystone sniffed, with a pointed look at her empty glass. Finn didn't quite hide a smile as she got up and refilled it, settling it carefully back in front of her and recorking the bottle. "You'll find a couple of cafés on the square, but most people eat in the pub a night or two a week." She glanced around at the empty room, dust hanging in the air as sunlight began to warm the windows that faced the square. "Or at least they used to."

Finn looked around at the worn tabletops and scuffed chairs. In the daylight the room seemed bigger than the night before, with a wide fireplace settled against the far-left corner and dartboards to the right of the bar.

"Of course, you'll want to replace most of the furniture. It's definitely seen better days, although the built-in snugs—"

"The what?" Finn cocked one eyebrow and directed her question at Aisling, who nodded to the velvet-covered seating on the opposite wall under the windows.

"She's talking about the half-circle booths that hold two, maybe three people. They're meant to provide a bit of privacy for the patrons who want to have an actual conversation, which is a joke. In a town this size everyone knows your business anyway."

"Right you are. Some things never change." Greystone nodded, picking up the stack of file folders on the bar and plunking them down in front of Finn. "But they do have history, so I'd recommend keeping them. The tables in front of them are made from the bedroom doors of a brothel at the outskirts of the village shut down by the church around 1790."

She nodded toward the wide mahogany pillars behind it on either end of the bar that supported the stained glass panes and mercury mirror backdrop, lined with glass shelves for the bottles. The bar itself was around twenty feet long, and slightly curved in a half-moon shape, with intricate carved-edge trim and handmade glass racks overhead.

"The entire town helped take the bar out of the brothel and fit it into the pub. The village priest at the time declared it God's work." She paused, looking at a long row of framed photos by the fireplace. "Nothing's been quite the same since it closed."

Greystone stood, shutting her briefcase with a snap and winding a tweed scarf loosely around her neck as she headed for the door.

"Wait," Aisling said. "Weren't we supposed to go over the details of how to order supplies and…whatever else we need to know?"

"Everything you need to know is right there." Greystone nodded to the folders as she slid her wool overcoat across her shoulders and buttoned it swiftly up to her neck. "The billing address to give to suppliers is in the first binder. All bills will go to your solicitor's office for the twelve months, which he will pass on to me. After that, you'll be on your own, so I recommend you find your feet before then." She paused, her hand on the doorknob. "I'd also recommend you open as soon as possible. Better to start turning a profit early, even if you're learning as you go."

"Wait," Aisling said as the door swung open and a gust of cold air swept in from the outside. "Is that all we need to know?"

"No," the older woman replied, with a long glance around the pub, as if leaving somewhere she'd lived all her life. "But that's all I'm going to tell you. The rest you're going to have to figure out for yourself." She paused for just a moment before she stepped out into the wind. "But I can tell you this: You'd be better off starting outside these doors, not inside."

The door squeezed shut behind her, and she was gone. Finn watched through the windows as she crossed the park in the center of the square, then disappeared into one of the tall Victorian row houses on the other side.

"Well," Aisling said. "That was the least helpful meeting I've ever sat through."

Finn thumbed through the folder labeled *Suppliers*. She looked at each page carefully before turning it, then closed the folder and walked to the window that looked out over the square.

"What?"

Finn held out her coat. "Let's take a walk."

Aisling looked around her, then picked up the folders and let them drop back down on the bar.

"Don't you think we should get started with this stuff?"

Finn smiled, then walked over and handed her the coat. "I think I'm going to starve unless I eat something. And it won't hurt us to see what's going on around here."

Aisling slid into her coat and shook her head as Finn turned out the lamp and held the door open for her. "I'm starting to think this is all just a bad dream. And I swear," she said with a glance skyward, "if I wake the hell up, I'll never kiss another bride."

❖

Directly across the square on the west side was a tiny café with two bistro tables out front and a glass door blurred from the inside by steam. The building was made of chipped, mossy brick, as most of the shops lining the square were, but the front had been painted a brilliant blue, with bright white trim and orange marigolds crowding the window boxes under the front windows. *Gryphon's Lair* was hand-painted in careful gold and black lettering on the door.

"Is this the café?"

"Nope, it's the glassblowing shop." Aisling pushed through the door and into the tiny seating area. "That's why you smell bacon."

Aisling looked around, but it didn't take long to take it in. The entire café was smaller than the living room of her apartment, and the open kitchen just behind the front counter was literally the size of a closet. An older woman was there taking orders and, apparently, also cooking the food.

"What can I get you, love?"

Her sharp accent was distinctly Welsh. Finn paused, looking for a menu until Aisling pointed at the wall beside the door. A chalkboard crowded with smudged white text teetered from a single nail in the wall, shifting with the wind every time someone opened the door.

"What's a jacket potato?"

The woman looked at her for a moment, then glanced behind them at the growing line.

"Lovely," she said, turning to Aisling. "And for you?"

"I'll have a bacon butty, please, with brown sauce. And two coffees."

She nodded and picked up two coffee cups from the shelf above her head. "That'll be eight pounds, twenty-seven pence, please."

Aisling pulled a ten-pound note out of her wallet and left the change on the counter as the server filled the mugs with coffee and pushed them to the edge of the counter, already shifting her attention to greet the customer behind them.

Finn found a tiny empty table near the window and edged in, coffee cup in hand. "What the hell did I order, by the way?"

"I'll wait to see if you like it, then I'll tell you." She smiled up at Finn while she poured milk into her coffee from the tiny stainless steel pitcher on the table. "But you've got to be quicker on the draw around here or you're going to be at my mercy permanently."

Finn laughed, rolling the sleeves of her red flannel shirt up to the elbows as she spoke. "Never gonna happen."

"What's not going to happen?" Aisling poured two packets of brown sugar into her mug at once. "You being able to keep up with me one day in the distant future?"

Finn looked up at her, then dropped her eyes. Aisling looked down to realize her emerald cashmere cardigan was buttoned just low enough to show the milky curve of her breasts, scattered with the faintest wash of freckles.

"I make it a policy not to be at any woman's mercy," Finn said, finally looking up and holding her eyes softly. "So don't get your hopes up."

The server slid their plates onto the table with a sudden clatter, then wove quickly back through the tables to the growing queue at the counter.

Aisling's plate held her bacon sandwich on toast, but Finn looked dubiously at her own.

"You're going to have to clue me in here. What the hell did you order me?"

"It's the special. A jacket—baked—potato filled with baked beans and coleslaw. It's one of my personal favorites, actually." Aisling tipped her head, her sandwich aloft. "What, can't handle it?"

"Just FYI, that's not a question you'll ever have to ask." Finn winked at her, stirred the fillings into her potato, and took a bite, followed quickly by another. "Damn. This is actually good."

Aisling smiled and peered out the window beside them. Blue-and-white-striped awnings lined both sides of the street on the opposite side of the square, and the space between them was filled with a few people, shopping bags on their arms.

Finn nodded toward the square. "What's going on over there?"

"A street market. I actually haven't seen one for a while." She leaned closer and squinted past the wide beams of sunlight hitting the window. "They used to be all over London, literally everywhere you looked, but since the bigger chain supermarkets have moved in, they just don't get the business that they used to."

"Where do you get your groceries in London?"

"Tesco, I guess. One of the bigger chains." Aisling looked back at Finn and stole a forkful of potato and baked beans. "I used to love the market when I was a kid, but it's just easier to get everything at once on the way home from work."

Finn quickly finished the rest of her potato and pushed her plate to the side. "You ready?"

Aisling popped the last of her sandwich into her mouth and sighed. "We're going over there, aren't we?"

Finn laid a pound coin on the table and slid out of the booth. "Yes, ma'am."

Aisling grabbed her jacket and followed Finn out of the café, pulling the door shut behind her. The air was cold but still, and the last shards of ice shimmered in the trees as they walked through the park to the market. Makeshift racks of clothing and costume jewelry occupied the first of the stalls, attended by a middle-aged woman in a long puffer coat, sliding more shirts from a box onto hangers as she talked to the customers. Under the next awning was an open vegetable cart with rows of fresh cabbages, carrots, and potatoes, topped by bunches of bananas hanging from string loops attached to the underside of the awning. Tin buckets of fresh herbs and flowers crowded on cascading display tables filled the area around the vegetable cart, and fresh baked goods wrapped in brown paper were just visible from the stall at the end of the row.

"Something smells good." Finn drew in a deep breath and looked around. "Like fresh bread and coffee."

"Could be coming from there." Aisling pointed at the tent with the bookshelf display of bread. Hanging on the front pole was a small handmade sign that read *Fresh Bread & Coffee*. "Either that or the fishmonger on the end. Can't decide."

"Smartass." Finn smiled back at Aisling over her shoulder as she wove her way toward the baked goods tent amid the shoppers swirling around them. "What did you do with your time before you had me to make fun of?"

"I really can't remember," Aisling said, smiling. "But it wasn't nearly as satisfying."

The rich scent of sweet pumpkin and earthy nutmeg swirled around them as they stepped under the stall awning. A plump older woman with gray hair and a wool overcoat sat in the only spot that wasn't covered in carefully wrapped loaves and baked goods, head bent close to an open book, pushing her glasses up on her nose. When she noticed them, she closed her book and smiled warmly, tucking a wool scarf the exact hue of her pale blue eyes into her worn pink wool overcoat.

"Would either of you like a tea or coffee to warm you up?"

She didn't wait for them to answer before she started toward the two carafes perched on a small table behind her, accompanied by a small bowl of sugar and an open pint of milk that looked to be from the local shop.

Aisling smiled. "A tea would be lovely, thank you."

"Coffee for me, please, just black."

Finn elbowed Aisling, pointing out random loaves of wrapped bread tucked into the piles of books in the shelves that lined the edges of her stall. Some were tipped on the side, with a book perched precariously on top, others just stacked into the books around them as if they were part of a series, but all were carefully wrapped in simple brown craft paper and tied with twine.

Aisling watched as she left her book on the table and edged to the front to join them, drinks in hand. The sun emerged just then, warming the air around them and illuminating the steam rising from the cups as she handed them over. Bright laughter floated over from another stall, and three boys in school uniforms raced down the center of the walkway on bikes, gravel crunching under the tires.

"Thank you so much," Finn said, reaching for her wallet. "How much do we owe you?"

"Nothing at all." She handed her a steaming paper cup of coffee. "I just keep drinks handy to warm people up while they shop."

Aisling looked around at the bookshelves, carefully stacked with the well-worn books and fragrant loaves, all carefully lettered with a fountain pen. Under each handwritten label was the name of the book displayed beside it and a single page number.

"My name is Maggie Hargrove, by the way," the woman said as

she straightened a loaf on the shelf beside her. She had a strong Welsh accent and a quick smile that instantly lit up the space around her.

Finn smiled and introduced herself and Aisling, then picked up a loaf and turned to it toward her. "I was expecting to see what bread is inside the wrapper." She paused. "But are these book titles on your labels?"

"Oh yes." She glanced over at the square and pointed to the small, neat shop beside the butcher. The inside was dark and the windows empty and papered over, some peeling at the edges. "I used to have a bakery just over the road, but I'm retired now. I've always loved books, so now I just read until I find something I want to bake, then I bring both to the market."

"That's a great idea, but..." Aisling picked up a tea-stained Frank McCourt book and the round loaf in brown paper beside it. "But this label only says *Angela's Ashes*." She hesitated. "How do you know what's inside?"

"Read the book," Maggie and Finn answered together, then laughed as Aisling tucked the paper-wrapped loaf under her arm with the book.

"How much do I owe you? I can't wait to see what I got."

"Three pounds for the bread, love." Maggie gave her a warm smile. "The book is free. Just drop it back by when you're done with it."

Aisling pulled a five-pound note out of her pocket just as Finn took off suddenly behind her, gravel spraying back from under her feet, and ran down the space between the stalls. Maggie and Aisling leaned into the aisle and watched as a lanky teenage boy shot out from behind the row of market stalls and tried to run. Finn took him shoulders-first to the road and held him there. They watched as she leaned down and spoke into his ear, still holding him firmly to the ground as he kicked and tried to get her off him.

"What did she say to him?"

Aisling looked over to her right at the man tending the stall with vegetables and fresh herbs for sale as he looked back to the boy. He was tall and handsome in a rugged sort of way.

"Whatever it is, I'm sure he deserves it." The man took off his tweed cap and shook his head, eyes still fixed on Finn. "He used to be a good lad when he was small, but for the last few years he's been a right eejit."

They watched as Finn finally stood and held her hand out to the boy to help him up. He paused, then took it and got to his feet, brushing dust off his jacket before continuing to walk in the original direction. Finn turned him back around with one firm hand behind his neck and walked him down the aisle between the awnings, stopping at Maggie's stall. He looked to be twelve, maybe thirteen years old, in ripped jeans and a black hoodie, with a cap pulled low over his eyes and unlaced, stained trainers.

Finn nodded at Maggie, then took the cap off the boy's head and handed it to him. "What's your name?"

The boy just shrugged, his eyes firmly fixed on the ground.

"His name is Barry Wright," the gentleman standing beside Aisling said. "And I'm Herschel Wright. He's my son, although I'd rather not admit that at the moment."

Finn elbowed Barry lightly, then nodded again in Maggie's direction. The boy sighed and pulled a worn blue wallet out of the front pocket of his hoodie. Maggie took it from him slowly, shock washing over her face.

"Barry! Where did you get my wallet?"

The boy made another futile attempt to jerk out of Finn's grasp.

"Barry," Finn said, her voice low and controlled. "Ms. Hargrove asked you a question. And we're going to be here until you answer her and act like the man I know you'll be someday."

A tense silence followed, surrounded by the stall owners jockeying to get a better look at the drama. When Barry finally spoke his voice was softer, younger than he appeared to be.

"I was walking behind your stall and I saw it on the table."

Maggie slid the wallet into the pocket of her coat and fixed her eyes on Barry. "So you just decided to steal from me?"

A long pause followed.

"I guess so," he said slowly. "Yes."

Finn cleared her throat beside him.

"I mean…yes, ma'am."

Barry paused. When he finally lifted his head to look at Maggie, Aisling saw the tears shimmering in his eyes.

"I'm sorry, Mrs. Hargrove. It won't happen again."

Finn let him go and stepped back. Maggie leaned into Barry and squeezed his shoulder softly, lowering her voice. "I've known your family my whole life. I know you can do better than this, son."

Barry nodded as a tear slipped down his face. Finn quietly stepped between Barry and the staring crowd as Maggie caught it with her thumb and whispered into the space between them.

"You *are* better than this."

Barry nodded. "Yes, ma'am."

She squeezed his shoulder again before he walked away and the other stall owners went back to what they'd been doing before. Barry's father stepped over into Maggie's stall and held out his hand to Finn.

"Thank you for what you did just there." He looked to be not much older than they were, but his face was creased with lines, and streaks of dirt crisscrossed his arms from his produce. He hesitated, then met Finn's eyes. "If you don't have children, you should."

Finn smiled. "Thank you, sir."

A young woman with a toddler on her hip stepped into his stall, and Herschel turned back to help her. Maggie pushed a bag of homemade chocolate cookies into Finn's hand and squeezed it. "Thank you, Finn." She shook her head and glanced from her to Aisling. "I just cashed my pension check on the way to the market. I don't know what I would have done if I'd lost it."

"I was happy to help," Finn said. "He actually seems like a good kid."

Maggie glanced toward a group of teenage boys hanging out by the train station down from the square and shook her head. "Teenagers are always a bit of trouble, but ours have been getting worse in the last few years. They're just always at loose ends these days. It doesn't surprise me they get themselves into trouble. There's nothing else to keep them occupied."

"What is there for them to do around here?" Aisling's voice was thoughtful as she glanced around the square.

"Nothing really, not since the businesses on the square started shutting down. Most of them used to have after-school jobs at the laundry service or the greengrocers, but the jobs disappeared when the shops closed down."

As she looked toward the empty storefronts lining the square,

Aisling realized that over half the businesses were closed, the windows papered over and dark, the signs tattered by the weather, torn awnings fluttering in the wind.

"Barry's a good boy." Maggie took Aisling's empty cup and refilled it, adding a cube of sugar and a splash of milk before she handed it back. "His mother passed away last year, God rest her soul, and since then Herschel's been doing his best to try to raise the four boys right, but it's no easy task."

"I can't imagine." Aisling glanced back at Herschel, who was sacking a handful of sweet potatoes for another customer. "How old are they?"

"The youngest is five, and Barry just turned thirteen. Herschel and his wife got married right out of school; he's only thirty-four."

"That's got to be tough," Finn said, glancing toward his stall. "He's got his hands full."

"We're all doing the best we can to help him, but it wouldn't hurt if the market stalls were as busy as they used to be." She paused and brightened, pushing a hairpin that seemed to appear in her hand out of nowhere into the bun at the top of her head. "But I don't mean to spoil your morning with all of that village doom and gloom. Are you here on your holidays?"

"Not really."

"Kind of."

Aisling and Finn looked at each other and tried again.

"Yes."

"Um...no."

Maggie laughed and said she'd just get the rest of the story the next time they stopped in. It took a while to get back to the pub, mostly because Aisling was determined to figure out what kind of bread was hidden in the wrapper and kept stopping to sniff it and peel back a corner of paper. Sunlight was streaming into the windows and dust hovered in the air as they stepped in and locked the door behind them. Aisling set her book and loaf of bread at the end of the bar and looked back at Finn. The air held an empty chill in the silence around them.

"I guess we should talk about how we're actually going to get this place up and running. Or," she said, looking around her at the threadbare upholstery and dated light fixtures, "if that's even possible. In any case, we need to call Mr. Clydd and let him know we're going to try." She paused, glancing toward the kitchen. "I just think that doing food is going to be too much. That's a whole different set of staff."

"I think we've got to do some food." Finn stretched her arms and interlocked her fingers behind her head. "If not, they'll have one drink and leave when they get hungry. If they can order food here, even just bar snacks, they'll stay all night and keep ordering drinks. And if we do actual food, from what Greystone said, we'll have entire families here two or three nights a week. That's where we're going to turn a profit."

Aisling paused, rubbing her temples. "I know, but it just seems huge. I don't know if I can deal with opening what's basically a restaurant on top of everything else."

Finn nodded, her eyes settling on the piles of paperwork Greystone had left for them on the bar. "Let's just focus on what we need to do to get that liquor license in place. That's the first thing we have to do. We can't open at all without that."

By the time they'd called Mr. Clydd, placed an ad for a bar staff in the local newspaper, figured out which supplier was which, and made a careful list of the furniture they wanted to replace for the opening, daylight was settling into dusk outside the windows.

"Well," Aisling said as she swiped the heel of her hand across the tired lines at the corners of her eyes, "that went by quickly."

Finn smiled, raking her hand through her hair. "Time flies when a dusty pub gets dropped in your lap."

Aisling looked over at her and picked up her bag. "When I went out to get us coffee this afternoon, I picked up some stuff for dinner on the way back and dropped it at the cottage. Hungry?"

"Actually," Finn said, walking to the door and holding it open against a sudden gust of cold wind, "I'm literally starving. Feed me and I think you'll find I'll do whatever you want."

Aisling stepped through the door and raised an eyebrow as Finn locked the door behind them and dropped the keys in her pocket with a clink. "Oh really?"

"Why the look?" Finn shot her a smile and fell into step with

Aisling as they walked by the park on the way back to the cottage. "I think you'll find I have skills the average jock does not."

A rugby ball flew suddenly out of nowhere and narrowly missed Finn's head, but as Aisling turned to look it hit her square on the cheek, and she doubled over instantly in pain. A scruffy-looking boy in tracksuit bottoms and a white puffer jacket immediately ran over and hesitantly picked up the ball.

"Um," he said, looking back at his buddies staring at them from the small rugby pitch at the end of the grassy park. "Are you okay?"

He looked cautiously at Aisling, who was starting to stand up again, brushing off Finn's attempt to steady her.

"I'm fine," she said. "Those balls are a lot to control. I used to play."

He let out an audible sigh of relief. "Are you sure?"

"I'm okay," Aisling said, smiling at him despite the swelling Finn could see already gathering in her cheek. "Or I will be in in a few minutes. Not your fault."

That was rewarded with a quick smile and a wave as he ran off toward his friends on the rugby pitch. Finn took the bag off Aisling's shoulder and tucked her loaf of bread under her arm.

"That was sweet of you to go easy on him," she said, dipping her head to get a closer look at the deep red mark under Aisling's eye. "But I'm a boxer, so you can stop pretending that didn't hurt like fuck."

"Maybe a bit," Aisling said as they rounded the corner of the church on the gravel road to the cottage. "But it was an accident. Those rugby balls are wonky. He couldn't have done that on purpose if he tried."

Finn insisted she sit down with some ice once they got into the kitchen, then opened the grocery bag Aisling had left on the counter earlier in the day. She pulled out a long orange box and held it up. "What the hell is a Jaffa Cake?"

"You've never had a Jaffa Cake?" She held her hands up and caught the box easily when Finn tossed it in her direction. "I think if I didn't have the occasional one of those, I might actually go mad."

Finn returned to the bag and found pasta, a can of diced tomato, a purple onion, some fresh basil and oregano leaves, and ground beef in the bottom.

"I was going to do a little Bolognese sauce for the pasta." Aisling put the Jaffa box on the table and started toward the counter.

"I think you'll find you're not going to do anything but sit your butt in that chair," Finn said without a hint of a smile as she nodded toward the abandoned bag of ice on the breakfast table. "I'm making dinner."

Aisling hesitated before she sat back down and watched as Finn chopped the onion and got it simmering with the tomatoes in a cast iron pot on the stove. When it started to bubble, Finn tossed in the torn oregano and some spices she found in the cupboard over the stove.

"That actually smells amazing." Aisling leaned back in the chair and let her hair fall out of the French twist it'd been wound up in all day. "I forgot. You were a caterer, right?"

Finn nodded as she glanced back in her direction. Another button on Aisling's cardigan had unbuttoned itself when she'd leaned back, revealing the gentle curve of her breast and just a hint of sheer nude lace.

"Yeah." Finn shook her head and made herself turn back to the sauce. "Somehow I managed to put together one of the top three catering companies in Brooklyn. I still don't know how I pulled that off." She tasted the sauce with a spoon and reached into the salt cellar on the counter, sprinkling a bit of sea salt into the pot. "I miss it occasionally. I'm actually looking forward to putting together a menu for the pub, provided I can talk you into it."

"Good luck with that. I'm seriously on the fence about the food in general." Aisling winced as she moved the bag of ice higher on her cheek. "I think I've just had such a hard time with idiot wedding caterers that I don't even want to touch that side of the business."

Finn smiled, one eyebrow raised. "Yeah, those idiot caterers can be a nightmare." She shot her a wink and searched through one of the top drawers for a corkscrew.

"God, I'm sorry." Aisling's cheeks flushed a deep pink as she spoke. "Let's blame that one on the blow to the head."

She put down the ice and found a spoon, then stood behind Finn to taste the sauce, leaning close enough to lightly brush her breasts against her back. Finn's breath caught.

"Delicious," Aisling said, dropping the spoon into the white ceramic sink on her way out the door. "I guess you do have some skills."

Finn watched Aisling walk down the hall and waited until she heard the sound of water filling the tub, then turned back to the pasta, fine-tuning the seasoning and garnishing it with torn basil leaves. By the time Aisling returned to the kitchen with wet hair and clean clothes, Finn had dinner dished up and steaming in wide glazed bowls on the table.

"Wow," Aisling said, looking at her plate with something like respect. "I'm impressed. This actually smells amazing."

"You sound surprised." Finn winked at her as she picked up her fork and twirled the pasta at the edge of her bowl. "Are you saying I don't look like I can cook?"

Aisling smiled, her eyes following the lines of Finn's shoulders and arms for a moment before she spoke. "I'm saying you look like a boxer."

"Yeah." Finn smiled. "I'll give you that."

Aisling savored her first bite with her eyes closed, then looked back to Finn. "So how did you get into boxing, anyway? Did you get tossed out of finishing school or something?"

Finn smiled and ran her hand through her hair, standing it all on end. "How did you guess?"

She got up and cut the foil on the bottle of cabernet they'd brought home from the bar. She uncorked it and poured two glasses, handing one to Aisling as she sat back down at the table.

"I don't know, really. I've always been athletic, but I never really fit in on the girls' teams in school and they wouldn't let me play on the boys' teams." Finn took a bite of her pasta and went on. "So one day I was coming home from school and saw a poster for a boxing match that Saturday night."

"Did you go?"

"Are you kidding?" Finn smiled at the memory. "Hell, yeah. I said I was going to the movies, took the train to Queens, and snuck in the back door."

Aisling took a sip of her wine. "So what was that like?"

Finn was quiet for a moment, pushing her pasta around in her bowl before she laid down her fork and looked up. "Honestly, I was in love from the first punch. I went to the boxing gym in Brooklyn the next day and begged them to teach me."

"Did they care that you were a girl?"

"Nah. Not really." Finn picked their bowls up and headed toward the sink, looking back over her shoulder at Aisling. "Women's boxing was just starting to be a thing. I started training, won a few fights, and went semipro after four years."

"So why did you stop?"

"I got hurt pretty bad in a fight and my equilibrium was never the same." Finn handed their glasses to Aisling and nodded her toward the living room. "And if you can't balance, you can't box."

Finn made quick work of the dishes, then sank down on the couch beside Aisling. She took the wineglass Aisling handed her, then put it back down on the coffee table and headed for the door.

"Where did you find that wood you started the fire with last night?" Finn opened the lock and paused, cold wind creeping around the edge of the door. "Around the side of the cottage?"

Aisling nodded hesitantly and Finn stepped out, closing the door behind her. Once outside, she held up her phone to illuminate one side of the cottage and then the other, but either there was no wood left or the wind had managed to push it over the edge of the cliffs to the sea.

"I don't see anything at all out there," Finn said as she came back, shoving the door closed against the cold wind and shrugging off her jacket. "Not even scraps."

"I must have gotten all of it last night." Aisling cleared her throat and fixed her eyes on the hearth. "But there might be some left in that copper wood bucket."

Finn found just enough wood there to start the fire, and soon the room was bathed in light, the sounds of crackling sap replacing words in the warming air. Aisling retrieved the bottle of wine and refilled their glasses.

Finn settled back into the sofa beside her and arched an eyebrow, taking her glass from Aisling when she held it out to her. "Are you trying to get me drunk?"

"Trust me, Finn," Aisling sank back into the pillows in the corner of the couch and tucked a stray wave of hair behind one ear, "if I wanted something from you, I wouldn't need to get you drunk to get it."

Finn threw her head back and laughed. "Okay, then. At least we know where we stand." She locked her dark eyes onto Aisling's and waited a few long seconds before she went on. "Or at least you seem to think you know."

"Actually…" Aisling looked up again and put down her wineglass. Her words were slow, as if they were finding each other and forming a thought in the air between them. "That gives me an idea."

Finn rolled up the sleeves of her navy plaid flannel shirt and waited. Firelight flickered against the black windowpanes as Aisling turned toward her on the couch.

"Perhaps we should make a little bet."

Finn swirled the wine in her glass. "Now, this is starting to get interesting. What are the terms?"

"Look, I know you want to serve food in the pub right away, and I know it's a disaster waiting to happen." She reached over and took Finn's wineglass out of her hand, took a sip, and handed it back. "First one to kiss the other loses. If you kiss me first, we do drinks only and scrap the food idea. If I kiss you first, which won't happen…" She paused, her gaze dropping to Finn's mouth. "Then I guess we'll be hiring some kitchen help."

Finn smiled and leaned back into the cushions, holding her eyes. "So what makes you think I want to kiss you at all?"

"Nothing," Aisling said as she turned her glance toward the fire. "But if you don't yet, you will."

Finn studied Aisling's profile as she ran her hand through her hair. "Let's see if you can back that up." She paused, her eyes dropping to the delicate slope of Aisling's shoulder. "You've got yourself a deal."

CHAPTER SEVEN

One morning a week later, Ms. Greystone was waiting for them in the pub when they arrived, scarf still primly tucked into her somewhat masculine herringbone overcoat, standing behind the bar.

Aisling shrugged off her own jacket and hung it on the row of hooks beside the door. "I'm sorry," she said, her voice a little too even. "Did we have an appointment?"

"No," Greystone said, glancing over at the dented retro coffeepot that hadn't been there before as it started to gurgle loudly on the counter. The scent of freshly ground Colombian beans and fresh percolating coffee warmed the air as Greystone sniffed and went on. "But you two need to settle on an opening date, so I came to get it."

"Like, when we're opening the pub officially?" Finn looked around at the mostly empty main room. After they'd decided which pieces to replace—which turned out to be almost everything not actually built into the walls—they'd donated the rest to a Cardiff charity. "We don't even have the furniture in yet. It's ordered, of course, and should be in tomorrow, but there's just so much to do before then—"

"So Friday is the opening date." Greystone pulled a creased notepad out of her pocket and jotted down a note with a glossy black fountain pen. "That's December thirteenth. Lovely."

She dropped the pad back into her coat pocket and stepped back behind the bar to pour the coffee into a cup with a pointed glance at Finn. The Irish whiskey had already been set out beside the coffeepot, so Finn took the hint, dropped her bag behind the counter, and poured a generous measure of Jameson into the cup.

"There's no way we can open that quickly," Aisling said with a panicked glance at the empty space. "We don't even have the liquor order in."

"Well, then I'd recommend you get that situation sorted before Friday. They can usually deliver in a day, but your temporary license expires this weekend, which I'm sure you remember." Greystone sipped her coffee and warmed her hands around the mug. "Keep in mind the liquor board are some right bastards, and they're based in Cardiff, so they don't give a toss whether you can open on time or not."

Finn coughed to hide her smile at Greystone's colorful choice of language, which was not successful and earned her a stern glance before Aisling started talking, the pitch of her voice spiked with tension.

"That's just not possible." Aisling slid onto one of the barstools and locked her eyes onto Greystone's. "We haven't even decided if we're offering food yet."

"Ms. Moss." The older woman took a long sip of her coffee and held it for a warm-up from the pot. Finn shot Aisling a reassuring smile and filled it to the rim, replacing the old-fashioned aluminum pot back onto its base. "I can tell by the look of you that you'll want things to be perfect before you even consider opening this place, but trust me on this, the sooner you open, the sooner you can turn a profit and give this…" She paused, searching for the word. "Little experiment a fair chance to succeed."

Then her face softened unexpectedly as she met Aisling's eyes, and the cup in her hand settled onto the counter with a soft tap.

"I promised your grandmother Joan that I'd do my best to help you both make a success of this place, and that's what I'm going to do." She winked at Finn as she touched up her coffee with a long splash of the whiskey Finn had set within her reach. "Even if you're determined to do the opposite."

"So what's your advice, then?" Frustration scraped through Aisling's voice. "Open up completely unprepared and have the place go tits up in two days?"

Finn shook her head and replaced the bottle behind the bar, then leaned back against the counter and waited. She knew better than to try to toss her two cents in when two spirited women were sparring, even if it was clear already who'd come out on top.

Greystone didn't miss a beat. "I'll get the word out about Friday, but you might want to get to the butcher and get some paper to cover these windows. People are already starting to talk, and as soon as they hear the pub will be reopening, you'll have some looky-loos." She swilled the last of her coffee and left the cup on the bar. "I left you a list of things on the bar you'll need to have in place before you open the doors."

Aisling looked at Finn, who just smiled and shook her head.

"And maybe," Greystone picked up her bag and headed toward the door with a pointed glance at Aisling as she buttoned her wool coat tightly to the top, "a little chaos would do you good."

The door clicked shut behind her and she was gone. Aisling's face was flaming as she unwound the scarf from her neck and picked up the list Greystone had left on the end of the bar.

"That woman," Aisling said, every word sharp and staccato, "is getting right on my tits."

"On your what?" Finn put down the coffee she'd just poured herself as laughter flashed across her face, wiping her eyes with the heel of her hand when she could speak again. "I can't wait to hear what that means, because I don't think it's remotely safe to take that literally."

Aisling looked up, distracted by the note in her hand. "It's just a Newcastle saying. It means she's on my nerves."

Finn shook her head, still smiling. "So what does the note say?"

"It says," Aisling shook her head slowly and read it aloud, "'Order crisps and nuts. Learn how to change a barrel. Do something with the patio out back. Open the damn doors.'"

Finn smiled. "I'm assuming she's talking about a beer barrel. That might be easier if we had some actual beer."

"I know we ordered it, but when are the deliveries from the breweries supposed to be here?" Finn watched Aisling's words turn into frost in the air as she walked over to the wall, dialing up the central heat system.

"I had them all scheduled this afternoon at four to simplify the process." Finn handed Aisling her coat, shrugging her own over her shoulders in the process. "So in the meantime, let's take a little tour of the shit we have to do."

Finn opened the back door for Aisling, and they walked out into the garden. A brick patio area surrounded by green-tinged brick walls made up most of it, with weathered wooden chairs scattered haphazardly about. A rickety roof was somewhat attached to the west wall of the pub, the slate tiles dripping with velvety moss. Under the roof was a tall statue of two women, naked, one holding the other's face in her hands.

"This is gorgeous," Aisling said, running her hand over the smooth ivory marble. Finn looked at her for a long moment, then pulled out her phone and snapped a picture. She slowly lowered the phone and walked over to where Aisling was standing.

"Look, the artist signed it with his initials. I can barely make it out, but it's H.G., I think." She paused and looked up at Finn. "Why did you take a picture?"

"I'll let you figure that out," Finn said, her voice suddenly soft as she handed Aisling the phone. "Tell me what you see."

Seagulls sailed overhead in a white V at that moment and the wind picked up, blowing leaves across the cracked brick floor. Aisling looked at the picture, shaking her head. "I don't see anything. What am I supposed to be looking at?"

Finn reached out and gently touched the honey-colored mole at the top of Aisling's left cheek with her thumb. She held her eyes as she pulled away, brushing Aisling's bottom lip before Aisling glanced back at the phone.

She studied it for a second, then reached up and touched an identical mark on the face of one of the two marble women beside them. She was quiet then, and when she finally looked back at Finn, her eyes were shining with emotion.

"She looks like me."

"She looks exactly like you," Finn said, reaching out and catching a tear on her cheek. "Her face, that wild hair...everything."

Finn leaned closer and pointed at the very top of the photo, just under the roof. "What's that?"

"What?" Aisling leaned closer. "I don't see anything."

"Right here. It looks like a lens flare, but there's two of them."

Finn watched as Aisling slowly raised her head and smiled, staring up at the underside of the patio roof. Finn followed her eyes and waited until Aisling looked back to her, the same soft smile still on her face.

"I guess it's a mystery." Finn shook her head and slid her phone back into her pocket. "Let's go see if we can figure out how to hook up the barrels in the cellar." She smiled. "Without the barrels."

❖

By the time they'd figured out that particular task was impossible, it was late afternoon.

Aisling brushed a stray wave of hair off her forehead and looked up the cellar stairs toward the door. "Isn't the brewery supposed to deliver at four?"

"Shit. I forgot about that," Finn said, starting up the stairs behind her. When they got back up to the bar, Aisling reached for a splayed pile of papers that had been pushed under the door. She picked them up, glanced at the first two pages, and held them out to Finn.

"It's the bill from the brewery, but I didn't even hear them up here." She leaned back over the bar and looked to both ends. "And I don't see any beer. Not that I'd even know what I'm looking for."

A loud knock on the door made her jump, and she looked to Finn with a raised eyebrow before she opened it. A stocky man in all white stood in the doorway, with a bloodstained apron down to his knees and a tweed flat cap perched atop his shiny bald head.

"Can I help you?"

"No, but I might be able to help you." The man stepped back from the door and gestured down the sidewalk. "Looks like you got some deliveries. And considering what it is, I give it about five minutes before the local hoodlums start carrying it off."

Aisling peered out the door. Twelve wooden barrels stamped with various logos lined the edge of the road, including one that had already tipped off the curb and was rolling at a good clip down the street. A slick blue Audi rounded the corner of the square just then, barely managing to swerve around the barrel as Finn and the man in the bloody apron took off to chase it down. Finn managed to gain enough ground to jump in front of it and slowed the roll, eventually bringing it to a stop before they started pushing the barrel in the opposite direction and back up to the pub doors.

"Thanks so much for your help," Finn said, holding out her hand to him after they'd managed to tip it back up on its end on the sidewalk. "I'm Finn Morgan, by the way, and this is Aisling Moss."

"Jack Evan. I own the butcher shop across the square." He shook Finn's hand and looked over his shoulder to the string of barrels lined up on the curb. "You buying the pub?"

"Something like that," Finn said with a glance in Aisling's

direction. "Hey, you wouldn't know how to hook these things up, would you?"

Jack looked at the closest barrel and shook his head. "If you need a pig slaughtered, I'm your guy. I don't know nothing about the pub business, though." He paused, then pulled his phone out of his chest pocket. "But I might know someone who does. My son worked at a hotel bar down the coast last summer. I bet he'd know a thing or two."

Jack turned to make the call and Aisling closed her eyes, rubbing her temples with the pads of her fingers.

Finn put her arm around her shoulders and pulled Aisling into her. "What are you thinking?"

"That there might not be enough beer in those barrels to get me through three hundred and sixty-five days of this."

Two hours later, all twelve barrels were safely in the cellar and hooked up, and Jack had even sent his son, Michael, back over to the shop for butcher paper to cover the windows. They both stayed to help put it up and Finn tried to pay them after, but they refused, only accepting a quick pint before they left.

The silence was suddenly heavy as Finn started a fire in the fireplace at the west end of the room using the pine logs and newspapers stacked on the hearth. She blew out the match, tossing it onto the grate as the flames caught and flared.

"How is it so cold in here with a fire, and the heat turned up?" Aisling asked, pulling the sleeves of her white button-down shirt over her hands. She'd taken the pins out of her hair, and it fell around her shoulders as if tossed by the wind in a still room. She rubbed her tired eyes with her fingertips and peered over at Finn.

"The fire will take the chill out of the air in a few minutes," Finn said, edging behind the bar. "Although I could definitely have packed more sweaters. When do you think the stuff we asked people from home to send will get here?"

"Shouldn't be more than a couple more months." Aisling paused, winking when she saw the flash of panic across Finn's face. "Kidding." She laughed, pulling herself up to sit on the bar as she glanced down at the calendar on her phone. "Really, they should be here any day. What did you ask your family to send you?"

Finn picked up six shot glasses in one hand and lined them up end to end on the bar. "My roommate, actually. I just had her send some warmer stuff and my boxing gear. I miss working out."

Finn turned around for a bottle of Irish whiskey and caught Aisling's eyes in the mirror.

Aisling pulled her hair over her shoulder and arched an eyebrow. "You're one of those butches that thinks they can flex and every femme will swoon, right?"

"Nah." Finn turned around and stepped up to where Aisling was sitting on the bar. She stood, hands braced on the mahogany on either side of Aisling's thighs, and held her eyes. "First of all, I don't 'flex.' Secondly, femmes don't often swoon, they're more interesting than that." She paused, the start of a smile at the corner of her mouth. "But I'm not blind."

Aisling rolled her eyes and leaned back on her hands. "Sorry, Boxer Boi. I don't care how ripped you are, you're not my type."

Finn smiled, then stepped back and poured Jameson into one of the glasses and topped it with a slow float of Baileys.

"What's that?"

"It's an Irish car bomb without the Guinness." She nudged the jigger toward Aisling. "Drink it."

"Why?"

"Because I'm going to try the three shots you make, too." She slid three of the glasses over to Aisling. "In a pub this small we have to watch how many bottles we have behind the bar, so we need to decide on a few shooters we want to highlight and stock just what we need for those."

Aisling tipped her glass and took the shot without a flinch, then scanned the bottles behind the bar as she set the glass back down.

"Hand me the Don Julio."

Finn turned to the bottles, her eyes scanning the labels. "The what?"

"The tequila. And while you're at it, hand me the Kahlúa."

Finn smiled and handed it over. "You don't strike me as a tequila girl."

"Well," Aisling said, layering the liquors smoothly into the shot glass and handing it to Finn, "then you haven't been paying attention." She smiled. "It's called a Brave Bull, but I'm making an executive decision and switching that to Boxer Boi."

Finn looked directly at Aisling as she tipped back the shot and set the glass back on the bar, eyes never leaving hers. They held the gaze for a moment until Aisling glanced over her shoulder at the hearth in the corner.

"Don't you have a fire to tend?"

"Damn, girl," Finn said, shaking her head and laughing as she headed for the fire. "You're hard work."

"Trust me, Finn," Aisling leaned back on her hands, looking over at Finn from her perch on the bar, "if I ever do decide to work you, you'll figure out pretty quick that this is nothing."

Finn smiled, tossing another split log on the coals and blowing on it until it flared and lit up the underside. Finn stirred the coals and waited until the flames had taken hold, then placed the poker back in the iron rack.

"Where did you get the wood for that, anyway?"

Finn stood, brushing the soot off her hands as she walked back behind the bar. "I ordered a load of firewood for the pub and another one for the house. They were delivered yesterday." She pulled three more bottles off the shelf and lined them up on the bar. "Ready for number two?"

Aisling smiled. "Hit me."

Finn poured and handed it to her. Aisling downed it with ease and clinked the glass back onto the bar with no change of expression.

"What do you think?" Finn said, setting her glass in the sink. "It's called the Three Wise Men. Johnnie Walker, Jim Beam, and Jack Daniel's."

Aisling slid the bottles down the bar with the tequila. "Not bad. I vote to keep that one and the Boxer Boi." She scanned the bottles on the shelf behind the bar. "Did we get the fresh lemons with the delivery yesterday?"

Finn opened the small fridge under the bar and held one up.

"Great. I'll need that and sugar."

"Jesus. I knew there'd be a girly shot that tastes like air freshener." Finn smiled at her as she sliced the lemon and poured a thin layer of sugar in a saucer. "This is a lemon drop, right?"

"Yep." Aisling pushed up her sleeves, a warm, deep flush moving from her neck to her cheeks. "Get the bachelorettes going and they'll drop a fortune on these."

Finn mixed Absolut Citron, fresh lemon juice, and sugar in a shaker, then strained it into a shot glass and downed it.

"You have sugar on your lips, genius." Aisling smiled, her eyes on Finn's mouth. "There's an art to these, and clearly that is not it."

Aisling leaned forward slowly and laid her hand on the base of Finn's neck, her tongue just touching the first grain of sugar on Finn's bottom lip.

When Finn closed her eyes, Aisling sat up, swiping her finger lightly across Finn's mouth.

She winked and licked the sugar off her finger. "What? You didn't think winning the bet was going to be that easy, did you?"

Finn shook her head and stepped back, rubbing the back of her neck with her hand. "Well played." She picked up an empty shot glass and rolled it smoothly through her fingers like a pen. "But I'm onto you now."

"Is that my last shot?"

"Something like that," Finn said. "Close your eyes."

"And why should I trust you?"

Finn turned back to the bottles and smiled back at Aisling in the mirror. "You probably shouldn't."

She watched from her perch on the counter as Finn poured a shot of Baileys. The fire crackled into the silent darkness at the end of the bar, and Aisling's breath caught as Finn edged her body between her knees.

Finn dipped her ring finger into the Baileys and ran it across Aisling's bottom lip, then across the tip of her tongue when Aisling touched it to her finger.

"You're holding your breath," Finn said, her voice slow and smooth as she took her finger away and put it into her own mouth. "Breathe."

Aisling took a deep breath, and as she let it out felt Finn unbutton the first of the delicate white buttons down the front of her shirt. Aisling bit her lip but said nothing.

"I'm listening," Finn whispered as she leaned in until there was only a breath between her words and the delicate skin of Aisling's neck, "for you to tell me to stop."

Aisling took a breath and leaned back on her hands as Finn unbuttoned every remaining button on her shirt, then flicked open the delicate gold bar at the front of her bra. It fell open to her sides and Aisling watched the sheer wash of golden freckles across her chest, like blown gold dust, disappear as Finn slowly poured the Baileys into the hollow of her throat and across her breasts.

Aisling's voice was a low whisper. "Jesus Christ."

She closed her eyes as Finn braced her hands on the bar and leaned in, tongue tracing the outside curve of her breast. She leaned in closer as she worked her way up, her mouth almost touching Aisling's as Aisling felt her nipples tense under the slick of Baileys. She arched her back as Finn pulled one of them into her mouth, achingly slowly, stroking it with her tongue. Her hand slid hard into Finn's hair, wrapping it around her fingers as Finn did the same to the other side, then followed the slope of her neck with the tip of her tongue until she was at Aisling's mouth, a single breath between them. Finn waited a long moment before she stepped back, then tossed her a clean bar towel from the stack under the counter.

Aisling caught the towel in midair and looked at Finn, shaking her head.

"Now it's on, Morgan."

"What?" Finn smiled. "It wasn't before?"

Aisling smiled. "Watch yourself. I might be a little more competitive than you're used to."

"And how would you know what I'm used to?"

Aisling looked her up and down. "Let's just say I can guess that the previous bar was attractive, but low."

Finn laughed, shaking her head as she turned. "Damn. You don't mince words, do you?"

Aisling slid off the table and buttoned her shirt back up as they headed for the door.

"Not usually."

She accepted the coat Finn handed her as she slipped off the bar and looked back to make sure that the fire had died. The hearth was dark except for a poof of fiery sparks that rose suddenly from nowhere and floated up the chimney. Aisling looked toward Finn, but she'd already stepped out the door and was holding it open for her. She watched the last few sparks rise into the chimney from the dark, silent fireplace and shook her head as she felt the door close softly behind her.

❖

The next day was Thursday, and the morning passed in a blur. If the pub was actually opening Friday evening at seven—which was what was printed on the flyers all over the village—they had an endless list of things to get done before they opened the doors. Even Aisling had to admit Greystone was right about the looky-loos; every few minutes someone looked through the loose corners of the butcher paper on the windows in hopes of getting the first look at whatever was going on inside.

Finn installed the new sound system first thing, and the Cardiff charity shop had come by to pick up the few tables and chairs still left in the pub by mid-morning. The new furniture they'd ordered was set to be delivered at 3:00 p.m., the temporary liquor license was in place, packets of crisps were stacked neatly behind the bar per Greystone's instructions, and every inch of the small pub sparkled. Finn had even managed to find some twinkling lights and Christmas decorations in the attic, which gave the seating area a warm, cozy feel. Except for the fact that there were no seats.

"Didn't they say they were coming with the furniture at three?" Aisling plumped the cushions lining the built-in snugs that hugged the walls.

"Yeah, I called and double-checked yesterday," Finn said as she hooked up the last of the twinkle lights that outlined the antique mirror behind the bar and plugged them in. The mercury backing had worn thin in spots over the years, but somehow the lights made it look romantic, as if it were meant to be that way. The tall carved pillars on both sides of the bar's half-moon shape were also warmed with lights, making it look even more inviting.

Aisling placed the last pillow and looked at her watch.

"Maybe we should call again. It's four thirty, and we have the final inspection with the rep from the alcohol council here at five. We have to pass it to be able to serve tomorrow."

Finn pulled her phone from her pocket and dialed as she walked back to the kitchen area with the stepladder she'd borrowed to hang the lights. As soon as she rounded the corner, there was a knock at the doors. Aisling twisted her hair into a bun as she walked toward the front doors, wishing she'd remembered to wear something that looked a bit more professional than the Levi's and cardigan she'd thrown on that morning. With any luck she'd have time to run home and change between the furniture delivery that was finally there and the inspection.

She opened the door, expecting to find trucks being unloaded and the first tables on the sidewalk ready to be brought in, but it was just one severe-looking older man. He was thin, with gray slicked over the top of his head from a deep part and a yellow ring around the inside of his collar.

"Can I help you?"

"I'm Harvey Donogan with the Cardiff Alcohol Board." He leaned in and peered at the bar. "I'm here to do the inspection of the premises to finalize your liquor license."

"Of course," Aisling said, taking his coat as he walked in. "But I hadn't realized you'd be here so soon. I thought our appointment was at five."

"Yes. I see that." He gazed intently at the empty center of the room. "I like to arrive a bit early to get a better idea of the preparedness of the applicants hoping to finalize their applications."

Finn returned from the kitchen, double doors swinging shut behind her, with a pointed glance at Aisling. Aisling introduced her to Mr. Donogan, who merely nodded as he scribbled on his clipboard, then took several pictures of the empty space on his phone before making more notes.

"So," he said when he finally lifted his head. "It says here that the maximum occupancy of this pub is two thirteen. I take it you're expecting all of them to stand?"

A sudden flush washed from Aisling's neck to her face and she took a slow breath before she spoke. "We're expecting our furniture delivery today. Around now, actually."

"That may be delayed a bit," Finn cut in. "I just got off the phone with them and it looks like they have a delivery schedule backup, but it should be resolved quickly."

Donogan looked up from his clipboard. "How quickly?"

"They don't know exactly, but I made sure they knew that we needed it yesterday."

Silence fell as Donogan thumbed through his papers. It was several long minutes before he found the one he needed, signed it with a flourish, and placed it on the bar behind him.

"You received the manual with the list of requirements for your conditional license when you applied, correct?"

"Yes," Aisling said. "It's behind the bar, I'd intended to go through it more carefully, but I just haven't had the chance with—"

"No matter. Unless your furniture is here within the next..." Donogan looked at his watch. "Twenty-four hours, your conditional license terms have been violated. Section thirty-three, article four states that there must be adequate seating for the full capacity of the venue or it's revoked. That's two hundred and thirteen individual seats, and each seat needs to have at least thirty centimeters of table or counter space."

"Revoked?" Finn laced her fingers on the top of her head and stepped back, locking eyes with Aisling as she searched for the words. "That can't happen. The whole village knows we're opening at seven tomorrow night. It's already been advertised."

"Well, there is *some* good news." Donogan smiled, dropping his clipboard back into his briefcase and buttoning his coat to his neck. "You're welcome to apply for a license again in a year."

Finn and Aisling looked at each other in shock as Donogan headed for the door.

"So if we don't get the furniture in time we won't even be able to apply for another license for a full year?" Aisling's spun around to face Donogan, her neck awash in crimson splotches.

He paused, his hand on the door handle. A long sigh filled the silence, along with a brief glance skyward. "If you can get it by noon, call me and I'll consider making an exception."

The door swung open, hitting the wall behind, and he disappeared around the corner.

"What the hell are we going to do?" Aisling said, looking around at the empty room. "Are we supposed to pull a pub full of furniture out of thin air?"

Finn was still staring at the door when she spoke. "You can tell that guy's from the city. He couldn't care less if the village has a pub or not. I feel like I'm back in New York." She shook her head and stepped behind the bar, picking up two shot glasses with one hand and the tequila bottle with the other.

"So what did they say when you spoke to them?" Aisling said, leaning against a barstool. "When did they say they'd have the furniture here?"

Finn filled the glasses and Aisling threw hers back in one go, nodding at the bottle the second she set it back on the bar. Finn smiled and refilled her glass, then clinked it to her own.

"Do you want the optimistic version?" Finn finished her shot and set her glass back down on the bar with a *clink*. "Or the truth?"

Aisling gave her a look and rubbed her temples. "The truth. Hit me."

"They won't have it here for a week. At the earliest."

"You're kidding me."

"Unfortunately, I'm not. They're backed up by a few days already." Finn hopped over the bar and walked over to the door, opening it wide. "And there's this, which I'm guessing won't help them get it here any faster."

Fluffy snowflakes were sifting through the trees in the center of the square, already gathering into soft drifts over the sidewalks and settling onto the black iron railing lining the park.

Aisling stared, her mouth open. "You're shitting me."

Finn laughed, letting the door swing shut as she walked back to the bar. "Such language, young lady." She looked over at Aisling with a wink. "And if I had to guess, I'd say you picked up that particular phrase from me."

There was a long pause as Aisling ran her hand over the top of the bar. When she looked up, tears spilled over onto her cheeks and she just as quickly swiped them away with the back of her hand.

"Hey," Finn said softly. "I was only teasing."

"I know." Aisling shook her head as she accepted the handkerchief Finn pressed into her hand. "It's not that. I guess I'd just started to feel..."

Her voice wavered and Finn pulled her to her chest, wrapping her arms around her, fingers warm around the back of her neck.

"Excited?"

Aisling nodded, softening against Finn's body. "Maybe. I guess the idea's grown on me."

Finn settled her hand on the back of Aisling's head and rested her chin on it. "Yeah. Me too."

Aisling stepped back after a moment and looked up at Finn. "What are we going to do? I won't be able to live with myself if we don't get this right."

Finn took her hand and led her to the door, handing her the coat hanging on the wall. "Let's go. I have an idea."

CHAPTER EIGHT

A few minutes later, they were back in the cottage, Finn digging in a large black duffel bag she'd grabbed out of an open box by the door and slung onto the couch.

"Is that some of the stuff you finally got from home yesterday?"

"How did you guess?" Finn held up a worn pair of boxing gloves. "The most important stuff, actually."

Finn unlaced the gloves and looked out the windows, where the reflection of the fire flickered against the panes. Beyond them, stars crowded the black sky, scattering moonlight that sparkled against the crests of the waves in the sea below. She looked back to Aisling, who was now staring at the gloves.

"What are you planning to do with those?"

"It's not what *I'm* going to do with these." Finn picked up the gloves again and tossed them in Aisling's direction, where they landed in a pile at her feet. "It's what *you're* going to do with them."

"You must be joking." Aisling paused, leaning back as Finn picked them up and motioned for her to extend her left hand.

"No, ma'am, I am not," Finn said, sliding the glove on Aisling's hand, then lacing the wrist as tight as possible before she covered them with wide Velcro straps. "Sometimes the best thing you can do is get out of your own head when you're trying to find a solution to something. And the only way to do that is to shift the focus from your brain to your body."

Aisling smiled and leaned close enough to Finn's ear for her words to hover warm against her neck. "I bet you say that to all the girls."

"Not true." Finn slid the other glove onto her right hand. "I usually tell them to shift the focus to *my* body." She winked. "But this time I actually mean it."

Finn stepped back and smiled at the combination of Aisling's scuffed boxing gloves and delicate sky-blue cashmere hoodie.

"I probably should have had you change before I put those gloves on you," Finn said as she reached back into the bag and pulled out two padded discs with straps on the back.

"Well, it looks like now you're going to have to do it for me." Aisling held her gloves out. "You might want to start with the buttons at the cuffs. If you unbutton all of them, it should give you enough room to slip it over the gloves."

"Jesus," Finn said, stepping closer to unbutton what seemed like a thousand tiny pearl buttons along the underside of each arm. "Why are there so many of these?"

"That was quick," Aisling said. "So you're admitting that you're having trouble getting my clothes off?"

"I can assure you, Ms. Moss," Finn finally slipped the last button out of the loop and carefully lifted the cashmere over Aisling's head and past the oversized gloves, "I'm thirty-four, and that has yet to be a problem for me even once."

Aisling was wearing a white ribbed tank underneath, and her shoulders looked even more delicate in comparison to the oversized gloves. Her skin was the palest ivory, scattered with a wash of pale freckles, the perfect contrast to the fiery waves of copper hair threatening to slip out of the scattered bun on top of her head.

"Okay, Boxer Boi," she said, blowing a stray curl out of her face. "You have me. Now what are you going to do with me?"

Finn smiled and shook her head as she slipped both hands into the straps at the back of what looked like circular baseball mitts, covered in soft black leather. *Morgan* was embroidered in the center of each in gold stitching.

"What's that?"

"These," Finn said, holding them at shoulder height between herself and Aisling, "are called punch mitts. And you're going to hit them."

Before the last word was out of Finn's mouth, Aisling had punched the mitt square in the middle with enough force to make Finn take a step back. Finn regrouped and braced her feet, taking every punch she threw at her until Aisling's face was flaming red and there was a fine mist of sweat across her shoulders and chest. Finn watched for signs that she was getting tired, but Aisling kept throwing punches past the tears that had started to flow down her cheeks.

"You don't have to keep going, Aisling." Finn's voice was soft, but she kept her hands up. "It's okay to stop."

Aisling swiped at her cheek with her arm and kept punching until her shoulders started to shake. Finn finally pulled her into her arms, slipping out of the mitts she was wearing, and held her as Aisling's shoulders dropped and shook with sobs. The fire sank into the coals with a sigh behind them as she held her, and a blur of snow brushed the windows as the wind picked up outside the cottage. After a moment Finn picked Aisling up, wrapping Aisling's legs around her waist, and sank back into the couch with her, pulling Aisling's head gently into her shoulder.

Aisling's arms were still trembling, and Finn wrapped her hands around them and rubbed them with her thumbs in a steady rhythm until they relaxed. When Aisling finally lifted her head from her shoulder, Finn unlaced Aisling's gloves and pulled a clean handkerchief out of her pocket.

Aisling smiled through her tears. "Do you always have one of these?"

"In my experience, femmes cry." Finn smiled. "So, yes."

Aisling pressed the handkerchief to her eyes for a long moment before she looked up.

Finn's eyes were soft, her hands warm and steady against Aisling's back. "You miss her, don't you?"

A tear slipped down Aisling's cheek and she nodded. "I don't know why I'm suddenly crying about it now." She looked at the ceiling, blinking back tears. "But I do miss her. Every day."

"Yeah, I get it," Finn said. "Me too."

"What are we going to do, Finn?" Aisling sat back and met her eyes. "For whatever reason, that pub was hugely important to them and they trusted us with it. We can't let them down."

Finn nodded, then stood and put her gently back down on the couch.

"Stay here, I'll be right back." Aisling nodded distractedly as Finn walked down the hall. When she returned a minute or so later, Aisling was still in the same position, staring into the fire.

"I ran you a bath. In the tub that only you fit into," Finn said, smiling and offering Aisling her hand. "Go get in. I'll make dinner."

❖

Aisling padded into the kitchen half an hour later wearing a white tank and black silk pajama pants she'd found in her box from home. Finn nodded her toward the table and sliced a thick grilled cheese sandwich into halves for each plate, then slid a steaming bowl of tomato basil soup beside it just as there was a knock at the door. Aisling reached for Finn's black leather jacket on the back of her chair just in case, but stayed in the kitchen when Finn went to answer it. She considered going to the door after a few minutes had passed, but Finn rounded the corner just as she was getting up. Whoever it was, Finn now had a face like thunder as she slid back into her chair.

"Who was it?"

"Remember the butcher who came by to let us know our barrels were rolling down the street? Jack Evan?"

Aisling nodded, melted cheese stringing from the sandwich to her mouth. She caught it with her finger and looked back at Finn.

"His wife works at city hall in Cardiff, and evidently Donogan stopped by her office before he left for the day and filed our license as 'canceled.'"

"What?" Aisling slowly put down her sandwich and stared at Finn. "He said we had until noon tomorrow to get that furniture." She shook her head in disbelief. "He didn't even wait until tomorrow morning."

"I guess he assumed we couldn't get it done and decided to file it early." Finn picked up her spoon, then put it back down on the table and raked a hand through her hair, staring out the window as she spoke. "At least Donogan had the courtesy to come tell us before we busted our asses trying to get it here tomorrow. Not that it would have worked anyway."

"What?" Aisling said, pushing her plate away and leaning back in the chair to look at Finn. "Why not?"

"I called again while you were in the bath and got someone different on the phone. Evidently, the 'transportation issue' they're experiencing is not an issue of getting the furniture to us, it's that it hasn't yet been delivered to them."

"It's not even there yet?"

"Nope," Finn said, her mouth set into tense lines. "Every bit of it is still at the fucking factory."

"Bloody hell." Aisling went to the cabinet and returned with a bottle of Jameson and two glasses, pouring three fingers of whiskey into each. "So even if we could have found a way to rent a truck and get all the tables and chairs from Cardiff to Cwylldbridge, it wouldn't have done us any good because they neglected to tell us that little fact."

"Exactly." Finn clinked her glass to Aisling's and sank back in her chair. She downed the whiskey in one shot and set her glass back on the table with a *thunk*. "Which means we're officially fucked."

The next morning, Finn and Aisling left the house just after the sun rose, the morning air hovering around their faces in a frozen fog as they walked to the pub. Sunlight glittered across a fresh inch of snow and had loosened the icicles just enough for two of them to lose their grip on the church eaves and fall like crystal daggers to the ground, shattering to shards and scattering across the stone path. Finn took a deep breath of the clean, icy air, wondering why New York never smelled this way after a first snow.

"So how's that couch in the living room working out for you?" Aisling glanced at Finn and kicked a twig out of the path. "Isn't that thing about three inches shorter than you?"

"Thanks for pointing that out." Finn looked over at her and smiled for the first time that morning. "But it could have been a room at the Four Seasons and I still would've been up all night."

Aisling slowed, putting her hand on Finn's arm and pointing into the distance toward the square. "What's going on over there? I know everyone's excited about opening tonight, not that that'll do them much good now, but it's only half six in the morning."

Finn followed her gaze to the pub doors, where the entire street and sidewalk was crowded with people milling around and chatting, the area blocked off at either end by ropes and two of the blue-and-white-striped market stalls. The scent of fresh coffee warmed the air, and Maggie Hargrove was scurrying about in one of the stalls, handing out coffee, scones, and what looked like thick slices of cinnamon bread wrapped in brown paper. The area around her stall looked like a pop-up café, with people sitting around tables in small groups, laughing as they talked, warming their hands around their steaming cups of coffee and tea. Children chased each other in the street, and there was even a group of sullen teenagers holding up the park fence. In the second stall at the other end of the street, another lanky teenager in a camouflage jacket and knit cap stood with a clipboard in his hand, speaking to people in a haphazard line, with several more walking toward the square from the park.

"This is our street, right?" Finn checked the green-and-white metal street sign attached to the iron park fence. "I know we've been wrapped up in trying to get this place open, but I don't remember seeing any flyers about a street fair or whatever this is."

They both caught sight of Jack striding toward them at the same time in a work jacket and leather gloves. Maggie called to him as he passed her stall and handed him two paper cups with a nod toward Aisling and Finn. Everyone seemed to notice at the same moment that they'd arrived, and swiveled to look in their direction, steam still rising from the cups warming their hands.

"Good morning, Jack." Finn held out her hand and Jack shook it, squeezing it in both of his for just a moment. "Whatever's going on out here looks way more fun than what we had in store. Room for two more?"

Jack smiled, sliding his leather gloves back on and looking back at the crowd. "Actually, we were hoping you had room for us."

Finn glanced at Aisling, but the look on her face told her that Aisling knew even less than she did.

"I hope I haven't overstepped," Jack said, looking behind him again with an excited smile. "But when my wife told me about what happened yesterday with Donogan, I started thinking. So over some scotch at the shop last night, a few of us put our heads together and..."

An older woman in a smart camel wool coat belted at her waist walked up just as he was talking and smiled, slipping her arm through Jack's.

"Well, that's where it started to get dangerous, but thankfully I was there to supervise," she said, giving his arm a squeeze.

Jack smiled. "Finn, Aisling, this is my wife, Marjorie. She works in Cardiff at city hall."

"It's great to meet you," Aisling said with a warm smile. "And thanks for sending Jack last night to give us the heads-up about the liquor license being revoked. It wasn't the best news, but I guess we'd rather know now than later."

"Actually," Marjorie said, looking up at her husband, "it hasn't actually been revoked yet. It landed on my desk late yesterday but I still haven't done anything with it."

"Wait," Finn said slowly, sudden possibility forming slowly in her mind. "So we might still have time to fix this?"

"It might as well be revoked, though, right?" Aisling's voice was soft, and she squeezed Finn's arm as she spoke. "Finn spoke to the supplier again last night. There's zero chance the furniture can get to us on time."

"Well, that might not matter." Marjorie's hazel eyes sparkled in the sunlight. "Because technically, your furniture is already here."

Finn and Aisling followed her eyes back to the growing crowd, who by this time were all picking up their chairs and carrying them to the sidewalk in front of the pub. As she watched, Finn realized that every piece of the furniture on the street looked like it had come straight from local homes. Coffee and end tables of all shapes and sizes were scattered among mismatched kitchen chairs painted in cheerful colors, chipped wooden patio furniture, and even a small recliner covered in faded rose-print fabric, complete with a large lace doily on the headrest. There was no mystery who that one belonged to; a feisty older woman in curlers and a pink tracksuit watched intently as two teenage boys carried it over to the sidewalk in front of the pub doors.

"So, everyone brought their chairs and tables from their homes," Aisling said slowly. "For us?"

"If you want them, that is," Jack said, beaming. "According to my wife, there has to be adequate seating for the permanent license to be issued, but the rules don't say anything about where it comes from or what it looks like."

Marjorie smiled. "When your furniture eventually does come in, we'll just get the word out and everyone will come back and collect what they brought." She turned as a portly man in worn construction overalls and a hard hat passed them carrying a leg lamp, complete with tassels and fishnet stockings. She turned back around with a wink. "Although you may want rid of certain items before others."

Aisling bit her lip and paused. "But isn't there a chance this might all go south when Donogan gets back Monday morning and figures it out? Could he revoke it then?"

"Well, that would have to go through his boss..." Jack smiled and nodded toward his wife. "Who happens to have a soft spot for me."

"Then what are we waiting for?" Finn said with a smile that instantly lit up her face. She dug the keys out of her pocket and headed for the crowd. "Let's set up a pub."

❖

Two hours later the furniture was in place, a cozy fire glowed from the hearth, and the space had taken on a homey, intimate atmosphere they hadn't expected. Finn and Aisling made the rounds and personally thanked everyone who'd brought something. The lanky teenager with the clipboard they'd seen as they walked up turned out to be Jack's son, Michael, who'd helped them hook up the barrels the day before.

"Okay, Mum," Michael said, joining Finn and Marjorie at the bar once most of the villagers had wandered back out the doors. "It looks like we have seats for two thirteen, including the snugs along the walls, but didn't you say each seat had to have a certain amount of table space too?"

"That's right. How much tabletop space do we have total?" Marjorie dug a stack of papers out of her bag and followed the page down with her finger. "Let's get that number first and see where we are. Let's see here...every seat has to have thirty centimeters of table or bar space."

"Oh, wow, I haven't even started measuring that," Michael said, looking around at the eclectic collection of coffee and end tables.

"Well, while you do that," Finn said, leaning out the door to look at the teenagers in the park. "I'm going to grab some sandwiches for lunch from the café. The very least we can do here is feed you."

"Cool." Michael took the tape measure his father handed him. "I should have the tables measured by then. Then before I go we can test your taps and barrels so you're ready for tonight."

Finn left and headed over to the park where Barry Wright, the boy who'd swiped Maggie's wallet that first morning at the market, was standing with a group of rough-looking older boys. As Finn approached, a disheveled boy in a tracksuit jacket with dirty cuffs and a long scar on his face looked her up and down. He took a deep drag off his cigarette, flicking the ash on the ground, and met her gaze.

"You lost, mate?"

Finn smiled, glancing at Barry, who quickly looked at the ground, gravel grating under the sole of his trainer as he turned it.

"Nope, not lost," Finn said, locking eyes with him. "Just have something over at the café I could use Barry's help with."

The boy held her gaze, his face stony, then looked at Barry with a raised eyebrow. "Whatever. Looks like you got chores to do, kid."

Barry hesitated, then fell into step with Finn as they walked across the park to the café, fists shoved hard into his pockets.

"Dude," he said, his eyes on the ground. "That was so embarrassing."

Finn laughed, opening the door of the café for him. "No, my friend, that was nothing. That haircut you've got going on is embarrassing."

Barry stopped in his tracks for a second, then broke into a genuine smile. "Whatever. You try getting a decent haircut around here, mate."

"But all is not lost." Finn followed Barry into the café, then stopped to hold the door inside for the woman behind her. "I may be able to help you with that."

By the time they made it back to the pub, Marjorie and Aisling had all the butcher paper torn down and the windows sparkling. Every table was topped with a different type of glassware: wineglasses, snifters, even rocks glasses, with an ivory votive candle in each.

"Where did you get those?" Finn asked as she and Barry came through the door loaded down with takeaway bags full of fresh sandwiches. "I leave for ten minutes and it already looks like a girl's been in here."

Barry's laugh came out as a loud snort, and he nearly dropped the bag he had under his arm. Jack grabbed it just in time and set it on the bar.

"I think what you meant to say," Marjorie flashed Finn a smile and started pulling sandwiches out of the bag and unwrapping them, "is that it looks lovely in here and you had no idea Aisling and I were so clever."

"Yes ma'am," Finn said with a wink in Aisling's direction. "That's exactly what I meant."

Finn and Aisling distributed the sandwiches, along with bags of crisps and soft drinks from behind the bar.

"I think I've got it." Michael walked slowly up to the bar from the back of the room, still staring at his clipboard. "But I don't know how to figure out if we have the right amount per person."

Marjorie twisted the top off a Lucozade and pushed it over the counter toward Barry. "Well, max capacity is two hundred thirteen people, so if everyone needs about thirty centimeters of table space, that's..." She picked up her phone and squinted at it, punching at the buttons with the tip of her finger. "Hang on. I swear I have a calculator on this thing somewhere."

"That's six thousand, three hundred and ninety centimeters." Barry made an unsuccessful attempt to catch a wet tomato slice as it slipped suddenly from his sandwich and plopped onto his lap. "Or sixty-three point nine meters."

Silence fell as everyone turned to look at Barry, until Aisling got a grip and handed him a stack of cocktail napkins.

"What?" Barry said, looking around and swiping at his face with his sleeve. "Do I have something on my face?"

Finn arched an eyebrow and smiled at Barry, still wrestling with the tomato, then got back to the business at hand. "And, Michael, how many meters do we have, total?"

"Right. I just wrote that down. I have it somewhere." He scanned his clipboard and finally found it near the bottom. "It looks like we have seventy-four point four meters of table surface area, including the bar."

Aisling looked at Marjorie. "So that does it, right?"

Finn nodded, a huge smile sweeping across her face, and Jack raised his bottle of Coke. "Here's to Gwenllian's Sword," he said. "Long may she prosper."

As everyone leaned in and touched their bottles to Jack's, the wooden wineglass rack above the bar started to shake, just hard enough to make the glasses clink. Finn and Aisling looked up together, but as soon as they did the motion stopped, except for one last clink from a sherry glass directly above their heads.

Jack laughed and turned to his wife. "Well, if that's not an endorsement from the prior owners, I'm not sure what is."

"What the hell?" Aisling stumbled over the words, still staring up at the glass rack. "What owners? What just happened?"

"This place is haunted, dear," Marjorie said, popping a crisp into her mouth. "Didn't they tell you that? It's been owned by only women since 1758, and the lot of them are still very protective of the place. They don't like just anyone running the pub."

"It's haunted? That's good to know." As she spoke, Finn slid the other half of her roast beef sandwich over to Barry, who picked it up immediately.

"Oh no," Aisling said, staring at the door. "Forget the ghosts, I just realized we forgot to get a sign for the door. How will people know we're open tonight?"

Jack laughed as he finished the last of his Coke. "I wouldn't worry. I can't imagine that will be a problem."

CHAPTER NINE

Finn watched as Aisling stepped into the dark, wet street after they'd finally closed the pub at 1:00 a.m., spinning around under the streetlights with her arms open wide, scattering the light dusting of snowflakes floating down from the moon.

"I feel like I should be shattered, but it's like I'm still high on our first night. I can't imagine going to sleep right now."

"I know," Finn said, pulling her jacket around her and buttoning it as she walked. "It couldn't have gone better. The way everyone pulled together so that we could actually open was amazing. I guess I didn't realize how important this had become to them, too." She glanced over at Aisling, who had fallen back into step with her. "And did you see Jack drinking his pint in that pink corduroy papasan chair someone brought? He didn't know what to do with that thing."

"It's a miracle he didn't tip it over into the table behind him." Aisling reached up and snapped off an ice-glazed leaf from a tree, glinting in the moonlight. "But aside from the papasan, it surprised me how comfortable everyone seemed all night. It's like no one even hesitated to sit in crazy chairs or rest their pint on one of their neighbor's bedroom nightstands." She jumped out of the way of a spray of sleet as a red Mini Cooper passed them leaving the square. "I was so nervous when we opened the doors, but five minutes later it felt like…"

Finn smiled. "Like we were just having people over for a party?"

"Yes!" Aisling said, tossing the leaf into a snowbank. "That's exactly it."

They walked past the church under the stars, then Finn held the cottage door open for Aisling and knocked the snow off her boots before she followed her in.

"Did you notice how many people brought in shopping bags that had to be from Cardiff, too? Like from that grocery store you said you shopped at in London...Presto?"

"Tesco."

"I mean," Finn continued, pulling her beanie off her head and running her hand through her hair, "I know some people must work in Cardiff, so that makes sense, but I must have seen a dozen shopping bags on people I know work here in the village."

"I think once people started shopping at the big stores, they just forgot about the village shops, like the butcher or stopping by the market stalls for bread and produce. It's a shame, actually." Aisling smiled, picking up the paperback on the table and turning it in her hand. "No one in Tesco is going to give you a book with your currant scones."

"Are you hungry?" Finn asked as she wandered into the kitchen. "I don't think I am, but I could use a drink after today. Everyone was drinking but us."

"Pour me one," Aisling said. "I'm going to get a quick bath and I'll meet you back here."

A few minutes later, Finn threw another log on the fire and Aisling got comfortable on her end of the couch, almost swamped by the plush navy velvet robe she'd wrapped around herself.

"So," Finn said, brushing her hands off at the hearth and handing Aisling her glass of scotch from the mantel. "Do you want to talk about how much more money we could be making if we were offering food at the pub?"

Aisling smiled, her eyes on the scotch swirling like firelight in her glass. "Do you want to talk about how that's never going to happen?"

"Are you seriously still holding on to that fantasy that I'm going to lose your bet?"

Aisling looked up with a smile, then held her eyes. "It's not fantasy if it's true. Or do you need a little lesson on the difference between those two things?"

"Why not?" Finn leaned back into the couch and set her glass down on the coffee table. "Hit me."

Aisling held her gaze for a moment before she also put her glass down on the coffee table.

"Give me two minutes," she said, glancing back at Finn over her shoulder as she padded barefoot down the hall. "And you may want to finish that scotch before I come back."

Finn laughed, downing her drink. "You talk some big game, little girl." She turned off all but one of the lamps by the couch, which made the room seem to glow with the firelight flickering on the walls, then settled back into the couch.

It was the stillness of Wales that had crept up on her. She'd started to forget the constant din of the Brooklyn streets, the late-night shouting, even the metallic screech of the trains braking against the rails as they came into the station by her apartment. When night fell here she heard only the ocean waves breaking on the shore below the cottage and the wind sifting through the trees behind the church. No voices, no taxi horns, no constant hum of the city. Something inside her that had always been on guard, always tightly vigilant, had loosened and was starting to be swept away by the sounds of the sea.

"Hey, Finn," Aisling called from the bedroom. "Do you have a sex playlist on your phone?"

Finn smiled. Of course she did.

"No," she called back. "What's that?"

There was a pause, then Aisling stuck her head out the bedroom door and peered down the hall at Finn on the couch. "Bollocks. You know you do. Put it on."

She closed the door and Finn smiled as she started her playlist, placing her phone beside the couch on the end table. Melissa Ferrick's "Drive" filled the room and Finn leaned back and closed her eyes. *This just got a lot more interesting*, she thought as she listened to the bedroom door open and Aisling's footsteps coming down the hall.

Finn opened her eyes when she felt Aisling step between her knees.

"Holy shit," Finn said, her gaze raking over every inch of Aisling, standing in front of her in an unbuttoned white shirt that was three sizes too big for her, barely covering a sheer black bra and panties.

"Is that my shirt?"

"Yes, ma'am," Aisling said, leaning forward and whispering the words against Finn's neck. "Do you want it back?"

Finn closed her eyes, breathing her in. "If it means it comes off your body, then…absolutely."

Her words hovered in the space between them. Finn turned her face, lips almost brushing Aisling's, and closed her eyes against the urge to wrap her hands around Aisling's ass and pull her onto her body. She slipped the shirt from her shoulders and listened to the sound of it falling, like a hesitant breath.

"That may not have been the smartest choice," Aisling whispered as Finn opened her eyes.

Finn felt her body respond quick and hard as she took in the sheer black bra made of lace so delicate she saw the soft pink of Aisling's nipples, with panties cut straight and low across her hips, highlighting the deep curve to her waist.

"Jesus Christ." Finn let her head drop back against the top of the couch. "You're killing me here."

"That was the plan, but you talk a big game yourself." Aisling braced her hands on each side of Finn's head and lowered her body so that her breasts just barely brushed Finn's mouth. "So you should be able to handle it, right?"

Finn slid her hands up the back of Aisling's thighs and drew in the scent of her skin, like fresh sea air mingled with the raw edge of cedar woodsmoke from the hearth. Aisling's hair fell around Finn's face as she traced the edge of Finn's ear lightly with her tongue.

"In fact," Aisling knelt, her knees at Finn's hips, then leaned back slightly, her ass warm against Finn's thighs, "I'm sure I can get even closer without it bothering you the slightest bit."

Finn held her gaze, hands sliding up the curve of Aisling's hips to circle her waist. In the fireplace, a log cracked and sank into the coals as Finn placed her hand lightly in the center of Aisling's chest, then wrapped her other arm tight around her hips and pulled Aisling into her body. Finn felt Aisling's heart speed up under her palm as she wordlessly reached up and flicked the clasp on her bra that instantly fell between them. Aisling bit her lip and watched as Finn brushed the backs of her hands slowly across her nipples before she leaned forward and took one into her mouth, working it with her tongue.

"Fuck."

The word was a whisper that barely reached Finn's ear as Aisling's hand slid around the back of her neck. Finn lightened the pressure to a slick swirl of her tongue, then paused before she claimed it again, hard enough to make Aisling arch her back and whisper something she didn't hear. Aisling pressed her hips into Finn and slid her hands under Finn's shirt, pulling it up and off, leaving them both bare to the waist. Finn wrapped an arm around Aisling's waist and stood, laying Aisling down on the couch underneath her. Finn sank slowly onto her, one thigh slipping between hers, leaning into her body, face buried in the warmth of her neck.

"Oh God, Finn, that feels…" Aisling's voice trailed off as she raised her hips to meet Finn's. Her breath deepened, fingers tightening around her shoulders as Finn gently worked her, leaning into her in a soft rhythm, the heat from Aisling's body damp against her thigh.

"Ready to give up?"

"It's cute that you think you're going to win that easily, Boxer Boi." Aisling smiled and arched an eyebrow. "So you're saying that's all you got?"

Finn laughed, touching her thumb to Aisling's lower lip as she spoke. "No, but I think it might be all you can take."

"You think?" Aisling whispered, her hand slipping between their bodies. Finn leaned up on her elbow and watched as the tips of Aisling's fingers slid slowly over the black lace, then disappeared underneath it. She was achingly perfect, with a tight waist and meltingly feminine curves, and it was getting harder for Finn not to touch her. By the second.

"Jesus," she said, watching as Aisling's fingers moved under the lace, stroking her clit, then dipping slowly inside. Aisling sat up, her face almost touching Finn's as she slicked her fingertips over her lips, then into her mouth. Finn took her hand and brought Aisling's fingertips to her own lips, watching Aisling's nipples tense as she pulled her fingers into her mouth, stroking them with her tongue, then slipped her hand around the back of Aisling's neck and brought her face to hers, as close as breath.

Then she kissed her. Slow, deep, and hard, pulling Aisling underneath her again and leaning into her body. Finn held Aisling's face with one hand, her thumb stroking her lip as she moved down her body, breathing in the scent of her skin.

The fire was dying in the hearth, sparks fading to embers, and the only sound was the wind brushing the windowpanes, the night black and dense beyond. Aisling's breath slowed and deepened as Finn kissed the inside of her thigh, slicking her tongue over the delicate skin then drawing it into her mouth, leaving her mark. Finn watched Aisling lean back into the cushions and close her eyes, biting her lip as the warmth of Finn's palm settled over her, her thumb stroking Aisling's clit through the lace. The texture of the fabric created the softest scrape against her thumb, hinting at the same sensation on Aisling's clit, and just for an instant Finn wondered if she'd be able to stop there.

Finn moved back up her body and kissed her for what seemed like forever, her thigh heavy and warm between Aisling's. Her voice was deep and raw around the edges when she finally spoke.

"You won."

Aisling smiled. "Are you surprised?"

"Not really," Finn said, leaning in to bite Aisling's lower lip gently before she spoke. "It was over as soon as you put those fingers in your mouth."

Aisling sat up slowly, then stood and held out her hand to Finn.

"Let's go to bed."

Finn smiled and led her down the hall to the bedroom, pausing only to light a small fire in the stone fireplace at the foot of the bed. She sat on the hearth until the wood finally caught and warmed the darkness, then climbed in and turned Aisling's body to wrap with her own from behind.

Aisling leaned her head back against Finn's chest. Firelight flickered on the plaster walls, painting them with copper light and shadow.

"I forgot to tell you something."

Finn slid her hand around her waist, pulling her closer. "What's that?"

"I actually decided we should serve food in the pub ages ago, after Greystone's visit."

Finn laughed, biting her shoulder playfully. "So I've been trying like hell not to kiss you this whole time but you'd already decided to go with the food idea from the start?"

"Yep." Aisling snuggled back into Finn's arms, her voice softened with sleep. "I just wanted to find out how long it would take me to win."

❖

The next night was Saturday and the pub was packed from the moment they opened the doors. Finn and Aisling spent most of the night behind the bar, setting up drinks as fast as possible, stopping only for occasional chats with the locals who stopped in for a pint and a giggle about the eclectic decor they'd helped create.

"I can't believe I was worried we wouldn't have any punters," Aisling said, reaching above Finn's head for the last clean wineglass. She nodded toward the opposite end of the bar, tucking her hair behind her ear. "I thought we were busy this afternoon, but now they're waiting three and four deep down there."

"Damn." Finn glanced back at the taps. "We're about to run out of Guinness. Can you hold the fort for a second while I go change the barrel?"

"Go," Aisling said, quickly pouring chilled chardonnay into the glass and recorking the bottle. "I got this."

As Aisling returned to the end of the bar to deliver the wine, a younger woman emerged at the back of the crowd, blond hair slicked back in a ponytail, wearing tall black boots, jeans, and a black turtleneck. Aisling handed over the wine and took the money, her eyes locked on the woman who had now leaned down to talk to the little girl at her side. The girl was holding the handle of an overfilled Dora the Explorer rolling suitcase and crying, shaking her head and swiping at her red cheeks with the sleeve of her coat.

Aisling turned back to the rest of the crowd, who by now were leaning expectantly against the stools, elbows on the edge of the bar, money in hand.

Aisling poured a shot of whiskey and handed it to an older gentleman in a green tweed coat, then glanced back at the little girl and turned to speak to the next customers standing in line.

"I promise to get right back to you." Aisling flashed them a smile as she pointed to the two nearly buried stools between them and the edge of the bar. "But would you mind stepping aside for a moment so these two seats are accessible?"

They stepped aside, as did the people behind them, clearing a path wide enough for Aisling to get the woman's attention and motion her forward. She looked confused and glanced behind her before she realized Aisling was actually talking to her. She took the little girl's hand and led her to the bar, lifting her up on one of the stools.

"Would you two like a seat?" Aisling asked, giving the little girl a wink. "It should calm down in a few minutes if you want to sit for a bit."

"Aye. Thank you so much," she said, pulling the suitcase up to the stools. "We're here to meet someone, but it looks like he's not going to show up."

"It's my daddy," the little girl piped up, followed by a long backward glance in the direction of the doors. "He's going to pick me up for the night and I'm going to stay at his house."

Aisling looked to her mom, who shook her head almost imperceptibly and then turned back to her daughter, smoothing stray wisps of white-blond hair off her face. "He was supposed to be here an hour ago, and Ella doesn't want to leave until she sees him." She lowered her voice to a whisper and caught Aisling's eye. "Again."

Aisling instantly understood and peered down over the bar. "Well, while you wait, why don't you hand me Dora the Explorer? We can keep it safe behind the bar so at least you don't have to worry about that."

She handed the suitcase up and over the bar to Aisling just as Finn came up from the cellars. Aisling leaned back against her and whispered into her ear for a moment, then turned her attention back to the punters who had made room for them.

"Hey, there," Finn said, leaning onto her elbows and speaking to the little girl. "What's your name?"

She didn't answer, just looked down at the bar, wiping her cheek hard with the back of her hand. Finn looked up to her mum, who mouthed *Ella* and looked back to her daughter.

"Hey, Finn!"

Finn's attention snapped back to the crowd, where Michael, Jack's son, was waving to her.

"Do you want me to step behind the bar?" Michael glanced around. "You don't have to pay me, but I've worked in a few pubs and could lend a hand if you need it."

"Dude, are you kidding?" Finn said, motioning him around the end of the bar. "You're a lifesaver. Are you sure you don't mind?"

"Well," Michael said. "It's this or watch my mum paint ceramic trolls in the kitchen." He looked to the door where a group of giggling young women were spilling in, looking more Manhattan than

Cwylldbridge. "And as fascinating as that is, your place has all the fit birds."

Finn raised an eyebrow at Aisling, who smiled as she snapped the cash register back open. "That's lad-speak for 'cute girls.'"

Finn laughed and stepped aside so Michael could get past her, then handed him the bottle opener from the back pocket of her Levi's. "You'll definitely need this, then Aisling can get you up to speed for the moment, anyway."

Michael headed toward Aisling, who had moved to the end of the bar to collect a stack of empty pint glasses. Aisling was almost finished giving Michael the lay of the bar and their shot specials when she saw Finn turn back to Ella and speak to the little girl. "Hey, have you ever seen anyone make a Princess Ella Secret Potion?"

Ella's head lifted and she looked at Finn suspiciously. "What is that?"

"I'm not gonna lie, it's pretty rare to find one," Finn said, leaning down to Ella's level, elbows on the bar. She looked around, making sure no eavesdroppers were lurking, and dropped her voice. "But I happen to know how to make them. Do you want to watch?"

"Yes!" Ella looked at her mum, suddenly excited by the tall, ornate glass Finn plunked down on the bar with a serious look. "Can I, Mum?"

"I'm Finn, by the way." Finn held out her hand to Ella's mum. "Is this okay with you?"

"Absolutely," she said, smiling as she shook her hand and looked back to her excited daughter, who seemed to have forgotten she was crying just a minute before. "My name is Olivia." She met Finn's eyes and paused. "And thank you for this."

"My pleasure," Finn said as she brandished a bottle of grenadine with theatrical flair. "Ella, are you ready?"

"Yes, please!"

Finn spun the bottle high into the air with one hand, catching it seamlessly in the other as it came down. She poured a small portion of the red syrup into the glass in front of Ella, then quickly lifted the bottle to her shoulder, dropped it down her back, and caught it with her other hand.

Aisling smiled as Ella clapped in delight, leaning forward to watch as Finn grabbed the gun that dispensed the drink mixers and ducked out of sight. An arc of soda water sprang suddenly from behind the counter and over Ella's head, landing safely on the floor in front of the snugs at the opposite end of the room as Finn reemerged as if nothing had happened, with three large ice cubes in a rocks glass. She tossed the cubes above her head and all three clinked into Ella's glass from an impossible height, prompting applause from the crowd.

Finn layered Ella's glass with club soda with a flourish, then caught Michael's eye, tossing the grenadine bottle in his direction. Aisling watched as he caught it with one hand and lofted it back to her, where she caught it on the back of her shoulder, rolled it down her arm, and spun it on the flat of her hand with dizzying speed, finally stopping to pour another bright red layer of syrup into Ella's glass.

"This is your moment, Ella. Are you ready?" Finn whispered, handing Ella a long glass swizzle stick from behind the counter that suddenly looked remarkably like a magical wand.

Ella nodded, tense with excitement. Finn put her finger to her lips, quieting the crowd, who by now were all watching the show with rapt attention.

"The magic potion can only be changed to the color of a rose by a true princess," Finn said, her voice somber. Then she leaned close to Ella, as if whispering a secret. "Do you want to try?"

Olivia smiled at Aisling as Ella hesitantly dipped the swizzle stick into the glass and stirred, instantly turning the red and white layers of liquid into a beautiful jewel-pink tint. The crowd erupted into applause again and eventually turned back to their conversations as Finn dropped three plump cherries into Ella's glass.

"Finn, thank you." Olivia caught her eye as Ella pulled the glass toward her like a freshly cracked treasure chest. "You have no idea how great your timing is."

"I'm happy to help." She glanced back at Ella, who was sipping her drink and looking up at her with a thrilled expression. "And princesses like Ella are welcome here anytime."

Finn went back to serving customers after that, and the next hour disappeared in seconds. Aisling had just rung the bell for last call when she saw Finn lift the small Dora the Explorer suitcase carefully over the bar to Olivia. She watched as Ella's arms circled her legs, and Finn crouched down to hug Ella back before she darted off for the door, dragging the suitcase behind her.

Michael watched as the door swung shut behind them.

"Mate," Michael said to Finn as she opened the cash drawer. "That was way cool. I haven't seen my little niece so happy in a long time."

"Whoa." Finn paused, then pulled a note out of the cash drawer before it sprang closed. "Olivia is your sister?"

"Yep, and her dickhead ex-husband keeps promising Ella all these things and then just never shows up. At least tonight she ended up feeling really special."

Finn nodded and handed him a twenty-pound note, which he tried to refuse.

"Dude, you saved our asses tonight," Finn said, glancing at Aisling, who nodded her agreement. "That's worth something. Besides, we might need you again sometime."

Michael reluctantly took the money and shoved it into his pocket. "Well, thanks again. I'll be happy to help any time you need me."

Within twenty minutes the last of the customers had finished up and headed out the door, laughing and talking, and the silence fell heavy across the room as the doors swung shut.

"So," Aisling said, plunking two rocks glasses on the bar and pouring a splash of scotch in each. "Why didn't you tell me you were some bartending rock star?"

"Well, primarily because I'm not," Finn said, clinking her glass to Aisling's. "I was always busy running catering for events, but I started as a bartender, so occasionally I'd still step behind the bar and do a little bottle work."

"Well, if you tell anyone I said this I'll deny it," Aisling said. "But that might have been a tiny bit hot."

"Why, Miss Moss." Finn smiled back. "That's shockingly close to an actual compliment, so I'm going to tell absolutely everyone."

Aisling hit her with a bar towel just as the front doors cracked open, letting in a rush of icy air. A thin girl leaned in, wearing a white jacket that was dirty around the cuffs. She held the door open against the wind, her hair blowing around her face as a slow trail of blood inched down her cheek and onto her coat.

"Sorry to bother you. I know it's late and you're closed," she said, looking behind her before she continued, her words tumbling out in a rush. "But do you think I could just use your loo to clean up? I can't go home like this. My mum will kill me."

"Alwen!" Finn hopped over the bar and guided her inside, locking the door behind her. "Are you okay? What happened?"

Alwen just shook her head, her face crumpling into tears before she visibly steeled herself and answered.

"It's nothing," she said, wiping her eyes with her fingertips, which only ended up smearing the blood across her face. "I'm okay. It was just a bunch of guys giving me a hard time at the store."

Aisling came around the bar with a damp towel as Finn guided her into a seat by the fireplace. The logs glowed with enough heat to relax Alwen after a moment, and she leaned back in the chair as Finn got a better look at the bruising on her face.

"I met Alwen the first five minutes I was in town," Finn said to Aisling, taking the damp towel from her and dabbing carefully at the worst of the dried blood that had collected around Alwen's hairline. "She took pity on me and saved me from getting a migraine."

"It was no big deal," Alwen said, glancing at Aisling and wincing as Finn located the cut just above her temple. "I just gave her some paracetamol from my purse."

Finn handed Aisling the bloody towel and disappeared into the kitchen. When she came back she was carrying a first aid kit from under the bar, a dish of hot water, and a stack of clean white bar towels.

"You don't have to make a fuss," Alwen said, her voice quavering as Finn went back to cleaning the cut, which turned out to have a large knot underneath it that was swelling at a rapid pace. "It's really not that bad."

"I'm Aisling, by the way, and it looks like this may take a while," Aisling said gently, her eyes dropping to the baby bump visible under Alwen's coat. "Can I get you a cuppa?"

Alwen looked at her for a moment before she nodded, shrugging off the coat as another drop of fresh blood hit the collar. Aisling took the coat and laid it across a chair, then went to the bar to get her the cup of tea.

"I'm not sure I'm the one that needs to be doing this, Alwen." Finn caught the fresh blood with a square of gauze and guided Alwen's hand to her cheek to hold it in place while she worked. "This might be serious."

"It's nothing."

"Well, it's definitely not nothing," Finn said distractedly, gently tucking Alwen's hair behind her ear and out of the way. "How about you tell me how it happened, and we'll go from there?"

Alwen started to say something but then went quiet until Aisling returned with two steaming mugs of tea and handed one to her. Alwen wrapped her hands around it, closed her eyes, and breathed in the steam rising from the surface. Her shoulders loosened slowly and she sat back in her chair.

Finn smiled. "What is it with the English and your endless cups of tea?" She finished getting the last of the blood from Alwen's hairline and picked up a new towel. "Evidently it's the same in Wales."

Alwen and Aisling gave Finn an identical look of mock disdain, then smiled at each other.

"So what happened?" Aisling pulled out a chair and handed Finn another damp towel.

"It's nothing." Alwen touched her forehead gingerly and winced. Finn guided her hand away gently. "Just some guys who saw me closing up and decided to come in and see what they could get."

Finn unwrapped another pad of gauze and pressed it to the wound. "Do you know them?"

She started to answer, then stopped herself and tried again with a glance at the window. "Not all of them."

Alwen was quiet again as Aisling tore off strips of tape and handed them to Finn, who was carefully bandaging the wound after she'd finally managed to get all the blood cleaned off.

"The cut itself is fairly small," Finn said. "But it's that knot on your head I'm worried about. Are you sure you don't want us to take you to the emergency room?"

"Aye. I'm fine," Alwen said. "I just couldn't go home covered in blood. That would have made everything worse."

"What do you mean?" Aisling asked, stirring another splash of milk into her cup. "Your mum would have been worried?"

Alwen shook her head. "Not really. It's just...complicated."

"Are you okay to go home tonight?" Finn's words were gentle, and she studied Alwen's face as she spoke. "Do you need a place to stay tonight?"

Alwen shook her head, then stopped and winced from the pain.

"God, no, I can't...but thank you. I'll be fine. I just need to get on with it." She stood carefully, handing her cup to Aisling.

"Thank you for everything." Alwen looked at both of them as she picked up her coat and slid her arms slowly through the sleeves. "You didn't have to do all this for me."

Finn glanced at Aisling and held her eyes for a moment before she turned back to Alwen. "Can you at least take a day off from work tomorrow?"

Alwen shook her head and gingerly touched the knot that was rapidly starting to bruise. "No, but it'll be fine by then, and those lads won't be back for a while. I can't lose that job. I need it for..." Her voice trailed off and she smoothed her hand across her belly. It was a moment before she spoke again. "I just need it."

Aisling looked at Finn, who nodded. "Listen, if you stay home and rest tomorrow, we'd love to have you work here with us after that. We'll match whatever they pay you there, plus some."

"You'd be doing us a favor, actually." Finn looked around at the smattering of glasses yet to be cleared from the tables. "You should have seen it here tonight. We were absolutely run off our feet. We ended up opening sooner than we thought, so we haven't had the chance to hire any bar staff."

Alwen looked slowly from one to the other.

"But I don't have any experience. I mean, I'm a quick learner, but you probably need someone who actually knows what they're doing."

"We can teach you," Aisling countered. "And we're open six nights a week, which means you can work as many hours as you want to get started putting money away. And we'll be serving food here within the next week or two, so you can eat here, too."

Alwen paused, then smiled for the first time. "Okay."

"Wait," Aisling said. "You have to be eighteen in Wales to serve—"

"Don't worry." Alwen smiled. "I look young, but I'm nineteen."

"It's a deal, then. I'll walk you home." Finn walked to the door and held it open for her. "Then we'll see you back here Monday?"

Alwen nodded and looked back at Aisling, mouthing *thank you* before she disappeared through the door with Finn.

CHAPTER TEN

The sun edged a wide beam of golden light through the curtains the next morning and warmed the air, melting silently across the sheets. Finn felt Aisling turn over and slide her hand under Finn's shirt, her fingertips grazing her nipples. Finn groaned and turned over on top of Aisling, capturing her wrists and crossing them over her head before she even knew what was happening.

"Watch yourself, little girl." Finn's gaze was intense. "I already have to look at that body all day. There's only so much I can take"— Finn leaned down and bit Aisling's lower lip lightly, stroking it with her tongue—"before I take you."

Aisling smiled and leaned up to kiss her until Finn let her wrists go with a low growl.

"Jesus," Finn said, rolling over onto her back and shielding her face from the sun with her arm. "I'm not exactly helping myself here, am I?"

"Well, we only get one day off a week, so I think you should be able to do anything you want." Aisling turned toward Finn, tracing the hard lines of her abs with a fingertip. "Don't you?"

Finn got out of bed and flipped the duvet back to cover Aisling. "I'm trying to be a gentleman here, but you're seriously killing me."

Aisling sat up, her lower lip making an appearance in a pout. She held the sheet around her bare breasts, wild copper waves of hair falling over her shoulders, and squinted up at Finn, her pale green eyes highlighted by a wide beam of sunlight.

"Look, if you don't fancy me, you can just tell me." For the first time, her voice lacked the confidence that seemed to come so easily to her. "I'm a big girl, I can handle it."

Finn climbed back onto the bed and over her body, kissing her neck softly until her lips reached Aisling's ear. Her voice was warm, more intimate than touch. Aisling held her breath, as if afraid to miss even one word.

"I do like you, Ms. Moss. A lot." Finn raised her eyes to Aisling's. "Which is why I'm waiting."

"Oh." A wide smile flashed across Aisling's face too quickly for her to hide, and Finn smirked as she dragged herself out of bed again with a wink in Aisling's direction on the way down the hall.

Later, rounding the corner onto the square on the way to the café for breakfast, they both noticed it at the same time: a woman with a slick blond bun and perfect red lips knocking aggressively on the pub doors. She held a sheet of paper in her fist, the wind whipping it loudly into a twist as she pulled her cell phone out of the pocket of her tailored black trench coat.

"Who is that?" Aisling whispered.

"I don't know, and I'm just taking a guess here, but she doesn't exactly look like a local." Finn watched as the woman fumbled with her phone and dropped it on one of her glossy nude high heels. It clattered onto the sidewalk and rolled off the curb. "Should we tell her we're closed?"

"You'd think that'd be obvious with the locked door and everything," Aisling said, her gaze moving quickly from the woman's scarf to her impossibly high heels. "But sure, why not?"

As they approached, it was impossible not to hear her hissing into the newly retrieved phone in a sharp American accent.

"Yeah, no shit," she said, knocking insistently on the door again for good measure. "I know that, Jason, but how am I supposed to do that when there's no one answering the freaking door?"

She looked up just then to see Finn and Aisling walking up the sidewalk to the pub doors.

"Oh, thank goodness," she said in a decidedly more friendly tone than they had just heard. She dropped her phone into her coat pocket. "I was starting to think that no one answers their doors here."

"The pub is actually closed on Sundays," Aisling said. "But we'll be open at noon tomorrow."

The woman looked Aisling up and down. "So this your little bar?"

Aisling glanced up at Finn and paused for a moment before she replied, as if choosing her words carefully. "The pub belongs to both of us. I'm Aisling Moss, and this is Finn Morgan."

"Oh, right," she said, smoothing the flyer in her hand and holding it out to them. "I was just telling someone how charming your little village is."

Finn took the flyer and smiled. "Is there something we can help you with?"

"Well, actually there's something we can help *you* with, I think." She paused, her gaze sweeping Finn's body in a single second. "And I didn't expect that accent. Are you from New York?"

"I'm from Brooklyn, but I'm here for at least a year," Finn said, handing the flyer over to Aisling.

"Well, I'm Kaitlyn Matthews with Rockfield Acquisitions Inc." She flashed a quick smile that didn't quite make it to her eyes. "Our company is interested in making a very lucrative offer concerning future development here in Coldbridge."

"Cwylldbridge," Aisling said. "Just like it's spelled."

"Of course," Kaitlyn said, dismissing Aisling with an impatient wave. Her eyes were locked on Finn as she smoothed her hair back with her hand, a fingertip grazing her lower lip slightly before she went on. "My number is on that flyer if you have any questions. Don't hesitate to call. I'm here to answer any questions business owners may have, and to hopefully get your support for the project before it goes for a council vote." She dug a business card out of her bag. "And you can feel free to call after hours as well, Finn. You'll find my personal mobile number on the back of my card."

Aisling visibly stiffened as they walked away, turning to look behind them as they crossed the square to the café. Finn followed her gaze, only to find Kaitlyn still standing at the doors peering back at them, mobile to her ear yet again.

"God." Aisling flipped her head back around and jerked the zipper of her bomber jacket up to her chin. "She couldn't be more irritatingly American if she tried."

Finn laughed, sliding an arm around Aisling's waist in an attempt to direct her attention back to the front. "I'm going to assume I'm an exception to that particular description?"

"Certainly not." Aisling smiled, arching an eyebrow as Finn opened the café door for her. "But that woman was beyond obnoxious. She didn't even look at me once she saw you."

The warmth of frying bacon and potato hash enveloped them as they walked in, pierced by the prickly scent of the black pepper the village postal delivery man to their left was layering onto his eggs as the women edged into the crowded line. They ordered quickly and slid into the only open booth by a window with their coffees, where Aisling dug through the sweetener packets before finally plucking them impatiently out of the holder and dropping them into a pile on the table. Finn reached across the aisle to another table, plucked three raw sugar packets out of their condiment stand, and handed them over to her.

"How did you know what I was looking for?"

"Aisling," Finn said, lifting her cup and blowing gently on the surface of her coffee to cool it. "We live together. How could I not have noticed how you take your coffee?"

"You are unusually observant." Aisling smiled, ripping the top off her third sugar and dumping it into her cup. "I'll give you that."

"Thank God she's got someone up there to help her today," Finn said with a glance toward the counter. "We may get our food quicker than usual. I have to get to the hardware store today. I need some bolts for the barrel racks in the cellar."

"Good luck with that." Aisling smiled. "Probably not smart to let me loose in a hardware store today. I'd probably come out with a chain for that American slag at the pub."

"You know," Finn said with a smile, glancing up at the counter for any sign of their food, "if I didn't know better, I'd think you were a tiny bit jealous."

"Certainly not," Aisling said, pulling her shirtsleeves down to matching points on her wrists. "I just don't like her. Already."

❖

As they passed the pub on the way home, they slowed to a stop on the sidewalk when they saw the door was ajar.

Finn put a hand on Aisling's shoulder to stop her, then walked into the pub and shut the door behind her. She was back in under a minute.

"Come on in." Finn smiled. "It's just Ms. Greystone."

Aisling bristled as Finn held the door tight to her shoulder and leaned into Aisling's ear. "She means well, she just isn't the most tactful of people."

"How does she even get in here?" Aisling whispered, angry red splotches beginning to rise on her neck. "Does she have a key? Didn't Mr. Clydd say we had the only one?"

"I have no idea. Let's just hear what she has to say, okay?"

Aisling took a breath, set her face to neutral, and walked in behind Finn. Greystone was perched on top of the bar with a bottle of sherry beside her, the same gray wool pantsuit buttoned to her neck but with an unexpected pair of glossy oxblood brogues on her feet. Judging from the half-empty bottle beside her and an empty packet of crisps, she'd been there for a while.

"Always great to see you, Ms. Greystone." Finn rounded the corner of the bar and stopped. Aisling followed Finn's glance to see that the ancient percolator Greystone had left in the pub last time had already been started. "Can I get you a cup of coffee?"

"Lovely." Greystone pulled a wrinkled piece of paper out of her bag, which was also parked beside her on the bar. "Thank you, Finn. And you'll be happy to know I took the liberty of dismissing that vile American woman you met this morning."

"She came back here?" Aisling slid onto one of the barstools and unwound the green cashmere scarf from her neck, placing it on the bar in front of her. "We spoke to her this morning when she was pounding on the door and told her to do one."

Finn looked up, coffee in hand. "'Do one'? What's the translation there?"

"It's the same as telling someone to get lost," Aisling said, tapping her nails impatiently on the bar. "And clearly she didn't get the message the first time."

"Well, this time she was looking for Finn, and that was a message I made clear again in far more colorful language than you did, I assure you." Greystone adjusted the shirt cuffs at her wrists and paused for emphasis. "And if she had any sense, she'd go back to wherever she came from, but I daresay we'll see her again." She held up the wrinkled paper. "She left this for you two to look at, by the way."

Finn slid the coffee over to Greystone and passed the flyer to Aisling, who noted that somehow she still managed to look prim while perched on top of the bar halfway through a bottle of sherry. At 11:00 a.m. On a Sunday.

Aisling scanned the flyer, shaking her head as she looked up.

"You talked to her when she was here, right? What is this all about?" Aisling leaned over the bar to grab a packet of crisps for herself and another for Greystone, who picked up her coffee cup and considered the question, her lips set in a thin, tense line.

"You haven't heard about the mining proposition? It's all everyone's talking about in Cardiff, and they're trying to get business owners in the area to sign off on it to make sure it passes the city council vote." She sniffed, opening the bag of crisps and plucking one out to examine. "You can't get a decent cup of tea without hearing about it."

"Mining?" Aisling twisted her hair into a bun at the base of her neck and secured it with a band from her wrist. "What would they be mining around here?"

"Crystals. Evidently, the land around Cwylldbridge village has a higher concentration of quartz than anywhere else in the world," Greystone said, abandoning her coffee cup for the bottle of sherry. "They want to dig them up and sell them to 'technology' companies, whatever that means."

Finn's smile faded and she raked a hand through her hair, standing it on end. "I saw a documentary about this last year. Acquisition companies mine the quartz crystals and use them in the production of computers and cell phones. Environmental groups aren't happy about it because it strips the land bare of everything, including trees, which is obviously devastating to everything around it."

Finn pulled her phone from her back pocket and pulled up an image of huge craters dug into red soil, half-dead trees hanging on by gnarled roots at the edge, surrounded by dead, blackened vegetation.

"Jesus," Aisling said as Finn put the phone down on the bar. "That looks like a war zone."

"The article said that's pretty much what it is after they get done mining. It can take up to a hundred years before the land recovers, but it's never really the same."

"I knew that woman looked shifty. No one is that bloody cheerful unless they want something." Greystone lofted an eyebrow. "What else does it say?"

Aisling picked up the phone and scrolled down. "It says here that the leakage of chemicals from mining sites can also have detrimental effects on the health of the population living at or around the mining site." Her voice slowed as the meaning of the words began to settle in. "Apparently, groundwater contamination is common, and increased rates of disease have been found in the surrounding populations, including certain types of incurable cancers."

Aisling laid the phone back down on the bar. "Why would anyone consent to that?"

Silence fell between them. They already knew the answer.

Money.

❖

After they'd finally locked up the pub, leaving Greystone inside to finish her drink, Finn left to do her errands. By the time she returned to the cottage, Aisling was curled up on the couch by the fire reading a dogeared novel from the above the mantel. Sap cracked and popped from green pine logs on the fire as Finn tossed her beanie on the chair, then knocked the snow off her boots just outside the threshold, cold air swirling through the opening until she finally stepped in, closing the door behind her. She shook the last of the snowflakes out of her hair and breathed in the scent of rich, buttery vanilla and baked sugar as she stepped in.

"What smells so good?" Finn said as she hung her coat on the hook, eyeing the saucer of crumbs on the coffee table beside Aisling's teacup. She leaned down and lifted Aisling's chin with her finger, kissing her then pulling away with a soft bite on her lower lip.

Aisling opened her eyes and smiled. "I made some of Grandma Joan's sugar cookies while you were out. They only have five ingredients, so we had everything I needed. They're mostly butter, actually."

Finn headed for the kitchen and returned with a handful of cookies in addition to the one in her mouth. As she sank into one of the chairs opposite the couch, Aisling asked her the question hanging in the air between them.

"Did you find out anything else about the mining proposition?"

Finn slid the handful of cookies onto Aisling's saucer and handed her the one on the top. "I stopped by the butcher shop and talked to

Jack and Maggie about it. They said almost everyone in the village is against it, which isn't surprising, but the bad news is that it's not really up to us."

"Why wouldn't it be?" Aisling said, sitting up and putting her book on the back of the couch. "Who's making the decision?"

"Cardiff City Council members. Maggie said the area they want to mine is right outside of the village itself and it's a gray area as far as jurisdiction. Cwylldbridge is actually part of the city of Cardiff, but they've historically let the village retain most of its independence."

"Until now?"

Finn nodded, brushing a cookie crumb from the front of her hoodie. "Exactly. According to Jack, they've always kept a respectful distance, but I guess now there's too much money at stake for Cardiff not to pull rank."

"And of course they want to jump on this." Aisling shook her head and glanced out the window toward the sea. "It's not polluting their water and devastating the landscape where they live. Most of them will probably never even know it happened."

"It gets worse. Evidently a public vote isn't required, and the final decision is made by Cwylldbridge Village and Cardiff City Councils at a meeting. They can then accept or reject the proposal, regardless of public opinion, although residents and businesses owners are invited to go to the city council meeting and speak their minds before the vote."

Aisling settled back into the pillows and rolled her eyes. "Which I'm sure is why that woman was at our door this morning, to drum up local support." She paused, looking over at Finn. "But if it's decided by both city councils, we have a fighting chance. No one in Cwylldbridge will go for it."

She spotted Finn eyeing the last cookie on the saucer and nudged it across the coffee table to her.

"Well, theoretically," Finn said, catching the cookie crumbs in her hand as she bit into it, "that's true. But I was speaking to Jack and Marjorie in the shop today, and Cardiff City Council members outnumber Cwylldbridge's three to one. So they're the ones making the decision, even though the dig site would be directly outside our village and nowhere near Cardiff." She paused, shaking her head. "They literally won't be affected at all, yet almost all of the money goes to them."

"Damn." Aisling sank back into the pillows and stared at the ceiling. "I can't believe this is happening so quickly. How much money is on the table?"

"Just over three million pounds, which is how this company is getting business owners to get behind the idea. They're obviously hoping for a cut of it and they don't have long to decide. The vote is next Friday." Finn paused and glanced at her watch. "Hey, are you hungry by any chance?"

"I'm starving," Aisling said with a sudden smile. "Please tell me you're making me dinner."

"Not even close. Go get dressed while I grab a few things to take with us, and wear something warm." Finn smiled. "And don't even ask where we're going because I'm not telling you anything."

Aisling asked twice before she disappeared down the hall to the bedroom, then emerged five minutes later in a slim black turtleneck and faded jeans that hugged every curve on her body, right down to the rip in the knee.

"Will this work?"

Finn put a hand at the small of her back and pulled her close, only a breath between her mouth and Aisling's. "You look beautiful."

She breathed in the scent of Aisling's hair as she spoke, a familiar silver swirl of winter air, woodsmoke, and sea salt. Aisling's scent and the whole of Wales was somehow the same—wild and still in the same breath.

Finn hadn't been able to sleep the night before. She'd pulled a sleeping Aisling close as the fire in the bedroom hearth was dying, just a few scarlet embers still glowing in the bed of velvet ash. A full moon filled the room with cool light, a backdrop for the swaying black outline of the branches outside casting shadows on the walls. Finn held her close for hours, her breath warming Aisling's cheek, and realized for the first time that the warmth between them was starting to feel like home.

She'd spent most of her childhood trying to spend as little time as possible at home in her father's tiny Brooklyn apartment. Even now the hollow *clink* of empty bottles reminded her of them falling from his hand to the splintered wood floor as he shifted on the couch in front of the TV. She'd find them there in the morning, jammed at odd angles under the coffee table or rolled toward the dirty metal edge of the kitchen linoleum. The apartment had always smelled like wet dust and desperation, something she didn't realize until she got older and started to breathe her own air.

Her dad had emigrated from Wales to New York in his early twenties and eventually bought one of the bodegas in his neighborhood. He worked long hours when she was growing up. When he got home at night, he'd turn on the fights before he'd even taken off his coat and stare into the TV, eyes glazed over until the alcohol lulled them shut; so as far as she was concerned, it was the same whether he was there or not.

She stopped going to school for a month in the second grade, just to see if he'd notice. When he got the letter threatening him with a fine for truancy, he crumpled it in his fist and threw it out the open window and down to the sidewalk. She watched him from the kitchen as he settled back onto the couch and turned up the volume to a deafening level. He didn't speak to her for the next week.

He had never hit Finn, but he'd never noticed her, either.

The summer she was eight, he went on a bender and closed the shop for nine days, drinking from one hazy dawn to the next in the ash-coated living room, dropping cigarette butts that burned black caterpillar patterns into the floorboards under the couch. She'd touched his shoulder after the fourth day, but when his eyes rolled in her direction, there was no one behind them. She'd pulled her hand back and shrugged on her jacket, closing the door softly behind her as she left the apartment.

She walked twelve blocks to her father's bodega because it was the only place she knew how to get to, then just kept going until she saw a Catholic church with the doors propped open. The sun was just rising in a rusty orange wedge beyond the bridge, and a rat scurried out of a bag of trash on the sidewalk then over her foot as she turned and climbed the steps to St. Brigid's Cathedral. It was heavily silent the second she stepped through the doors. Finn tried to breathe silently, but emptiness amplifies everything around it.

As she got closer to the sanctuary, she saw an older woman with a rose headscarf and thick wool coat kneeling beside the rows of flickering candles at the altar, carved teak rosary beads slipping silently through her fingers. Finn walked slowly toward the flickering candles in the red votive holders until she stood beside her, but the woman didn't notice Finn beside her until her lips had stopped moving. When she finally opened her eyes and looked up, the words Finn didn't know she still had came tumbling out.

"Can..." She paused, searching the woman's face. "Can you see me?"

The woman's gaze settled on the broken zipper on Finn's jacket, then the jagged tear on the sleeve where the white stuffing inside had started to escape.

"Of course I can," she said in a thick Jersey accent, lighting a final candle and shaking out the match before putting it in the small silver dish by the donation box. "What kind of a question is that?"

Finn didn't answer, not even when the woman's eyes softened and she asked gently if Finn needed help. She just turned and walked down the aisle and out the wide double doors of the church.

It was enough to know she still existed; that someone had seen her.

"So where are you taking me, Finn Morgan?"

Finn winked in Aisling's direction as they passed the square and walked almost to the edge of the village. "What, you forgot? We're supposed to meet Kaitlyn for dinner to talk about how we can help her with the mining proposition."

Aisling stopped in her tracks and shoved her hands down into her pockets, eyebrows pushed together in a scowl.

"Kidding," Finn said, laughing and reaching for her hand. "I'm just yanking your chain. She's gone for the day by now, probably fucked off back to her fancy hotel in Cardiff."

"Well, if she has any sense she'll stay there. I can't imagine anyone in the village is going to be tempted by this proposition, although I can see why Cardiff business owners might be tempted since the dig site is over forty minutes' drive from them."

"Yeah." Finn squeezed her hand. "But all that devastation will be right in our backyard."

Aisling stepped aside as a woman with a stroller passed them with a silent wave. "I can't believe I'm saying this, but Cwylldbridge is starting to feel like..."

Finn smiled. "Home?"

Aisling smiled back. "Yeah. That's exactly it. Not that I don't miss some things, not the least of which is my favorite Indian restaurant in London, but this place is kind of growing on me."

Finn stopped and pulled her close, then let her go slightly and squinted into the distance over her shoulder.

"What?" Aisling said, straining to see what Finn was looking at through the falling dusk. They'd walked past the village and started into the field surrounding Dun Laoghaire castle, where the only sounds were silence and the sea crashing onto the shore in the charcoal darkness at the edge of the village. Somehow darkness always magnified the sound of the waves, even at the cottage, as if the rising moon emboldened it.

Then she saw what Finn was still looking at: scattered, flickering pinpoints of light in every window of the abandoned castle. Aisling had caught a glimpse of the castle several times in the last few weeks, but it never seemed the right time to go and see it again. At the back of her mind, she was hesitant to experience the same magic that she'd seen as a child. Or maybe she was afraid she wouldn't.

Finn was still staring into the distance. "What the hell?"

Aisling looked back over her shoulder, slowing to a stop just before the field. "It's Dun Laoghaire Castle," she said. "Have you never seen it?"

"I have, it's just..."

Finn's voice trailed off. She paused, then took Aisling's hand as they walked into the field, long grasses swaying in the breeze around them, their silvery tips illuminated by the last traces of evening light. They brushed Aisling's outstretched palm as she walked, listening for the faint evening sounds of the forest that hovered in the air, just under the molten sunset that had melted and dripped through the trees.

Finn squeezed her hand and Aisling looked back toward the castle. One by one, candles were swooshing to life along every window opening, even glowing around the turret at the top, illuminating the stone walls within with flickering candlelight. By the time they arrived at the doors, every available window frame was crowded with dripping ivory candles in all shapes and sizes, as if they'd been burning all night, glowing from top to bottom with rich, warm light.

"You saw that, right?" Finn whispered, still holding Aisling's hand. "We just watched every one of the candles light themselves." Finn's words were slow and deliberate, as if still sifting through any possible explanations. "But that's impossible, right?"

CHAPTER ELEVEN

A s Finn and Aisling stood in front of the castle, the only sound was the owls calling to each other within the darkening forest at the edge of the field. A flock of silent white birds rose from behind the trees and flew overhead in the direction of the sea as the wind picked up suddenly and blew Aisling's hair softly against her face. She smiled, climbed the steps to the open Gothic doorframe, and held out her hand to Finn.

"Ready?"

Finn hesitated, watching candlelight flicker onto the rough stone walls inside, then took her hand and they walked into the great room of the castle, the navy night sky above them awash with the haze of a million stars. They turned slowly in different directions, taking in the hundreds of candles all around them, some glowing within antique iron lanterns or perched on handmade black iron candlesticks, others crowded together and dripping on bare stone landings and windowsills. The massive stone fireplace and mantel were ablaze with candlelight, and at the other end of the room was the spiral staircase, each step illuminated with a glowing lantern. The castle was nearly silent, the only sounds the wind scraping against the turrets outside and the occasional drip of melting candle wax splashing onto stone.

"This is gorgeous," Aisling said, still taking in the scene. "You did all this?"

"Well, yes and no." Finn led her over to the hearth and spread the blanket she'd carried from the house out in front of it. "I was here earlier and delivered this basket, but everything else is a mystery. I didn't bring even one candle with me, much less hundreds of them."

Aisling leaned into Finn's body and slid her hands under her sweater, tracing the strong lines of her back with the tips of her fingers. "I'm okay with a little mystery."

Finn's fingers rested light and soft around the back of Aisling's neck as she tilted Aisling's face up with her thumb. She kissed up the side of her neck, then whispered warm and slow against her ear, "I've already forgotten. I can't see anything but you."

Aisling rested her forehead on Finn's chest, then gave her a distracted kiss as she glanced toward the basket.

Finn leaned back and smiled. "You're wondering if I brought you any food, aren't you?"

Aisling nodded, and Finn threw her head back and laughed, the sound echoing against the stone walls around them.

"Well, you're in luck," Finn said, her dark eyes sparkling in the candlelight. "Because I had Maggie make us dinner and it's in that basket."

Aisling dug into the basket, pulling out thick roast beef sandwiches on homemade baguette topped with sautéed mushrooms and sage, and a rich brown gravy to pour over them. An entire apple pie was hidden beneath, still warm from the oven, along with a small dish of vanilla custard, wedges of sharp cheddar, and a tiny jar of winter currant jelly. A small stack of plates and cutlery lay at the very bottom of the basket, along with some sky-blue cloth napkins and a handwritten note from Maggie tucked into the paperback she'd said had inspired their pie.

Finn reached carefully into the clusters of candles on the mantel and retrieved a dark bottle of malbec.

"There are so many of these candles, it's warming the air like a fire." Aisling shrugged off her coat and carefully cut her sandwich in half. "It's actually nice in here."

"And very romantic." Finn handed her a napkin and draped another over her knee. "Which I'd love to take the credit for, but this is like that wine rack shaking on opening night at the pub. I wouldn't have believed it if I hadn't been standing right under it."

"Grandma Joan used to tell me that 'magic is everywhere if you look for it.'" Aisling smiled, looking around her, suddenly awash with the memory of being in the very spot she sat now. "Maybe she was right."

"So," Finn said, taking a sip of her wine and setting the glass back down on the hearth. "Tell me about your family."

"We haven't really had the chance to talk about any of that, have we? The last few days have been a blur."

Finn nodded, adding a bit more gravy to her sandwich and replacing the lid on the thermos. "What are your mom and dad like?"

"Very sweet." Aisling paused, shaking her head. "Annoyingly perfect, actually, but they've always been supportive of me. I haven't really seen them much in the last few years. I was busy constantly with my job." She hesitated and took a long sip of her wine. "What about you? I know your dad moved to the States because of that big falling-out our dads had in their twenties. I can't believe they never saw each other again."

Finn nodded. "It was over your mom, wasn't it? That's the only thing he ever said about it."

Aisling settled her empty plate onto the hearth with a soft clatter and refilled their wineglasses. "As far as I know, they were both in love with her, and she chose my dad."

"There has to be more to that story, although I'm sure no one else knows what it is." Finn leaned back on her hands, her jaw flexing as if struggling to hold back words. "Dad never talked about it."

When Aisling spoke, her voice was gentle. "Your mum died young, didn't she?"

"When I was five years old. She had an aneurysm." Finn's voice caught and she cleared her throat. "She died in her sleep, and Dad had a neighbor take me to school the next morning. I never saw her again."

"What happened after that?"

Finn took a deep breath, as if filling her lungs for the last time before being plunged into the sea.

"Dad disappeared."

"What do you mean?"

"He just…" Finn paused, and Aisling noticed her hands were tense against the floor behind her, the fingertips white against the gray-striped wool blanket beneath them. "Disappeared. I mean, he was there, but it was also like I never saw him again, either. He started drinking." Finn's voice cracked and she leaned her head back to look at the sky. "And just never stopped, I guess."

Aisling lifted Finn's forgotten plate to the hearth beside hers and scooted closer to her, hands resting warm and soft against Finn's knees. "You were so young. Was it just you and him after that?"

Finn nodded, a tear slipping down her cheek and dropping onto her shirt. "He was my dad, so I think everyone just assumed I would be fine with him. No one ever really checked on us after that."

"When did he pass?"

"When I was nine. He drank himself to death." Finn's eyes were locked onto the wall behind Aisling. "How did you know he was gone?"

"I don't think they intended for me to know, actually," Aisling said, picking up the extra folded blanket Finn had brought from the house and left on the hearth. She shook it out and wrapped it around both of them. Finn leaned against the hearth and Aisling sat beside her, her legs tangled into Finn's, mirroring their fingers.

"When Grandma Joan called with the news, my dad was shattered." Aisling paused, recalling the conversation she'd had with her father when she'd called to tell them she'd be staying in Wales. "And then when he tried to make arrangements to bring you to the UK, he found out your dad didn't leave a will. They were not blood related, so that meant he had no right to take you out of the country."

"I never knew that." Finn looked at Aisling, tears shimmering in her eyes. "I went into foster care right after he died. I didn't know anyone wanted me."

Aisling leaned into her and gently caught the next tear with her thumb.

"He actually just told me that recently, which makes something that happened when I was a kid make a lot more sense. When he found out they didn't consider him family, he didn't come out of his room for four days, although at the time I didn't know why. When he finally did, he tried for years to find you—"

"But I was already in the foster care system." Finn's body stiffened as she said the words. "I wish they would have told me. I knew I had an uncle, but when I never heard anything...I thought maybe they'd found him and he just didn't care."

"He cared." Aisling laid her hand over Finn's heart. "In fact, he was never the same again. When I spoke to him after we found out about the pub here, he told me that he thought about you every day. And I know he still does."

"Did he say that?"

Aisling nodded as tears flowed down Finn's cheeks and her shoulders shook with sobs. She wrapped her arms around Finn, fingers sifting through the layers of her hair as she cried. She was quiet, careful not to try to wrap words around Finn's memories. She had enough sense to know that there just weren't any words to make something like that better. Not now.

After a few minutes, Finn wiped the tears from her cheeks, then leaned slowly back against the hearth and pulled Aisling into her chest. Aisling slipped her hands under the hem of Finn's sweatshirt, fingertips light and warm against her skin. A cluster of bats swooped across the sky, dipping just for a moment to swirl within the walls of the castle before they disappeared beyond the open wall toward the dark forest beyond. Finn's breath slowed eventually as she held Aisling close, resting her chin on the top of her head. It was a long time before she spoke.

"Thank you," she said. "For telling me."

Aisling trailed her fingertips across Finn's chest. "Do you want to meet him someday?"

"Who?" She leaned back and looked in Aisling's eyes. "My uncle?"

Aisling nodded. "When I told him what we were doing the day after we got here, he didn't know what to say, I think. But Mum told me he's driving her crazy ever since, asking if I've told her anything about you."

Finn laughed and leaned her head back, looking at the sky.

"Of course I'd like to meet him. Someday."

A few drops of melted wax sizzled and dripped down the edge of the mantel and splashed onto the hearth beside them. Finn lay back on the blanket and Aisling settled closer into her arms, the stars dense and scattered in the black night sky above where the crumbled stone walls formed a makeshift frame around them.

"Do you remember anything about your mom?"

Finn settled one arm behind her head, eyes fixed on the endless black sky. "Not much. But from the pictures I've seen, I look just like her. Same dark eyes, dark hair. She was an immigrant from Cuba. She'd only been in the country a week before she met my dad."

"And they fell in love?"

"Yeah. I think that's why it was so hard for him when she died." She paused, her words slowing as if they were piecing together for the first time. "Maybe he wanted to die too."

Finn ran her fingertips lightly over Aisling's cheek and pulled her closer. The only sound was the wind through the tall grasses outside the castle, the rustling coming through the open spaces where windows had been centuries ago. Finn started to say something, then looked back at the sky and stopped.

"What?"

"I do remember something about her." Finn's voice softened, as if the memory was shimmering into existence in front of her. "The scent of her. Like roses. She loved them. She had them in little pots everywhere there was a spot of sunlight in the house, then when the petals fell she'd scoop them up and set them out to dry on the windowsills."

Aisling bit her lip softly until she spoke again, holding a space in the silence for Finn's memories.

"I think she might have made perfume out of them as well. I was too young to remember. But when she tucked me in at night, she sang me songs in Spanish, and I remember the scent of them on her skin."

Finn's fingers sifted through Aisling's hair. "When Dad died four years later, the first night I was in a foster home, I think I was in shock. I remember being huddled in this tight little ball under the covers. The room was pitch-dark, too dark, and I just wanted to go home."

Aisling traced Finn's palm with her fingertips, listening. "But there wasn't one anymore."

"Exactly." Finn's voice was low and steady, like she was reading a story that had happened to someone else. "When social services came to get me, I remember looking back at the apartment as we walked out the door. I knew I'd never see it again, and I didn't."

"And you went into foster care that day?"

"Yes, that night." She drew a long, slow breath. "I was scared out of my mind."

Finn stopped and was silent for so long that Aisling wondered if she was going to go on. She started to speak twice, then hesitated.

"Tell me."

"And then something happened." Finn held Aisling closer and whispered into her hair. "But if I tell you, you're going to think I'm crazy."

Just then, Aisling caught a glimpse of a golden ball of light, barely peeking over the top of one of the stone walls but so bright it lit up its own little corner of the night sky. "You might be surprised," she said, smiling. "Try me."

"I was lying there under the covers so no one would see me cry…" Finn's breath slowed with the memory. "And I felt her."

"Your mum?"

"Yeah, it was like she was suddenly there with me, holding me. I felt her arms around me. I even smelled her. She held me until I fell asleep, I think." Finn paused. "I should have been scared, but I wasn't."

"I don't think you're crazy," Aisling whispered.

Finn tensed suddenly, then leaned up on her elbow. "What the hell was that?"

"What?"

"I just saw something." Finn sat up and shrugged on her jacket. She nodded toward the far corner of the castle. "In that corner."

"Like something glowing?" Aisling said, sitting up beside her and peering into the sky. "An orb?"

"Yes, exactly like that," Finn said, her voice dropping to a whisper as she pointed to where the top of the castle wall met the sky. "And now there's more."

Several golden orbs were hovering just above the top of the wall, as if waiting for permission to enter.

"Finn," Aisling whispered. "This may get a little weird. I should tell you…"

But Finn wasn't listening. Her eyes were fixed on the golden orbs that were now slowly dropping into the room like a waterfall, hovering and glowing in the open space. Aisling's voice trailed off. It was too late for words. She glanced over and tangled her fingers into Finn's.

"Breathe," Aisling whispered, waiting until she heard Finn take a long, slow breath beside her. "They won't hurt us."

"What are they?" Finn whispered.

"I don't really know." Aisling smiled as a few orbs dropped lower down the wall. "But I think it may be closer to 'who' rather than 'what.' "

Finn turned to look in her eyes. "It's not the first time you've seen them, is it?"

"No." Aisling turned back to the orbs, glowing even brighter now. "It's not the first time."

Finn found Aisling's hand and they looked up together as more orbs spilled over the top edge of the castle wall and hovered, the liquid light within them in constant motion, waxing and waning, casting a translucent gold wash over the castle walls. The candles around them seemed to glow more brightly as they watched a single orb sink slowly beneath the others, the light undulating within it like water, as if asking permission to come closer. It dropped slowly, the color changing from gold to a pale, warm pink, hesitantly sinking until it was only slightly above Finn, where it shifted to a deep, velvety rose hue.

Aisling felt Finn hold her breath, saw her close her eyes when the orb floated just above her face, and heard the sob that caught in her throat as it dipped to touch her forehead. It stayed there for a long moment, the rose-tinted light becoming brighter, warming Finn's face, then Aisling watched as it rose slowly and disappeared over the edge of the castle and into the sky with the others.

Finn opened her eyes as the last of the golden lights floated away and pulled Aisling into her arms, cheeks wet with tears, and just for a second, Aisling thought she heard her whisper something in Spanish.

❖

When they finally got back to the cottage, it was nearly midnight and so cold their breath turned to frost in the living room as they walked in. Finn started fires in the main room and their bedroom, and the air warmed quickly with the sound of Scottish green pine popping and crackling in the fireplace. She rubbed the sap off her hands and hung her coat by the door, breathing in the scent of crushed pine needles and fresh earth the wood gave off as it flamed to life.

"Will you go start us a bath?" Aisling said from around the corner, unpacking the basket onto the kitchen table. "I'll be there in just a minute."

As Finn leaned into the kitchen to kiss her, Aisling caught her hand. "Hey," she said, her eyes soft. "Are you okay?"

Finn leaned in to kiss her slowly before she stepped back, thinking before she answered. She felt suddenly softer, more relaxed, as if her body was a fist she'd just unclenched.

"For once in what feels like forever, I'm more than okay," she said, lifting Aisling's chin with her thumb and kissing her softly. "Way more."

A few minutes later, Finn was luxuriating in the bath when Aisling entered, wearing her navy velvet robe and carrying a tea tray with an enormous slice of Maggie's apple pie drenched in vanilla custard.

"Sorry," she said. "I tried to be cool about it, but I couldn't wait a moment longer."

Finn laughed as Aisling handed her the tea tray. She slipped out of her robe and hung it on the back of the door before she sank down into the water in front of Finn, leaning back against her in the steam with a long sigh of contentment.

"Jesus Christ," Finn whispered, lowering the tea tray and balancing it on Aisling's knees in front of them. "You are…beyond beautiful."

"Well, if you're trying to sweet-talk me into getting a bite of this pie," Aisling said, handing her the fork loaded with flaky crust and cinnamon-scented apples, "it worked."

Finn ate the bite of pie and another before she handed the fork back to Aisling, who started with the crust edge, dipping it in the custard.

Finn dipped her head to whisper in Aisling's ear. "That's the first time I've seen you naked."

"Aye," Aisling said, looking back at her with a wink. "Lucky you."

The water cooled quickly in the chilly air, and they managed to stay in the tub only long enough to finish the pie before Finn stood up and reached for a towel, wrapping it around her hips and running her hands through her wet hair. When she was done, she took another towel off the stack and offered it to Aisling along with her robe.

"Wow." Aisling took the robe and stared. "You…"

"What?" Finn smiled, arching an eyebrow. "Never seen a naked boxer before?"

Finn watched Aisling's gaze as it moved over shoulders and chest, then lingered at her abs before she finally smiled and stepped out of the bath and into her robe.

"Not one that looks like you." She stood on her tiptoes and kissed Finn. "Where have you been hiding that body?"

"Well, until the last few days, folded up on the couch."

Finn snapped her with the towel and headed to the kitchen with the pie plate. When she got back to the bedroom, the fire was still crackling in the small fireplace at the foot of the bed, and a single lamp with amber glass panels was lit up on the nightstand. Aisling was already in bed, tangled in the duvet, her shoulders delicate and bare. "Come to bed."

Finn unwrapped the towel, and time stopped as she memorized every inch of Aisling's naked body in the flickering firelight. The lightest drift of amber freckles was visible across her breasts, like an ocean wave had left them there, washed across the pale pink of her nipples. Finn felt Aisling's fingertips at the back of her neck as she dipped her head and touched them only with her breath, then kissed up the side of Aisling's neck to her ear.

"Tell me what you want."

It was a moment before she answered, and when she did, it was a whisper that just brushed Finn's lips.

"This," she said. "Us."

Finn kissed her then, strong and deep, lifting Aisling's hands above her head and holding them there with one of hers. She traced the edge of her ear with her tongue and kissed slowly down her neck to her breasts, warming her nipple with her breath and a hot swirl of her tongue before she pulled it into her mouth with a slick, sudden intensity.

Aisling's breath caught, and Finn watched wild copper waves fall back from her face as she arched her back, her hands light and tense on Finn's shoulders. Finn rolled her hardening nipple in her mouth, stroking it with her tongue, then brushing it achingly slowly with just the tip before she moved down her body, kissing every freckle.

"God." Finn's words melted into the warmth of her skin, her tongue tracing the curve of Aisling's hip as she took her in. "You're just so fucking beautiful."

She felt Aisling's hand in her hair as Finn drew in the scent of her skin, her hand smoothing around the curve of her hip then settling between her thighs. She looked up into Aisling's eyes as she slicked her thumb lightly over her clit, watching as Aisling tilted her hips up and her breath caught. Finn listened as Aisling's body begged her to deepen her touch, then dipped her head and traced the edges of her clit with the tip of her tongue. She felt Aisling's thighs tense, then open for Finn's long, slow strokes, tongue suddenly swirling and surrounding her clit, until she heard Aisling hold her breath, fingers tangled hard in Finn's hair.

Finn raised her body and settled her hips over Aisling's. She slipped one hand between their bodies and cradled her face with the other, holding Aisling's eyes. She stroked Aisling's bottom lip with her thumb, and when she spoke her voice was a deep scrape, a whisper like gravel across concrete.

"Do you want me inside you?"

Finn parted Aisling's thighs with one of hers as she spoke, her fingers warm and soft against the heat of her. Aisling nodded, but Finn waited until she heard the words.

"Finn, please." Her voice was a restless whisper. "I need you."

Finn leaned forward and bit Aisling's neck gently as she slid two fingers deep inside, stroking her slowly, eyes locked on Aisling until she arched hard against the bed and wrapped her hands around Finn's hips, pulling her deeper. Finn leaned into her and moved her hand with her hips, face buried in the heat of Aisling's shoulder. She closed her eyes, memorizing the feel of Aisling's body under hers until Aisling's lips moved against her cheek.

"More."

It was only one word, but the desperation in it swept away all restraint Finn had left. She added another finger and thrust deeper inside, the heel of her hand sliding strong against Aisling's clit. She shifted her body so that her own clit rode the back of her hand and their bodies moved together like rolling ocean waves, smooth and strong, as Aisling reached for the pine headboard behind her. Finn watched a slow flush move across her breasts and wash scarlet across her neck. Aisling's arms were tense, her fingers pressed hard against the wood behind her head, her breath quick and shallow.

"Finn. Don't stop. Please don't stop."

Finn wrapped her other hand around the back of Aisling's neck and slowed her hips, moving in direct strokes over Aisling's clit, slick and tight under her hand. Aisling groaned, a fine mist of sweat covering her chest as she whispered into Finn's neck. Finn leaned into her, deep, fucking her slowly, curving her fingers up to stroke the tense spot inside her. She felt Aisling's orgasm build quickly and shake the breath from her body when it finally washed over her, her thighs trembling against Finn's hips as she came. She was still arched and breathless when Finn came hard with a low growl, Aisling's legs wrapped tightly around her waist.

Her hips slowed until Finn sank to the bed beside Aisling and caught her breath. After a few minutes, Aisling rolled over on her side and traced the tattoo just under Finn's left shoulder. It was hand drawn, two simple triangles with a tree between them, the roots reaching deep into the earth, topped by branches stretching toward the sky.

Aisling's voice was soft, intimate, as if she knew the words were a secret.

"When did you get this?"

Finn pulled her closer and closed her eyes. "It's the first tattoo I ever got. I don't know where I saw it, but I've dreamed about that pattern since I was a kid."

"What does it mean?"

"I don't know." Finn's whisper was warm against her cheek. "I just knew it was important."

She was almost asleep when she felt Aisling's lashes flutter closed against her shoulder.

"It was us." Aisling's voice fell into deep breath as she stirred in her arms. "It's always been us."

CHAPTER TWELVE

The next morning the sun was shining as they walked to the pub, snow melting into lacy patterns at the edges of the path, pierced by icicles from the trees above that dropped and splintered along the path.

"So, what do you think the chances are we'll see Kaitlyn at the door when we round the corner?" Finn said, unzipping her jacket as they neared the square.

Aisling tangled her fingers into Finn's and pulled her sunglasses down over her eyes.

"Well, she may have gotten the message from Greystone, but if not, you're American, right?" Aisling peered up at Finn, sunlight glinting off the blue reflection on her aviators. "So I'm sure you have a gun somewhere."

"Simmer down, babe." Finn laughed, squeezing her hand. "I think we should let Greystone take her out, don't you? It's only polite. Something tells me she might want to have a shot at that."

As they rounded the corner there was indeed someone by the pub doors, but it wasn't a tall California blonde, not by a long shot. Barry Wright sat on the sidewalk tying two ends of a broken shoelace together and trying to yank the knot through the eyelet on his worn trainers.

"Hey, Barry. Good to see you," Finn said as they walked up. "What can we do for you?"

"Hi." Barry's eyes darted to Aisling, then back to the concrete as Finn turned the key in the lock. "I was just wondering…" His voice trailed off and he looked over to the park in the center of the square as if contemplating an escape.

Aisling glanced at Finn, then took the keys and ducked through the door, closing it behind her. Barry pulled off his beanie, tucking it in his back pocket.

"Do you remember the other day when you said something about my haircut, that you might be able to help me with it? That day we set up the pub?"

Finn nodded.

"I might need a haircut, but I don't want to bother my dad about it. He's got enough on his mind with my brothers." He glanced over at the market stalls, the blue-and-white-striped awnings blowing up into the wind on the next street over. "I can't pay you, but I was thinking maybe I could help you with something instead." He paused, pulling his beanie back onto his head and shoving his hands deep into his pockets. "Like last time?"

Finn nodded. "You've got great timing, man. I've been thinking about starting a project I can use your help with."

She held the door open and pulled out her wallet. "Why don't you go over to the café and get us three bacon sandwiches while I run home and get my clippers?" Finn handed Barry a twenty-pound note. He flashed a sudden smile and took off in the direction of the café, running through the park, icy slush splashing in every direction.

"Aisling?" Finn said as she came through the door, turning on the lamps in the corners she'd forgotten. "Are you here?"

"Aye." Aisling popped up from behind the counter and plopped an enormous box of crisps on the bar. "I've been wrestling with this stupid box since I got in here. I don't know why they tape them up like there's military secrets that might spill out. I can't get into the stupid thing."

Finn walked over and pulled out her pocketknife, flipped it open, and split the box down the center. Bright packets of crisps spilled out onto the bar, and Aisling grabbed Finn's shirt and pulled her over the bar for a kiss.

"Thank you. Another second and I would have lost my mind."

Finn kissed her again and sat down on the nearest barstool. "I have two questions for you."

"Hit me."

Finn smiled. "The first one is, do you want a bacon sandwich from the café?"

"I can't believe you even asked me that. It's like you don't know me at all." Aisling sniffed as she sorted the bags of crisps by flavor and tucked them behind the bar, grabbing the register money while she was down there. "What's the second?"

"The second thing is a little more tricky." Finn glanced back at the door and checked her watch. "I told Barry once that I'd cut his hair if he wanted me to, and he's taking me up on it. So I sent him for the sandwiches while I go grab my clippers from home."

"Why in the world do you have clippers?"

"I had my roommate throw them in with my stuff from New York." Finn raked her hand through her hair and checked herself out in the mirror behind the bar. "There's no way in hell I'm trusting some random Welshman to give me a decent fade."

Aisling smiled and raised an eyebrow. "I have no idea what that is, but knock yourself out." Pound coins clanked into the register drawer as she counted out the day's starting cash. "That's sweet of you to do, actually. I know his dad can't have a lot of money laying around for stuff like that with four boys in the house."

"That's what I was thinking." Finn reached over the bar for the mixer gun and a glass and filled it with Coke. "But he offered to help me with something around here since he couldn't afford to pay me." She smiled and replaced the mixer gun. "Not that I would have let him pay me at all."

"You know, there's something about that kid that I like, and I don't say that very often." Aisling stopped counting and looked up. "What are you going to have him do?"

"Well." Finn paused, pulling up a picture on her phone and holding it out to Aisling. "Tell me what you think of this idea."

❖

A few minutes later, Barry was back with the sandwiches and carefully laid out every penny of the change they'd given him, organized by descending value in tiny, even stacks on the bar.

"Thanks, Barry," Aisling said with a wink, opening her sandwich and breathing in the crisp, smoky scent. "Ah, bacon. Scent of the gods." She paused, nodding in Finn's direction. "Hey, do you think you can get Finn out of my hair for a bit while I get everything ready to open? I'll bring you guys a stool out back if you want to start… whatever it is you're going to do with these." Aisling picked up the clippers cautiously with her thumb and forefinger off the barstool and held them up. "I don't even want to know why these look like they've been through a war."

"Hey, those are vintage Wahl Pro from the sixties. That's like the Maserati of hair clippers." Finn winked at Barry, who giggled into his bacon sandwich.

Aisling held them up by the cord at arm's length. "Well, they smell like motor oil, so the sooner you get them out of here, the better."

Finn grabbed a barstool on her way out and nodded to Barry to go on outside to the patio.

"Thanks for this," Finn said, lifting the stool to her shoulder. "It won't take long."

Aisling smiled, twisting her hair into a knot at the back of her neck. "We left everything pretty much ready to go Saturday night, so there's not that much to do. Take your time. Alwen's coming in today anyway when it starts to get busier, so we're all set."

Finn gave Aisling a quick kiss and walked out to the back patio area to find Barry kicking rocks scattered across the bricks, his beanie in his hand.

Finn had him take a seat on the barstool and ran her hand through the long, uneven layers of Barry's hair. "So, what are you thinking for your cut, man?"

The back of it was well past his collar, and even the front layers were almost long enough to tuck behind his ears, which, she realized, was probably why he wore a beanie constantly.

Barry looked up, confused. "What do you mean?"

"I mean how do you want it to look? We could do pretty much anything here, you've got a lot to work with."

Barry paused. "I don't know. I don't think anyone's ever asked me that. My mom always cut our hair, but then I—" He stopped abruptly, looking off to the side. "She died last year."

"I'm sorry, Barry." Finn stepped to the side and squatted down beside him. "I can't imagine how much that sucked."

"Yeah." Barry looked up at the sky. It was a moment before he spoke again. "It feels like it just happened."

"I know how that feels, and it's overwhelming sometimes." She paused. "Let's just think about what we can handle right now, okay?" Finn stood and pulled a pair of silver scissors out of a leather pouch she'd laid on the table by her clippers. "And we can definitely handle this hair situation."

Finn started by cutting some of the length off the back, Barry's light brown hair falling silently to the brick patio, some lying around his trainers in a downy pile, some swept away by the breeze. When Finn got to the crown, she stepped around in front and looked at Barry.

"Do you want to leave it longer in front, or short all over?"

"Um...I don't know." Barry hesitated. "Not long, though. I kind of hate it right now."

"Okay." Finn ran her fingers through her own hair, standing the top layers on end. "Is there anything you don't like about my hair?"

"Nothing." Barry looked at the sides of Finn's head and she turned so he could see the close cut at the back. "I like it. It's cool."

"Okay, we'll start there."

Finn stepped around behind the stool again and started cutting, the weightless layers falling through her fingers as she took them gradually shorter.

"So how did you learn how to cut hair?"

Finn handed Barry the scissors and leaned over to pick up her clippers, setting the guard to a level two with the dial on the side.

"When I was younger, I used to box—"

"Whoa." Barry turned to look at her. "Like in fights?"

"Yeah, I did semipro boxing until I was twenty-four. Hold still." She turned on the clippers and cut a careful, clean arc over Barry's ear to just below his crown. Barry caught a long chunk of it in his palm and held it for a moment before he let it float to the ground. "And when I got hurt and couldn't fight anymore, my coach paid for me to go to barber school."

"Wow." Barry was quiet as Finn shaved the other side of his head. "So you're a barber?"

"Well, I never ended up doing it professionally, but I've always liked it. It's a good skill to have. There's something about a fresh haircut that just makes everyone feel better, you know?"

Finn buzzed the second side with clean lines, stopping a bit lower than she had on the first side and fading it into the top.

"I know you're a girl," Barry said, then paused. "But you're not like most girls. You're different."

Finn laughed, adjusting the setting on the clippers again and tapering the back of his hair into a perfect fade to match the sides. "You're right there. I've never been like other girls, not even when I was your age." She put down the clippers and brushed the hair off Barry's shoulders. "But it's okay to be different. You can't let other people tell you who you are."

Barry was quiet as Finn took the scissors back from him and sliced choppy layers into the front of Barry's hair, pulling it up through her fingers and cutting the ends with a subtle V shape to help them hold some height. When she was done, she pulled out the small container she'd stashed in her pocket when she grabbed her clippers at home.

"What is that?"

Finn held up the tin for him to see. "This is a styling wax, although most guys just call it 'product.'"

"What does it do?"

"Well," Finn said, warming a dab in her hands before she rubbed them together and ran them through her own hair. "Do you see what I'm doing here? You just want to warm a little bit of this, about the size of a penny, in your hands, then just play with it until you get the look you want. Keep it about an inch from your roots, though. You don't want to weigh those down."

She scooped out a bit more and did the same to Barry's hair, handing him the tin. "You can keep that. I brought it for you. I always have product lying around."

"But," Barry's smile faded to worry, "I can't pay you for it. It looks expensive."

"First of all, it's not expensive. I don't buy it if it is." Finn stepped back to look at the shape and pulled several pieces up in front to work with. "And you shouldn't either. The cheap stuff from the drugstore in town will work just as well when you run out of this. Just try to get something with the same texture as this one."

She picked up her phone and scrolled through some pictures. "Look at this." She held the phone up to Barry and he leaned in to look, a smile instantly lighting up his face.

"That's so cool! I love that."

"See where they parted his hair here and razored in a shaved line?" Finn widened the picture and pointed to the perfect part at the side of the head. "That's called a hard part. I just styled the rest of your hair to look like this picture, so if you like the way that part looks, I can do that too."

Barry nodded and sat back in his chair while Finn switched her clippers back on. It took less than five seconds to cut in a perfectly straight part on the side of Barry's head. Finn set her clippers down when she was satisfied with it, then pulled up a mirror app on her phone and handed it to him.

"You look five years older, dude," Finn said, smiling. "It looks great on you. You're not a kid anymore, and now you don't look like one."

Barry stared at his reflection like he was looking at someone he didn't know, then lowered the phone. Tears were welling up in his eyes, and he aggressively swiped one away with his sleeve.

"Hey, what's wrong? You don't like it?"

"No, I love it." Barry's voice caught when he answered. "I don't know why I'm crying. I'm just stupid, I guess."

Finn crouched down and looked Barry in the eye, her hand warm on his shoulder.

"Listen, you're not stupid, far from it. Everyone cries sometimes, including me."

Barry met her eyes. "Really? You don't look like you cry."

"Yeah, really," Finn said. "Strong people deal with how they feel, and sometimes that means we have to cry a little bit. That's a sign of strength, not weakness."

Barry nodded, then looked at his reflection again before he handed the phone back.

"Thank you. I know it's just a haircut, but it's kind of a big deal to me."

Finn smiled, handing him the clippers and scissors to carry back in. "When you need a cut, you come to me, right? I have too much to do on my own with this place, so I'd be pretty excited if you're serious about helping me out some."

Barry beamed, straightening his shoulders and sliding the product tin into his back pocket. "Christmas is in ten days, so I'm on my school holidays. When do you want me?"

❖

By the time Finn returned inside, Aisling had opened the doors and there were already a few punters in the pub laughing at one of the back tables by the windows.

"Finn," Aisling said, turning when she caught sight of her coming through the doors. "You should have seen Barry leave just now. He walked like a totally different kid."

"Really? That's good to hear. I enjoyed it." Finn stashed her clippers and scissors behind the bar and started washing the two wineglasses in the sink. "I guess their mom used to cut their hair before she died last year. I didn't realize how rough everything had been for them."

"People don't usually surprise me." Aisling smiled. "But you seem to have quite a few hidden talents."

"Well, someone's got to keep you on your toes." Finn winked in Aisling's direction. "So are you good with him helping me out for a few hours upstairs tomorrow for that project?"

"Honestly, this place is super easy to open. It only takes one of us to do it now that we're set up anyway, so take as long as you want."

"Great," Finn said, leaning back on the counter and folding her arms in front of her. "Now all we need is someone in the kitchen."

Alwen showed up right on time later that afternoon. After they'd given her a tour and showed her how to run the cash register, she blended right in, laughing and talking to the locals at the bar. It took her exactly three minutes of practice to pull a better pint than Finn, so Finn retreated to the kitchen to try to do some work on the menu and supply lists. By the time she'd gotten through most of it, she could tell by the music and laughter that the pub was nearly at capacity and the evening was in full swing. When she'd finally wrapped everything up and returned to the bar, she was just in time to catch Aisling coming up from the cellar with a case of orange juice bottles and took them out of her arms.

"Why don't you go home and put your feet up for a few hours? You've been working all day. I've got this."

"You've been working too, silly," Aisling said as Finn plunked the box onto the bar and started unloading it. "And it's actually been an easy afternoon. Alwen is a natural and somehow knows every single person that comes through the door."

"What would you think about hiring Michael, Jack's son from the butcher shop, just part-time to give Alwen a hand? If she starts coming in later and closing for us, that means she wouldn't have to be here alone."

"That sounds like a great idea. He's actually sitting at the end of the bar right now if you want to chat with him." She leaned to the left and peered down the bar. "If you can get those girls to let him go for a second, that is."

"Look at that." Finn caught his eye and headed around the corner of the bar to talk to him, winking in Aisling's direction as she went. "A boy after my own heart."

Aisling tossed a bar towel in her direction, and the rest of the evening sped by in what seemed like five minutes. Right before last call, Alwen stuck her head into the kitchen where Finn was showing Aisling some of the possibilities she'd come up with for the menu.

"Hey," Alwen said, looking back toward the bar. "There's a lady out here that wants to see Finn."

Aisling shot Finn a look. "What does she look like?"

"Um…" Alwen considered that for a moment before she answered. "She looks like she doesn't live around here."

Aisling smiled. "Gotcha."

Alwen went back to the bar, the kitchen door swinging shut behind her.

"One guess who that is," Finn said, heading for the door with a wink in Aisling's direction. "Let's see what she's got to say for herself. Anything you'd like me to tell her?"

"Let's see…" Aisling paused. "If you get a moment, you can tell that bunny-boiling American slag to get the hell out of our town." She smiled sweetly. "Or at least out of our pub."

Finn laughed out loud, shaking her head as she pushed through the swinging kitchen doors and found Kaitlyn sitting at the table closest to the fire. She was wearing a sleek black pinstripe skirt and jacket, but she'd taken the jacket off and draped it across the back of her chair. As Finn walked up, she saw that the silk blouse underneath was unbuttoned more than enough to show the curve of her breasts in a translucent bra.

"Ms. Matthews." Finn pulled out a chair opposite her at the table and nodded toward the bar. "Can I get you something to drink?"

Kaitlyn crossed her legs slowly and met Finn's eyes.

"I'm actually here about business, so not at the moment." Her eyes dropped to Finn's shoulders and down to her belt, where they lingered until her eyes swept leisurely back up. "But if you want to hit me up later, we can get a drink somewhere more private."

"Kaitlyn," Finn said, her voice low and strong as she sat down and leaned back against the chair. "I think it's pretty clear that Aisling and I are together, so that's not going to happen."

Kaitlyn pulled a lip gloss out of her bag and slicked it across her lips, then pressed them together and leaned forward as her blouse fell dangerously close to open.

"Look, Finn. Let's cut the bullshit. I think you're hot as fuck. And no one else ever has to know."

Finn glanced toward the ceiling and reminded herself to be polite. For the moment anyway.

Kaitlyn took out another business card and jotted something on the back.

"I'm at the Dalton Inn in Cardiff, and this…" She held Finn's eyes as she pushed the card toward her. "Is my room number." Her fingers brushed Finn's as she gave her the card, which Finn immediately pushed back in her direction.

"Ms. Matthews." Finn's head snapped up when she heard Aisling's voice and she pulled out the chair beside her at the table. Aisling continued as she sat down. "I wasn't sure we'd be seeing you again."

Kaitlyn dragged her eyes over to Aisling and paused. "I'm sorry, your name slipped my mind. What was it? Ashlee?"

Finn laid a soft hand on Aisling's knee under the table.

"Aisling Moss." Aisling's voice was cool. "We met the other day here at the pub."

"Well, it looks like we're going to be seeing a lot more of each other."

Kaitlyn pulled out a short stack of stapled papers and handed them to Finn with a smile. Finn passed them to Aisling without looking at them.

"The mining proposal for Rockfield Acquisitions passed this morning, so as the Community Liaison Director, I'm going around to local businesses and giving out this information packet that will let you know what to expect as far as changes in the next few months. The support of the community is essential to the success of this project." She paused, her eyes dropping again to Finn's mouth. "And, of course, as the Community Liaison, I'll be here for the next few months to answer any questions you may have and make sure your every desire is taken care of."

Finn felt her neck grow hot as she sensed Aisling fuming beside her. She cleared her throat and sat back in her chair. "That vote was scheduled at Cardiff City Hall for Friday. What happened?"

"An emergency meeting was called this morning and the proposal was passed."

"Let me guess." Aisling thumbed through the papers Kaitlyn had given them as she spoke. "Because it was an emergency meeting, there wasn't time to notify the Cwylldbridge councilmen."

Kaitlyn raised an eyebrow, her smile fading. "I've been assured they were notified by email a few hours before the vote."

"So that email would have gone out in the middle of Sunday night," Finn said, holding Katlyn's gaze and leaning back in her chair. "And how many of them actually saw it in time to show up?"

Kaitlyn shifted in her seat and looked longingly at a line of shots being poured at the bar.

"You'll be happy to know that there was a representative there." She dug in her enormous leather bag, finally producing a copy of the minutes from the meeting with a flourish. "It looks like Herschel Wright was there to represent Coldbridge."

"Well, I guess it doesn't matter." Finn tensed and set her jaw. "It's done now. But I understand the actual mining will be done right outside Cwylldbridge city limits. Is that right?"

Kailyn nodded, pointing to a map on the stack of papers she'd given Aisling.

"So the environmental damage, negative effect on tourism, and threats to our groundwater are only an issue for our village, right?" Finn waited until Kaitlyn nodded reluctantly before she went on. "Cardiff is over forty minutes away from the dig site. They won't even know it's happening…except the city will be millions of pounds richer."

"Forgive me for asking," Kaitlyn said, a knife edge glinting in her voice. "But why is this so important to you? I mean, I get why this would affect Ashlee, she's Welsh or British or whatever." She paused, eyes still focused on Finn, and lifted an eyebrow. "But when we spoke previously you said you were only here for a year."

Aisling stood up and extended her hand. "Miss Matthews, we

appreciate you coming by, but this is our home. There's no way in hell we'd ever get behind this project, so let's not waste each other's time."

"Well," Kaitlyn said, ignoring Aisling's hand as she stood and slid on her suit jacket and caramel cashmere overcoat. She tied the belt around her waist and pulled it tight as she locked eyes with Finn. "As I said, if you ever want to…bury the hatchet, you've got my card."

She picked up the bag and walked away, with one more long glance in Finn's direction before the doors shut behind her.

CHAPTER THIRTEEN

Jesus Christ, that woman is shameless." Aisling felt her neck and face flaming, her words instantly melting into a low hiss. "I'm surprised she didn't just lie on the table with her legs in the air and hand you an engraved invitation to fuck her."

"Well, it wouldn't have done her any good." Finn picked up the papers Kaitlyn had left them. "Which I'm happy to clear up for her if she has any doubt." She got up from the table and checked her watch, then walked over to ring the large brass bell behind the bar.

"Last call, lads. Drink up!" Alwen shouted, weaving in and among the tables like a pro, a stack of dirty pint glasses in each hand.

Aisling watched as Finn collected glasses from the back tables as the customers left, setting them behind the bar by the sink. *The nerve of that...woman. She couldn't have been more obvious if she'd been sitting in Finn's lap for the entire conversation.*

Aisling was still fuming silently a few moments later when Finn caught her by the elbow as she passed. "Let's get everyone out of here and we'll talk about it."

Cleanup was quick with three of them, and Alwen even did the prep for the next morning before she picked up her coat to leave. As she headed for the door, Aisling called her over to the register.

"You smashed it tonight, girl." Aisling smiled and handed her an orange juice from the cooler under the bar. "I don't know how we ever did this without you."

"Thank you." Alwen touched the mark on her forehead from the weekend. "I still don't believe this job is real. There's never any jobs going in the village anymore, so I feel really lucky."

"If you don't mind my asking, what did you make at the shop?" At Alwen's response, Aisling touched a button on the register and the door sprang open with a clatter. "That's barely minimum wage, right?" She picked up a few bills and folded them into a small brown envelope from under the drawer. "Let's add a couple of pounds an hour, shall we? Plus your tips, of course."

"You really don't have to give me that much." Alwen took a knit beanie out of her jacket pocket and pulled it onto her head. "I'm just grateful for the job."

"I'm not giving you anything. You deserve this." Aisling pressed the envelope into her hand. "You being here means Finn and I may not actually have to be here until close every day. And you're great at it. Everyone loves you."

Alwen smiled, slipping the envelope into her pocket.

"So, let's do four till close, Sundays and Mondays off?"

Alwen just looked at her for a moment, letting her words sink in before she pulled Aisling into a hug. When she let her go, there were tears shimmering in her eyes. "That sounds brilliant. I won't let you down, I promise."

Aisling hugged her back, laughing when she felt the baby kick between them.

"You may have a future football star on your hands there. How far along are you?"

"I think about seven months, maybe more."

Aisling hesitated, choosing her words carefully. "You haven't been to the doctor yet, have you?"

"It's not that I haven't tried." Alwen picked at a loose thread on the sleeve of her jacket. "I've had three appointments for a scan in Cardiff but had to cancel all of them because the owner of the shop needed me to come in."

"And you live with your mum, right?"

Alwen nodded, the thread finally coming loose in her hand. "But she's not...involved. I don't really bring it up to her anymore."

Aisling squeezed her hand. "Do something for me, okay? Make another appointment so they can get you registered with a midwife. Tell them how far along you are when you call."

"Okay. I'll try to get one on a Monday."

Aisling shook her head, meeting Alwen's eyes. "Take the first appointment they have. I'll shut the pub if I have to. You're not missing this one."

Alwen smiled and promised to call in the morning as she rounded the corner of the bar, waving to Finn as she left. Aisling wiped down the spotless bar as she watched Finn throw another log on the fire and replace the grate, the iron scraping on the rock hearth as it slid back into place. She turned out most of the lamps and came back around the bar, reaching underneath for a small cardboard box she handed to Aisling.

Aisling shook it twice before she sat on the counter. "What's this?"

"Just something for us." Finn smiled. "Open it."

Aisling arched an eyebrow until Finn reached for her pocketknife.

"That's right. I forgot about your complicated relationship with packing tape."

Aisling reached into the box and pulled out two heavy crystal whiskey tumblers, both etched on the side. One was engraved with *Moss* and the other *Morgan*, and underneath, *Gwenllian's Sword* and the date.

"These are amazing," Aisling said, turning hers in light that caught and sparkled in the cut crystal. "How did you find these?"

"I had them made for us, at a shop in town that sells local crystal, then had them engraved."

"Thank you, Finn." Aisling pulled her close and stood on tiptoe to kiss her. "They're beautiful. I love them."

"I can't lie," Finn said, rounding the bar and picking up her favorite scotch, Laphroaig Ten Year from the isle of Islay in Scotland. "I love this place, but I'm pretty excited to have Alwen here. I know we're both used to long hours, but an extra evening off every once in a while wouldn't be terrible."

Finn pulled the cork out of the bottle with a pop just as they heard a knock at the door.

Aisling shot the door a withering glance. "Finn, I swear to God, if that is that American slapper here to—"

"Then I'll tell her to get lost. Believe me, I've had enough of her for the day, too," Finn said over her shoulder as she headed to the door. Herschel Wright was there when it swung open, and Finn waved him in out of the midnight mist that was gathering and turning to a cold rain.

"I know it's late," Herschel said, pulling off his cap and brushing the raindrops off his jacket just inside the door. "I was hoping I'd catch you before you closed, but I just now got everything finished for the market tomorrow."

"You have perfect timing, actually." Aisling motioned him toward the bar. "We were just about to pour ourselves a drink." She grabbed an extra glass off the rack and set it on the bar. "Can we persuade you to join us?"

"Well, it would be impolite to turn down good scotch." Herschel smiled, shrugging off his jacket and draping it over a barstool. "But I can't stay long."

Aisling poured and the three of them clinked their glasses.

Finn swirled the amber scotch around the side of the glass and looked up. "You're here about the mining proposition, aren't you?"

Herschel nodded. "I am. But more importantly, I'd like to thank you for what you did for my boy today." He paused, staring into his glass, then looked up at Finn. "He's been having some trouble dealing with his mum passing last year, and for some reason, I think that hair was his way of hanging on to her."

Herschel leaned back on the barstool and set his cap on the bar. "He's a smart kid. Smarter than a couple of his brothers put together, if I'm honest."

Aisling laughed at that and he looked up with a wide smile.

"Anyway, I didn't even recognize him tonight when he came through the door. He usually goes straight back out after dinner with those teenagers that are always hanging around in the park, but tonight he said he was helping you with a project first thing in the morning and just went to bed early."

"I wasn't thinking. I should have asked you first—"

"No. Not at all." Herschel shook his head. "I'm a good judge of character, Finn, and I trust you. Simple as that." He took a sip of his scotch. "I just wanted to say thank you. You've been there for him a couple of times now. If there's anything I can do to repay you in the future, consider it done."

Finn smiled and promised she would keep it in mind.

"We heard about what happened at the city council meeting this morning," Aisling said as she leaned against the back of the bar. "Sounds like a setup to me."

"That's putting it lightly. They didn't even try to hide it." He paused. "I just happened to see the email in time to get there, but it didn't really matter if I was there or not. There wasn't anything I could do."

Finn shook her head. "You were completely outnumbered."

Herschel nodded, and Aisling noticed the tired lines around his eyes. "To say the least."

He looked around him at the pub, his gaze lingering on the fireplace, coals still glowing red below the fresh log Finn had added. Green sap popped and crackled in the quiet of the empty pub. "I hope you two don't let this discourage you. It's done a lot for the town, reopening this place, and I know everyone is hoping you'll stay."

"No worries." Aisling leaned over and topped up his glass. "It'll take a lot more than this and a few ghosts to run us out of the pub."

"Ah, so you've met the famous Tribe?"

Finn glanced at Aisling, and they both asked the question at the same time. "The *what?*"

"The Tribe," Herschel said, nodding toward the stairs leading to the second level of the pub. "What? You haven't been upstairs yet?"

"We checked it out when we first got here, just long enough to see the flat that needs some work, and that there were some tools and lumber left in one of the bedrooms," Finn said. "I think we've both been avoiding it. We've had our hands full down here."

"There may be something up there that you missed the first time." Herschel set his glass down on the bar and headed toward the stairs. "And it's the only way to explain the Tribe."

Finn and Aisling followed him up the narrow black staircase tucked behind the bar. The old wood stairs creaked as they climbed, the curling edges of faded wallpaper brushing their shoulders as they passed. The top of the stairs opened up to a long landing with five evenly spaced doors. A combined kitchen and living area with a fireplace stood on the right, a bathroom in the middle, and three small bedrooms down the left side. Every room had basic furniture and fixtures; all they needed was a lick of paint and some homey touches.

"It's over here." Herschel stepped into the living room and opened a small door on the right wall. "I've never actually been up there; my wife worked here at the pub for years and told me about it. Have a look." He smiled, holding the door open. "I can see myself out."

Aisling looked at Finn and started up the short staircase that was barely wide enough to pass through. The walls and stairs were all made of the same glossy mahogany as the bar below, and the corners of the stairs were coated in dust. They both paused as they heard the front door downstairs close behind Herschel, the air around them still and expectant.

Finn put a hand on her shoulder.

"Babe, I know you're a little badass, but step behind me this once and let me go first. We have no idea what we're walking into." Finn climbed ahead and stepped into an area the size of a large closet, Aisling close behind her. It was dark, the only light coming from an alley streetlight that shone through the dusty window illuminating the pub patio below. The air was cold and silent, heavy with the scent of old paper, as if they'd opened a forgotten book found in the attic after a century.

"I've seen this window from the patio," Aisling said, peering down into the courtyard below. "But there's no third story, so I just assumed it was decorative, or maybe just part of the flat."

"Is this a closet?" Finn turned slowly in the dark room, fingertips brushing the wall around the doorframe. "It seems odd to have one upstairs and off the living area. Let's see if we can find the—"

Just as she said it, a light switched on over their heads, the silver ball chain still swaying and dangling between them exactly as it would if one of them had just pulled it to turn on the light. Except they hadn't.

"Did you..." Finn's voice trailed off as Aisling shook her head. They turned slowly to find a small wooden desk with an inkwell and blotter. A brass candlestick holder with a small loop handle sat on the edge of it, white candle wax still pooled in the dish at the base. But when Aisling looked closer, it looked soft, as if someone had just blown out the candle. Aisling touched it gingerly with one finger and left a soft dent in the warm wax.

"Holy shit," Finn said. "Look at that."

Aisling turned to find Finn staring at the wall over the desk. Photos of women, some single, some coupled with other women, hung in identical frames on the wall. Aisling leaned in to read the small brass plate on the first photo in the row.

"Colette and Darby Collins, 1866."

The photo itself was a crude daguerreotype in black and white, with aging sepia edges. One of the corners had broken off and fallen to the bottom edge of the frame behind the thick, settled glass. The woman on the left wore an ornate corseted dress, her brunette spiral curls swept into a high, glossy bun. The other wore more masculine trousers, suspenders, and a striped waistcoat. Her hair, twisted into a knot at the nape of her neck, was almost hidden under a black top hat.

"Look," Finn said, leaning closer to the photo. "Do you see that?"

"What?"

Finn stepped back, smiling. "Look at their hands."

There was a small table between them, and each rested a hand on it. When Aisling looked closer, she saw that the woman in the top hat had placed her hand slightly overlapping her partner's, fingers slightly entwined.

Aisling smiled. "That's the sweetest thing I've ever seen."

"And brave," Finn said, stepping back, her eyes sweeping down the line of photos. "Considering what society must have been like back then."

Other photos followed, some women standing alone in front of the bar downstairs, a few posing outside the pub's front doors, squinting into the sun. One couple in the early twentieth century stood together in the pub's back patio, the brick walls barely visible behind cascades of colorful flowers and ivy, dripping with bright yellow roses and silvery lavender. It was dated 1910.

Aisling smiled suddenly. "Look, do you what I see?"

Finn leaned in, studying it closely. "Not really. What am I supposed to be seeing?"

Aisling traced the outline of the fountain with her fingertip. It was placed in the exact spot as it was downstairs today, although nearly hidden by all the flowers.

"It's the fountain." Finn smiled. "And look at the woman on the left. She looks just like you."

"She does," Aisling said slowly, as if examining the faded image of a distant memory. "We could be twins." She stood back up and nodded to the next frame in the row. "This one is dated 1922 on the brass plate underneath, but it doesn't have a photo or a name like the others."

"That's strange." Finn peeked behind the frame's edge. "Why take the photo and leave the frame?"

Finn lifted it carefully from the wall and turned it over in her hand. "And I'm not quite sure how someone would have even taken the actual photo out of the frame." She handed it over to Aisling and pointed to the sealed edges of the backing paper. "That was sealed by the photographer when it was framed. Look, the same date and his name are stamped on the bottom edge. It would have had to be torn to remove it."

"And it's perfect," Aisling said slowly, running her fingertips across the edge. "It hasn't been touched."

Aisling carefully replaced the photo on the wall, then lifted the one before it. She turned it over and held it out for Finn to see. The same photographer's signature was stamped in gold at the bottom left edge and the edges of the paper sealed by the same method.

Aisling shook her head and rehung the photo on the wall. "Why would there be a date but no name?"

Finn shook her head, her eyes scanning the row to the last frame. "Looks like the last one in the row is missing a picture, too." She leaned in to look closer. "No nameplate or date. I wonder—"

"Finn."

Aisling took a step back, her hand covering her mouth. She pointed to the photo next to the blank frame Finn had been looking at. It was in an identical frame, and the picture inside was of two older women standing at the bar downstairs, smiling at each other with genuine happiness, like a candid snapshot taken by a photographer they hadn't noticed was there. It was Joan and Rose.

Finn looked at Aisling after a moment and smiled, bringing her hand up to kiss it. Aisling smiled, her gaze turning back to the picture of their grandmothers. "This was much more than a piece of property to them." Her gaze moved down the row to the first picture. "To all of them."

Finn nodded and pulled Aisling into her arms as they took a long last look, then turned and walked back down the stairs to the pub. They shut off the remaining lights, gathered their things from under the bar, and stepped out the door together. Finn turned the key in the lock and slipped them back into her pocket.

"Oh no," Aisling said, glancing up suddenly. "We forgot to turn the light out in the room upstairs."

Their eyes met for a moment, then Finn unlocked the door again.

Instead of going upstairs, they both walked straight out the back door to the patio. The light behind the highest window was on but clicked off as soon as they looked up, seamlessly replaced by the reflection of the silver crescent of the moon in the night sky.

CHAPTER FOURTEEN

The next morning Finn left Aisling at the cottage to get ready and walked to the pub early to meet Barry. He was sitting on the sidewalk when she arrived and, from the look of his reddened cheeks, had been there for a while.

"Hey, man," Finn said. "You ready to get started?"

Barry flashed her a smile as he got up and waited as Finn unlocked the door.

"Hit some of those lamps by the snugs over there for me, okay?" Finn pointed to the left as they walked in. "We need to get some light going in here before we can do anything else."

It took a while to get all the lights and heat turned on and a pot of coffee fired up, but finally the air was warming and the room looked cozy and bright. Finn glanced through the kitchen doors and turned back to Barry.

"Have you eaten yet?"

"Um." Barry shook his head. "I guess I forgot this morning."

"No worries. I didn't have time either." Finn headed back to the kitchen and motioned for Barry to follow. "I had some groceries delivered a couple days ago to try out some of the things we're putting on the menu. How does a breakfast sandwich sound?"

"That sounds so good." Barry smiled and followed her every move with his eyes as Finn got out a dozen eggs, a hunk of Irish cheddar, and a package of bacon rashers out of the fridge and tucked them under her arm. "But you've gotta stop calling them sandwiches, mate. Nobody says that."

"See?" Finn smiled as she fired up the grill. "This is the information I need. So tell me, what do people call them around here?"

"Well, if it's regular it's either a butty or a sarnie, but if it's toasted it's a toastie."

"Do you make them at home?"

"No, my dad always cooks now." Barry pulled a stool over to the prep table and sat down to watch. "I think he misses the café."

"Why is that?" Finn said, carefully pulling the bacon slices apart and slapping them down on the sizzling grill. "Does he not eat there anymore?"

"Well, no, but I mean I think he misses owning it. He and Mom bought it when I was eight and they worked there until the business on the square really slowed down and they had to sell it. Some guy from Cardiff bought it. It's still okay, but it used to be a lot busier."

"Oh, wow, I had no idea." Finn handed two eggs to Barry and nodded toward the grill. "Do you know how to crack one of these?"

Barry tapped an egg gingerly on the edge of the counter but dropped half the shell into the yolk when it hit the surface of the grill.

"Oh no," he said, panic flashing across his face. "I did it wrong."

"Hey, that's okay." Finn cleared the mess with one quick swipe of her spatula and handed him another egg. "Mistakes are what happen right before you learn how to do it like a pro. If you don't make mistakes, you're not trying hard enough."

She picked up one more egg from the carton and spun it, perfectly balanced, on her spatula.

"And I'm about to teach you how to crack that egg one-handed like you're a short-order cook from Brooklyn."

Later that afternoon, Aisling pushed open the door to the butcher shop, the brass bell clanging against the glass. Jack came around the corner and greeted her, his white apron pristine and starched over his ample belly, green wool cap perched slightly askew on his head.

"Jack," Aisling said. "Nearly every time I see you, your apron is perfectly clean. How exactly does a butcher do that?"

Jack leaned toward her over the counter, his voice a conspiratorial whisper. "A smart butcher hires his son to do all the actual butchering in the back. I just consider myself the...spokesmodel, shall we say."

"Now, that's genius. Don't tell Finn, but I'm hoping to do the same thing at the pub."

Jack laughed as he filled a small bag with pork cracklings and handed them over the counter to her.

"I should refuse," Aisling said, crunching into the first one and closing her eyes to savor the rich, salty rush of flavor. "But I just can't bring myself to do it."

"Marjorie keeps threatening to make me eat kale." He shook his head, one eyebrow cocked like a hammer. "I mean, why would any sane individual eat kale? It looks exactly like the bushes outside the church, and I'm sure it tastes about the same."

Aisling tucked the bag into her coat pocket.

"I actually came over here to ask a favor. We got the call this morning that the pub furniture is ready to be delivered, and we wondered if you'd help us get the word out that anyone who let us borrow theirs can come pick it up?"

"Absolutely. All I have to do is get Marjorie to tell her book club ladies, and everyone in town will know before you make it back to the pub."

"Perfect. You're a lifesaver." Aisling smiled, sneaking one more pork crackling out of her pocket and crunching into it with relish. "They can only hold the new furniture for two days, so we thought maybe if people wouldn't mind dropping by tomorrow evening to collect their pieces, we'd have a little spread of food out and some free drinks to thank them. Maybe around seven?"

"Oh, I do love a party!" Jack rubbed his hands together and beamed. "Consider it done. What can I do to help?"

"Well, your son mentioned the other day he'd be happy to help tend bar if we needed it, so if you don't mind asking him when you see him, that'd be great."

"He'll be excited, I can tell you that." Jack looked back toward the door to the prep area and grinned. "Just between you and me, he hasn't stopped talking about it since. I'm still finding little scraps of paper with phone numbers written on them all around the house."

"He was a huge help, and he's a great kid. You and Marjorie must be very proud."

"We are indeed. I couldn't ask for better." Jack smiled. "Now if we could just get Olivia sorted, we'd be set. She won't admit it, but I know she hates having to live at home. Bless her, she just wants to find a decent chap and settle down."

They chatted for a few more minutes before Aisling thanked him again for the pork cracklings and pulled her beanie out of her pocket and onto her head on the way out. Rain had begun to fall while she was in the shop, and darkening storm clouds rumbled and shifted overhead. When she looked across the park to the street market, the awnings covering the stalls were being whipped around and several merchants had already started to pack up to leave.

She'd always despised the rain in London. Getting a taxi was next to impossible, and her hair had always sprung defiantly into deep waves as soon as the first drop hit the ground, so her expensive sleek blowouts disappeared instantly. But it was different in Wales somehow.

Everything was different. Her hair, and her life, were suddenly as wild as the Welsh storms, and she barely even noticed anymore. She used to have her future mapped out by the week, down to the minute, but at this point she didn't even know where she'd be this time next year. More than once she'd started to ask Finn if she was considering staying in Wales, but she hadn't decided herself, so it hadn't seemed fair to ask. She'd worked for ten years building a career she loved, and after the dust settled she could always try to open her own company. The thought had been at the back of her mind for days now. Did she really want to step away from the industry she loved, permanently, to run a haunted pub in wild Wales?

Finn could hear that the rain had begun in earnest when the pub doors blew open and Aisling ducked inside, running smack into her as she was hanging mistletoe over the inside threshold.

Aisling picked up the mistletoe that landed on her boot and handed it to Finn, laughing, but Finn just pulled Aisling close and locked the door behind her, pressing her into the entryway wall.

She whispered into her ear as her hands slipped under Aisling's shirt and circled her waist. "Don't worry. Barry left a few minutes ago, and we don't open for another half hour."

Aisling melted against her as Finn kissed her neck, then with one flick of her wrist popped open every snap on the front of her denim shirt. She edged her thigh between Aisling's and kissed her, one hand at her waist, the other at the back of her neck.

"Fuck."

Aisling's word was a whisper as Finn edged down her bra, pulled a nipple into the swirling heat of her mouth, and pushed her skirt up around her waist. She wrapped one of Aisling's legs around her hips as her fingertips brushed her inner thigh, then stopped and smiled as her forehead sank down onto Aisling's shoulder.

"Jesus Christ. You're not wearing panties."

Aisling smiled. "I was wondering when you were going to notice that."

"So you're wearing knee-high leather boots and a sexy-ass pinstripe skirt with nothing underneath it." Finn leaned in and bit her bottom lip, letting it go slowly as she held her gaze. "How the hell am I supposed to keep my hands off you all night in the pub?"

"I don't know, Boxer Boi." Aisling took Finn's hand and slid it around to her bare ass. "Maybe a little challenge is good for you."

"Or maybe," Finn said, the warmth of her hand sliding up Aisling's inner thigh, "I can just take you right now and have that image to think about all night."

Finn sank to her knees and lifted Aisling's thigh over her shoulder. She slicked her tongue over Aisling's clit, then surrounded and stroked it in a steady rhythm until Aisling moaned, her fingers tightening suddenly around her shoulder. When Aisling's breath turned to begging, Finn sank her fingers deep inside, curving them just enough to weaken her knees.

"Finn..." Aisling's voice faded and Finn watched her slip her hand into her bra. "If you keep doing that, I'm not going to be able to stand up."

Finn met her gaze and started on Aisling's clit again with long, intense strokes, flicking just the tip of her tongue across it in a quick rhythm until she felt Aisling tighten around her fingers and hold her breath, balanced on the knife edge of orgasm. Finn slowed, looking up to watch Aisling roll her nipple with her fingers before returning to the long, slick strokes she knew would push her over the edge.

She slowed her hand as she felt Aisling's orgasm building, until Finn felt her hips start to move and heard a single whispered word.

"Finn."

She took Aisling over the edge then, fucking her deep and strong, catching her when her thighs gave way and she started to sink down the wall. A few seconds later Aisling came, arched hard, but Finn just picked her up as the waves of it faded, wrapped both legs around her waist, and kept fucking her until Aisling was lost in the next orgasm before she'd even stopped trembling from the first.

Finn held Aisling as she caught her breath, then gathered her close as she rested her head on Finn's shoulder.

"That," Aisling whispered into Finn's neck, still flushed and breathless, "had to be the best kiss in the history of mistletoe."

By six o'clock that evening, the pub was packed and word had already gotten around about the party the following night. The locals poured through the doors the minute they opened, as if they couldn't bear the thought of their lives after the leg lamp was returned to its rightful owner.

"You know," Alwen said, reaching past Aisling for another pint glass behind the bar, "I don't think I've ever seen this much of the village in one place."

"I know." Aisling handed her the glass with one hand and finished pulling a pint of Guinness with the other. "When we started I was worried we wouldn't get enough business, but I can't say that keeps me up at night anymore."

She looked out over the bar to see the village priest laughing and sipping a pint in the pink glitter Hello Kitty lawn chair by the windows. Beside him Jack and Marjorie were having a lively discussion with Olivia and little Ella at the table with the red velvet seats, and a couple in their eighties held hands by the glowing coals in the fireplace at the end of the room, matching glasses of red wine on the nightstand between them.

Aisling shook her head, plunging glasses into the warm soapy water that threatened to overfill the sink in front of her. Wales was getting dangerously close to feeling like the home she assumed she'd never want. She washed the other glasses slowly, trying to picture herself back in London, until Finn's touch startled her out of her thoughts.

"Hey, gorgeous. Do you think you two can handle this for a half hour or so?"

Aisling nodded as she scrubbed the glass in her hand and eased it into the rinse sink.

"This lot are talking too much to drink at a decent clip tonight." Aisling smiled. "And Michael is right over there if we need him, so take your time."

Finn's hand lingered at the small of Aisling's back for a moment before she edged through the crowd and out the front doors.

"Hey," Alwen said over her shoulder as she tore the paper from a new roll of pound coins and dropped them into the register, nodding toward the end of the bar, near the entrance to the hall. "Isn't that the same lass that was in here the other day?"

Aisling looked up from the sink and followed Alwen's gaze. The American slag was back, and this time she was staring at her and Alwen with her hand in the air, snapping her fingers.

"You've got to be bloody joking me. She's snapping her fingers?" Aisling took half a step toward her, then paused and pointed under the counter at the full racks of crisps in every flavor. "Would you look at that? We're out of crisps. I'll just go to the back and grab us some more."

Alwen slid behind her and laughed, moving toward the end of the bar. "I'll come get you when she fucks off back to America."

"Give her my regards." Aisling winked at her as she headed toward the hall. "And by that, I mean aim and fire with the mixer gun until she does."

Aisling slipped into the hall behind the bar where they kept all the extra boxes of crisps, nuts, and racks of backup mixers. She grabbed a bag of Walkers Cheese & Onion and slid down the closed door to sit on the floor, but when she tore the bag open, the contents flew into the air like they'd been shot out of a cannon.

"Bollocks." Aisling shook her head and spoke to the wayward crisp packet on the floor. "That's all I need."

Aisling made an attempt to pick them up, but it was clear this was going to require the brush and pan stashed behind the bar. Just as she was about to round the corner into the bar area, she heard Kaitlyn's voice rise well above the others.

"What do you mean you don't know where she is?"

Aisling guessed Alwen was giving her the brush-off based on the sudden desperation in Kaitlyn's voice when she tried again. Aisling leaned in as close to the door as possible to listen.

"Wait, can you at least give me her number?"

Aisling heard Alwen pause before she answered. "And why would I do that?"

Kaitlyn forced out an exaggerated sigh. "Because I'm supposed to be meeting her. We've done it before, but this time somehow I deleted the number from my phone, and now I can't call her to see where she is. She's waiting for me right now."

"Oh right." Alwen passed by the hall doorframe and Aisling watched her grab a pen and a scrap of paper from underneath the register. "Hang on and I'll just write it down for you."

There was a pause, then Kaitlyn's voice again at a much higher volume, teetering on the edge of shrill. "What the hell does this mean? 0800 SODOFF?"

As Aisling rounded the corner into the bar area, Alwen had already turned to help the next punter, and several more were laughing as they watched Kaitlyn crumple the paper in her hand, toss it on the bar, and stomp out the door, blond hair flying.

A few minutes later Finn walked out of the park into the rain where the wind whipped around the corner of the building like thrown knives. She ducked down a rain-slicked alleyway and walked to 71 Merryvale Street, a tall, narrow, semidetached house on one of the streets leading down to the docks. She stopped in front, pulled a scrap of paper out of her jacket pocket, and checked the address again before she knocked.

There was a small window in their bright blue door, and Finn watched as a lanky teenager in a sweatshirt loped down the hall and pulled the door open. He had a slice of toast in his other hand and took a leisurely bite of it before he spoke.

"Um, can I help you?"

"My name is Finn Morgan. Is your dad home?"

The teenager looked Finn up and down before he stepped aside, pointing down the hall.

"He's in the kitchen at the end of the hall."

Finn nodded her thanks and rounded the corner into the kitchen at the far end of the hall. The scent of warm butter, fresh thyme, and slow-simmered sauce enveloped her as she knocked on the doorframe and leaned in.

"Herschel?" she said, hoping not to startle him as he pulled a tray of broiling garlic bread slices from the oven. "I hope it's okay that I just dropped by. Barry told me this morning you might have a minute to talk while you're cooking."

Herschel turned around with a wide smile, extending his hand to Finn before he realized he was wearing an oven mitt. He laughed, tossed it on the counter, and offered Finn a seat at the table.

"Of course I do." He glanced at the opposite kitchen counter. "Can I get you a cup of tea? I can just pop the kettle on."

"I wish I could, but I can't stay long," Finn said as they pulled out their chairs and sat at the simple wooden table, worn smooth at the edges. "The pub is getting busy, so I should get back. I just thought I'd come ask if you might have time to help me with something tomorrow."

Herschel nodded. "That's actually perfect timing because I'll be at loose ends. It's supposed to storm until late afternoon and then get worse, so I won't be setting up for the market at all." Hel smiled, reaching over from his seat to stir the sauce bubbling on the stove. "What can I do for you?"

Finn leaned back in her chair and ran her hand through her hair. "We're having a little get-together tomorrow night to thank everyone for loaning us their furniture—"

"Everybody in town is talking about that," Herschel cut in, leaving the spoon in the sauce and turning back to Finn. "I saw Olivia putting up some flyers at the shop this afternoon, and they're plastered all over the outside of the café."

"That's great to hear. We figured it was the least we could do to thank everybody." Finn shrugged off her jacket and laid it on the chair beside her. "Barry told me today you used to own that place?"

Herschel nodded toward a framed photo on the counter of him and a young brunette woman. She was laughing, the wind blowing her hair in every direction around their faces. "My wife and I owned it together.

I cooked for the most part and she worked the front. Back when people actually did their shopping in town, they'd stop in for a bite to eat or a cuppa nearly every day. We were always busy."

"Aisling mentioned that the street markets used to be a lot busier in London as well. Where do people shop now?"

Herschel shook his head. "Most people order everything and have it delivered to their homes, or they do a big weekly shop at Tesco in Cardiff. The market stalls and little shops on the square just aren't nearly as busy as they used to be, and a couple of them that have been open for fifty years have had to close their doors."

Finn started to say something but was interrupted by a deafening thump coming from the ceiling. Herschel rolled his eyes.

"Pay no mind to that. My oldest boy, Paddy, has taken up weightlifting. He can't actually lift them, so he ends up just dropping them on the floor." Herschel glanced above his head. "Someday he'll figure it out." He paused, still looking at the ceiling. "Or at least a father can hope."

"So," Finn said, "do you ever miss the café?"

"Every day." Herschel's smile faded for the first time and he nodded. "I have the market stall now, but it doesn't pay the bills. I do odd jobs around town as well, whatever I can get."

"That has to be tough with four boys. The older they get, the more expensive they are."

"That's the damn truth." Herschel smiled again and nodded, pulling out his wallet and holding up a picture of himself and the boys on the front step of the house, red and gold autumn leaves lying in drifts on the edges of the stairs. He looked at it for a moment and tucked it back into his wallet, letting out a long, slow breath. "Most of the time we manage to keep our heads above water, but it keeps me up most nights."

"They're happy and healthy, though. You must be doing something right." Finn paused and peered over at the pot on the stove. "But it looks like your pasta might be threatening to boil over."

Herschel hurried to lift it off the stove and poured the steaming pot into the waiting colander in the sink.

The tall teenager Finn had met at the door leaned into the kitchen, eyeing the garlic bread still on the tray. "When's dinner?"

"Finn, this is Barry's brother, Conor." He looked up at his son.

"This is Finn Morgan. She's the one that did the woodworking with Barry today at the pub."

"Yeah? That's cool," Conor said, meeting Finn's eyes for the first time. "He's been talking about that all day. And some spinning egg or something."

Herschel looked up from the sink at his son.

"Dinner's in a few minutes." He poured the steaming pasta into a wide serving bowl and topped it with a few ladles of the sauce simmering on the stove. "Go tell your brothers to wash their hands." Conor disappeared around the corner as Herschel called after him. "With soap!"

Finn laughed, getting up from her chair and reaching for the pasta tongs Herschel had just managed to pry out of the drawer.

"Here, let me mix this while you get the plates. If your boys are anything like me, they'll be down here in about thirty seconds."

Herschel pulled a stack of plates from the cupboard and a handful of silverware from the basket on the counter as Finn closed her eyes and breathed in the earthy scent of the sauce. It looked like a basic puttanesca, but the scent was complex, layered with savory heat and the freshness of chopped oregano as well as the spice of the traditional dried chilis.

"This smells amazing," Finn said, looking back over her shoulder at Herschel. "And that reminds me. I actually came over to ask if you have time to give me a hand in the kitchen at the pub tomorrow afternoon. I have everything I need for the spread but not nearly enough time to get it done."

Herschel was tucking a folded cloth napkin under each plate as Finn talked, then paused as a wide smile flashed across his face.

"I'd love to." He placed the last napkin as the clattering thunder of eight feet started to pound the stairs. "That sounds like more fun than I've had in a long time."

"It's a deal, then," Finn said, picking up her jacket from the kitchen chair. "I'll see you tomorrow, about noon?"

"I'll be there, for sure. But are you sure you can't stay for dinner?"

Finn glanced down and realized he'd set a place for her.

She hesitated. "They can probably spare me at the pub, but Aisling might be jealous if I eat something that amazing without her."

A scruffy pile of boys poured through the door all at once, scattering around the table, the chairs scuffing the floor as they hurriedly pulled them out and plunked down into the seats. Barry flashed Finn a smile and grabbed the bowl of garlic bread just before Conor got his hands on it.

"Sit. Eat," Herschel said with a smile, reaching across and serving her a huge helping of steaming pasta. "Then I'll pack up some leftovers for your Aisling."

Once she got back to the pub, the rest of the evening flew by, and by the time Finn looked up, Alwen had just closed the door behind the last of the customers. She gathered the last few glasses on her way back and set them on the bar, rubbing the back of her neck as she headed back toward the sink.

Finn shook her head and handed Alwen her coat as she rounded the corner. "No way you're cleaning up tonight. We were slammed all night, and you barely had a chance to take a break."

"Finn, don't be silly." Alwen took her coat and stashed it back under the bar. "I'm fine."

"Sorry, I'm afraid it's two against one," Aisling said as she emerged suddenly from the hall with an armful of crisp packets. "The two of us can clean up and be ready for tomorrow in less than an hour. You need to go home and get your feet up."

Aisling spilled the crisps across the top of the bar just as a cell phone rang by the register. Finn hurriedly shook the water off her hands and reached for it.

"Go ahead and take it," Aisling whispered as Finn clicked it on and put it to her ear. "I'll walk Alwen home."

Finn shook her head. "This is Finn Morgan," she said quickly into the phone before turning back to Aisling, her hand over the speaker. "Are you sure? I can call her back."

Aisling smiled, but it quickly faded as she found her coat and bag under the bar.

"It's okay. I need some fresh air anyway."

Finn squeezed Aisling's hand and shot her a tense smile as she turned back to her phone and walked toward the back stairs.

❖

"You really don't have to walk me home," Alwen said as they stepped out and Aisling locked the door behind them, dropping the key in her pocket and falling into step with Alwen on the wet cobblestone street. "I just live around the corner."

"Are you kidding?" Aisling glanced back at the pub, trying to push thoughts of Finn and Kaitlyn together out of her mind. "This is great. If I time this right, Finn will be done with all the cleaning by the time I get back."

Alwen laughed, the only sound on the quiet, icy square, which reminded Aisling why she'd brought her bag with her.

"Finn's already started making food for tomorrow, so I packed some up for you." She pulled a large plastic container out of her bag and handed it to Alwen. "It's nothing too special, just some meatballs in sauce and some American thing that looks like just the skin sliced off a jacket potato, but with cheese, bacon, and spring onions of all things, baked on top. It should crisp up if you pop it into the oven. I snuck one when she'd just pulled them out today, and it was delicious."

Alwen laughed as she peeked underneath the lid. "I distinctly remember you saying that American food is hideous."

"It *is* hideous," Aisling said as they turned onto a dark street just past the square. "Just maybe not these jacket potato skins or whatever she calls them."

Their laughter echoed in the empty street, and Alwen slipped her arm through Aisling's as they walked. The half moon was high in the sky, blurred to a silver smudge by the last of the storm clouds that broke up just over the sea, clearing a space for the stars in the black night sky. The air had the scent of rain turned to ice, and tree branches were glossed with the sleet that was starting to gather on the edges of the street.

"So that American asked me for Finn's number."

"I know," Aisling said, steadying her other hand on Alwen's arm as they neared a slick section of cobblestones. "I was listening in the hall. Nicely handled, by the way. I couldn't have said it better myself."

Alwen shot her a grin and they chatted as they walked to the very end of the road, until Alwen stopped hesitantly at the last house. The concrete block walls were coated with peeling gray paint, and plastic flowerpots in waist-high piles were stacked around the door, the frozen brown remnants of the plants flattened to the sides. An abandoned mop bucket with a gaping crack down the side sat by the door, surrounded by scattered paint cans coated with rust and broken lawn furniture piled under the dark, still window.

"I'm okay from here," Alwen said, her voice tight. She glanced at the window and searched her pocket for her keys. "I just need to find…"

Her voice faded away as a light switched on in the house and the porchlight over the door blazed to life. The inside light through the window was barely visible behind a chaotic mountain of clothes, empty soda bottles, and twisted plastic bags rising almost to the top of the window frame. Everything was smashed hard against the glass, and from what Aisling could see from the one gap in the pile, that was because there was more of the same on the other side, nearly filling the room completely.

She jumped as the door opened just enough to reveal a very obese woman in black tracksuit bottoms and a stained T-shirt. Her hair had been dark at some point, judging by the thin, greasy clumps around her shoulders, but had grown in gray down to her ears.

"Alwen!" The woman paused, as if she'd forgotten what she wanted to say. Then her gaze swiveled to Aisling and she narrowed her eyes. "So now you're bringing someone else to steal from me too? Filling your own pockets isn't good enough?"

Time seemed to slow down, and Aisling saw the frozen cloud of Alwen's breath slow to a stop beside her. The woman kept hurling insults, but Aisling didn't hear what she said. She turned to Alwen and watched her hand slide slowly over her belly. The woman shouted again, spittle flying from her mouth, and Alwen flinched as she shuffled back through the door finally and slammed it behind her.

"Aisling, I'm so sorry. I had Finn drop me off at the top of the street. We were just having such a good time talking that I forgot." She stopped and looked down at her feet, then seemed to steel herself and go on. "Anyway, I'd better get in there."

"Alwen." Aisling held her eyes. "Are you safe in there? Do you want to come home with us?"

"You two have been so kind to me." She paused as a tear slipped down her cheek and dropped off her chin. "But I'm fine, I promise."

Aisling hesitated and looked again at the window. A seagull called overhead and swooped in to land on the top of the chimney, scattering a group of velvety gray doves into the darkness.

"I know how strong you are." Aisling paused and pointed to the church steeple rising above the rooftops into the sky. "But do you know that little cottage behind the church?"

Alwen nodded. "That's where Rose and Joan lived, isn't it?"

"Rose was Finn's grandmother, and Joan..." Aisling stopped herself and smiled. "Well, that's a story for another time. But that's our house, and you're welcome there, anytime, day or night."

Alwen nodded and turned to go in, then paused on the step and looked back.

"I used to spend every day just wondering what was going to happen next." She turned the doorknob and smiled. "But now I'm not so scared anymore."

She opened the door and slipped in, closing it quietly behind her.

Aisling lingered outside the house, her breath frozen and still around her, trying to imagine what Alwen was walking into. A mouse scurried across the inside windowsill between the piles of trash and the glass, and the light went abruptly dark a few minutes later. She turned and left, closing the gate behind her and hurrying up the street. The pub was only a five-minute walk away, and she could see the park from where she was. She'd never been scared in Wales, not as a child or an adult, but now she'd seen the shadows lurking in the corners of the village, and even the air felt different.

She hurried up to the square and through the park but stopped short when she looked up and saw the pub. Kaitlyn was walking out of the doors again, blond hair flying in the wind, wrapping her coat around her and tying it at the waist. She paused and looked back at the door before she got into the black BMW parked in front and drove away, her tires kicking up a blur of water from the rain-slicked street as she turned the corner and drove out of sight.

CHAPTER FIFTEEN

After the car sped away, Aisling stared, frozen, at the pub doors, then sank to the cold, wet edge of the park bench beside her. Kaitlyn's voice played in an endless loop in her mind, when she'd told Alwen in the pub that Finn had met her outside the pub. She'd pushed it out of her mind at the time, but now that was no longer possible. And it never would be again.

Her phone buzzed in her pocket, but she couldn't move her hand to get it. Time slowed to a stop as she sat breathing in the icy darkness, as still as the trees around her.

Her phone buzzed again, then pinged with a text. She slowly took it out of her pocket, numb, then threw it as hard as she could into the trees. It landed with a crunch on the frozen grass and flipped a few times before coming to rest in the shadows just as Finn stepped out of the pub doors and locked them, turning down the street in the direction of Alwen's house. She stopped short after only a few steps and stared into the park, then ran across the wet street, calling Aisling's name.

She didn't answer, not even when Finn got to her and knelt down in front of her on the bench, her hands warm on Aisling's bare knees.

"Baby, what happened? You're freezing out here."

Finn shrugged off her jacket and wrapped it around Aisling's shoulders.

"Did something happen?" Finn looked her over, then took Aisling's hands in hers to warm them. "Talk to me."

Aisling finally looked at Finn. "I saw her."

Finn glanced around the dark, deserted park and met her gaze, confused. "You saw who?"

"Kaitlyn." Tears burned behind her eyelids and she shut them tight as she spoke. "I saw Kaitlyn coming out of the pub. She was in there with you."

Finn waited until she opened her eyes and held them softly with hers.

"You're right." She paused. "She was there but she left about twenty minutes ago. She called right as you left with Alwen and said she had something for us, some kind of liability paperwork they want all the business owners to sign."

"So you told her to meet you there? Without me?"

"Hell no." Finn lifted Aisling's chin with her fingertip until she looked at her. "Baby, I told her I was locking up and she could come by tomorrow during the day so we could both look at it."

"Finn, I saw her leave the pub." Aisling sniffed and wiped her cheeks with the back of her hand. "If you told her that, then why was she there?"

"That's a great question, and it was the first thing I said when she walked in." Finn reached into the inner pocket of the jacket she'd draped across Aisling's shoulders and handed her a clean, pressed handkerchief. "When I figured out she didn't even have a bag with her, much less paperwork, I told her to get the hell out. She was there less than two minutes."

Aisling looked up at Finn, the faintest hint of a smile on her lips. "Really? You just told her to get out?"

"Absolutely. I think she was there for me, but I didn't give her the chance to even start. She never got within five feet of where I was standing behind the bar."

Aisling's shoulders sagged with relief and she leaned into Finn's arms. Finn pulled her up from the bench and held Aisling's face in her hands.

"Aisling Moss, I'm in love with you. I have been for a while now. There's no way in hell I'd let anything mess that up."

Aisling wrapped her arms around Finn's waist and buried her face in her shoulder as Finn kissed the top of her head. When she finally looked up, she smiled and looked into Finn's eyes.

"Do you remember the spider?"

"What spider?"

"That first day in the pub. I walked into that spiderweb and started having a panic attack."

"I do." Finn pulled her close, wrapping the jacket tighter around her. "And you let me hold your hand over my chest. I remember you tried so hard to follow my breaths."

Aisling looked up and held Finn's eyes. "I knew that day that I'd fall in love with you. And that it would turn my life upside down."

Finn smiled and kissed her softly. "And did you?"

Aisling nodded, laying her hand over Finn's heart and then her own. "I can't even remember my life before you."

Finn hugged her close and lifted her off the ground, turning her in circles in the icy air.

"Then what are we doing standing around in the cold?" She laughed, setting her back down gently and taking her hand. "Let's go home."

After a few minutes of searching for Aisling's phone, Finn wrapped Aisling's frozen fingers in hers for the walk home, but by the time they'd gotten past the church and onto the cottage path, Aisling's teeth were chattering and she was shivering from head to toe. As they walked to the gate, gold light shone behind the cottage windows.

"We're almost home," Finn said as she pushed the gate open for her and it creaked loudly, the hinges expanded from the cold. "I'm worried you may actually have some frostbite. I'll try to get the house warmed up as quick as I can."

They hurried up the walkway where Finn opened the door into warm, cedar-scented air and glowing firelight. Aisling stood there for a moment, taking in the cozy blanket thrown over the back of the couch and the blazing fire that snapped and popped in the hearth as they closed the door against the cold wind whipping around the cottage outside.

"How did you…" Aisling's voice faded as she realized what might have happened and smiled at Finn. "You didn't do this, did you?"

"Nope," Finn said, laughing. "And I'm now officially at the point where nothing surprises me. I don't even know where that blanket came from, but I'm about to wrap it around you."

Finn took their coats and hung them on the wall as Aisling walked over and ran her hand over the soft, charcoal wool throw trimmed with ivory and navy stripes at the edges. "It's my Grandma Joan's. I haven't seen it since I was little."

Finn sat her down on the hearth and wrapped it around her shoulders, the flames crackling behind her on the iron grate.

"You're still shivering." She warmed Aisling's frozen cheeks with her hands. "If you saw Kaitlyn coming out of the pub, you must have been outside for the better part of an hour with walking Alwen home. I kept trying to reach you on the phone, but you never picked up, so I was headed to Alwen's house when I saw you."

When Aisling finally started to warm up enough to leave her seat on the hearth, Finn ran her a bath and Aisling sighed as she leaned back and sank down into the violet-scented bubbles, her hair scooped into a wild bun on the top of her head. Finn perched on the sink across from her.

"So," she said, rolling up the sleeves of her plaid flannel shirt, one side of the hem tucked into her faded jeans. "This afternoon when I left the pub, I went to Barry's house to speak to his dad."

Aisling wiped the bubbles off her chin and looked up at Finn. "Oh no, did something go wrong this morning?"

"Not at all. We started on that woodworking project upstairs and he was a huge help," Finn said, dropping her shoes and resting her feet on the end of the tub. "But he told me today that his parents used to own the café, so I swung by to see if Herschel had time tomorrow to help me put together the food for the party."

"Good thinking." Aisling leaned back farther into the bubbles and stretched out her toe to touch the tip of the brass faucet. "If today is any indication, we may be busier than we thought tomorrow, even before the party."

Finn nodded. "He was cooking for his boys when I got there, and I tasted the pasta that he sent back for you." She shook her head. "It was beyond good. He's got some real talent."

Aisling smiled. "You're thinking about having him cook at the pub, aren't you?"

"Maybe, but I didn't say anything to him about it. I wanted to talk to you about it first."

"Well, unless you find out tomorrow that he doesn't know how to turn on an oven, I'm all for it. We need someone in charge of the food, and if you think he's the one, that's good enough for me."

Finn's eyes followed the wet curves of Aisling's shoulders and breasts as she reached into the cabinet behind her for the soap. "I figure if we get someone experienced to take over the kitchen and ordering, that frees us up for the bar as we get busier in the spring."

Aisling wondered again if Finn was considering staying past the year but quickly pushed the thought to the back of her mind.

"So." Aisling brought her knees up in the tub and wrapped her arms around them. "Do you remember when Alwen showed up at the pub the other night? After she got roughed up at the shop?"

"Yeah, and it's a good thing I never found out who did it." Aisling watched as Finn's hands tightened around the edge of the counter. "What kind of a person hits a pregnant girl?"

Aisling stood and reached for her towel. "Well, from what I saw of her home tonight, I think she's not much safer there than she was at the shop."

"Seriously?" Finn stood and handed Aisling her robe. "What happened?"

Aisling wrapped the robe around her body and pulled the pins from her hair, copper waves falling like water over her shoulders.

"Finn, it was awful. I think her mum might be one of those people you see on the telly, the ones that never throw anything out..."

Finn's eyebrow shot up. "A hoarder?"

"Yes. I only got to see from outside, but trash was piled literally to the top of the front window on the inside. And when her mum opened the door she shouted at Alwen and accused her of bringing me to the house to steal things. I felt so sorry for her." Aisling paused and shook her head. "She was mortified."

"Poor Alwen. That's crazy."

Finn walked down the hall with Aisling to the kitchen. The fire was still sparkling in the fireplace, and Finn pulled out a bottle of French chardonnay and two glasses while Aisling settled into her chair and tucked her feet underneath her. "No wonder she wouldn't let me walk her past the top of the street."

They were quiet as Finn poured the wine and laid out some wedges of soft cheese and crackers on a plate, setting it between them on the table with a jar of fig jam. Aisling cut a thick slice of the cheese, topped it with a dollop of jam, and handed it to Finn.

Finn smiled. "How do you know I don't like crackers?"

"I guessed." Aisling leaned forward and kissed her cheek. "Well, that, and you never eat them when they come with the soup at the café."

Aisling watched Finn pop the cheese into her mouth and stare off into the living room. After a minute, a brilliant idea struck her like a lightning bolt, and she spun around in her chair. Finn turned to her with an identical expression.

Aisling smiled. "Are you thinking what I'm thinking?"

Finn's face broke out in an excited grin and she nodded. "I just can't believe we didn't think of this sooner."

The weather that morning included another storm warning for the evening, so Finn and Aisling got to the pub a bit earlier than usual to get a jump on preparations for the party that night. Aisling got a start on hanging the rest of the Christmas decorations, and Herschel turned up right on time and hung the highest lights for her before he and Finn headed back to the kitchen.

After they'd gone over what prep they wanted to do first, they fell into an easy rhythm right away. Within five minutes it was clear to Finn she'd made the right decision, but Herschel seemed a bit more subdued than usual. She was just about to ask what was wrong when he looked up at her from the onion he was chopping at lightning speed.

"Did you see the heaving equipment moving into the field on the other side of the village this morning?"

Finn shook her head, rinsing a knife in warm water before she used it to slice through the cheesecake she'd made the day before.

"No, but let me guess. They're going to start digging the mine?"

Herschel tossed the onion skin into the trash at the end of the prep table. "Worse than that. I heard from Marjorie this morning that Dun Laoghaire castle is set to be demolished in just a few days. Evidently, the area they want to mine is right underneath it."

Finn stopped, her knife still poised over the cheesecake. "They can't do that, can they? Isn't it a historical building or something like that?"

"Well, yes and no," Herschel said, sliding the minced onion into a prep bowl and picking up a tomato. He sliced it in half and diced it, picking up the next before he went on. "Dun Laoghaire Castle was actually privately owned until about fifty years ago—actually by distant members of my family—but at some point they sold it, and the land it sits on belongs to the city of Cardiff. Long story short, it was never declared a protected historical monument, so if they want to knock it into a pile of rocks, they can."

Finn paused. "I know none of us want to see the castle demolished, but that's why this is more personal to you, isn't it?"

"Aye." Herschel paused long enough to pick up another tomato, turning it over in his hand a few times before he looked back up at Finn. "I've always loved it, even when I was little, and then when I grew up and had my own kids, my wife and I were proud to have it as a part of the family history. Our family's connections to it can be traced back to the late seventeenth century. I'm just having a hard time wrapping my head around the fact that it won't be there anymore."

"I can't believe any of this is happening." Finn picked up her knife again and scored the cheesecake into eight perfect slices. "Aisling loves that place too, and I don't have a clue how to tell her."

Aisling walked through the double doors suddenly, carrying two bottles of Coke for Herschel and Finn. "Tell me what?"

"That the cheesecake is ready." Herschel flashed her a smile as Aisling stuck her head back through the doors to ask Alwen if she'd like a slice. Finn mouthed *thank you* and had slid the second slice onto a small plate by the time Aisling ducked back in.

Aisling smiled. "Alwen says yes, please."

Herschel slid a perfectly fanned sliced strawberry onto each plate as Finn handed them to Aisling. Aisling kissed her on the cheek and backed through the doors, a plate in each hand.

"Thanks, man." Finn ran her hand through her hair and backed up from the prep table. "How in the world did you think of that so quickly?"

Herschel winked in her direction. "Sixteen years of marriage, mate."

A timer went off and Finn leaned into the oven, emerging with a tray of bite-sized calzones. She set it on the grill and leaned against the oven, arms crossed.

"Herschel, I'd love to run something by you. See what you think of it?"

"Sure." Herschel put his knife down and dried his hands on

a kitchen towel before he cracked the tops off two Coke bottles and handed one to Finn.

"So, would you consider working here in the kitchen full-time?" Finn paused. "I know you do the market most days, but if you're interested, Aisling and I talked about it, and I think we can make it worth your while to switch."

Finn took a piece of paper and a pen out of her pocket and slid it over the prep table to Herschel. He smiled, and jotted something underneath the numbers before handing it back.

Finn read it and laughed. Under the salary she and Aisling had jotted down earlier, he'd written: *Fuck yes*.

❖

A couple of hours later the party was in full swing. The bar was covered in food and drinks, and what seemed like the entire village stood shoulder to shoulder in the pub, laughing and swapping stories about whose piece of furniture had seen more action over the years. Even Kaitlyn was there, nursing a glass of white wine and generally being ignored by most everyone there.

"Should we tell them now?" Aisling whispered to Finn as she passed carrying two perfect pints of Guinness and handing them over the bar.

"Do you want to do it?"

"Sure." Aisling smiled and attempted to pull her hair into a twist in the mirror behind the bar and keep it there with a ballpoint pen from the register. "Can you get their attention for me?"

Finn whistled and everyone turned to look, the noise slowly quieting to a low murmur.

"Can we have your attention?"

Finn led Aisling to a small coffee table near the front of the seating area, wrapped her hands around her waist, and lifted her up onto it. "Aisling and I have something to say."

The pen she was using to hold her hair back slipped out and bounced off the coffee table with a *ping*, and everyone laughed as Aisling shook her hair out and compared it to taming wild Welsh horses, which made everyone laugh again. She leaned down to take a hair tie Olivia handed her and looked out at her neighbors' expectant faces, ruddy from lager and laughter.

"First of all, Finn and I want to say thank you for the incredible support you gave us as we opened. If you hadn't pulled together and figured out a plan to come to our rescue, we wouldn't be standing here today, so thank you."

Cheers and clapping commenced until finally Michael let out a commanding whistle from the back and pointed back up to Aisling.

Aisling looked out at all the kind faces she'd come to love in the short time they'd been in the village and took a deep breath.

"We all know Cwylldbridge Village is facing some challenges right now with the mining proposition, so Finn and I wanted to show our support."

Aisling paused and motioned for Finn, who set the pint of cider in her hand down on the bar and looked out over the crowd.

"Starting tomorrow," Finn said with a glance at Aisling, "any time you spend thirty pounds or more here in the village, whether it's in the butcher shop, the café, or even the hardware store, bring the receipts to the pub with you and we'll buy your first pint that night."

Aisling smiled at Finn and continued. "We all want our village to stay strong, and the only way to do that is to pull together like..." She paused. "Well, like you did for us when we opened. And it can't hurt to start keeping our money in Cwylldbridge where it belongs."

A cheer went up as Aisling hopped down from the table. They spent the rest of the night enjoying the party with everyone, occasionally jumping behind the bar to pour a drink, but Michael and Olivia handled most of the orders. There was even a special request for a Princess Ella Potion, so Finn made one with ice-flying fanfare and carried Ella around on her shoulders the rest of night so she could drink it and survey her royal subjects.

As the night went on, the storm sweeping in from the sea intensified, and the freezing wind started blowing so hard at one point toward the end of the evening that the gusts whipping around the corners of the building shook the windowpanes in their frames. When everyone started to leave around eleven o'clock, each one stopped and hugged Finn and Aisling on their way out, thanking them for the evening. As the last guests left with their furniture lofted onto their shoulders, Finn opened the door for them, and the wind swept in with enough force to push them back a couple of steps before they managed to get outside and close it behind them.

Aisling stepped behind the bar and picked up her phone. "They expect seventy-kilometer-an-hour winds along the coast," she said to Olivia, who was wiping down the bar. "I sent Alwen home a while ago so she could get off her feet, and now I'm glad I did. I'm not even sure she could get to her house safely if she'd waited until this point. She lives at the very end of the row, so there's nothing blocking the wind."

Olivia screwed the cap back on the jar of cherries by the sink and looked up.

"I sent Ella home with her nana too." She fiddled with the jar for a moment, then asked, "Have you been to Alwen's house?"

Aisling nodded, dropping her voice almost to a whisper. "Last night. I almost didn't want to leave her there."

"You must have met her mum." Olivia sighed, turning around to lean against the bar, cherry jar in hand. "She hasn't always been this bad. But over time, the hoarding has gotten worse and I think her mental state has deteriorated. No one really knows because she hasn't left the house in years."

Aisling poured two small glasses of sherry and handed one to Olivia. "Is there anything we can do to help? Honestly, the way she treated Alwen last night…it was awful. I just stood there outside the house awhile, just wishing I could do something for her."

"Alwen is so loyal, and at this point, that's the problem." Olivia wiped the sticky cherry jar with a damp towel as she spoke. "She feels like if she leaves, she'd be abandoning her mum, but I can't imagine bringing a baby into that house." She clinked her glass to Aisling's and took a sip, worry creasing her forehead. "I had a quiet word with her about it a few weeks ago when I ran into her in the café, and she feels the same way. She didn't really want to talk about it, though, just said she'd sort it out somehow."

Aisling shook her head. "She's probably just overwhelmed. I can't imagine being in that situation. I don't know what I'd do, either."

"I've actually been speaking about it to my mum since we had that cuppa in the café, and I think she's finally managed to find Alwen's mum a place in a Cardiff mental health facility if someone can convince her to go."

Olivia stacked the last of the bottled beer into the coolers behind the bar and turned around as Aisling finished up the register count and flipped the drawer shut.

"So what's the story with the blonde that works for Rockfield? Katie?"

"Kaitlyn." Aisling laughed. "You saw her tonight too? Holding up the wall in the back?"

"She was hard to miss. Basically, she just followed Finn around with her eyes like she was the prom king or something." Olivia rolled her eyes and held open the bank bag while Aisling slid in the starting money for the next day. "When I refilled her wine, I asked how she knew you guys, and she said that she and Finn had history. What's the deal with that?"

Michael and Finn came through the kitchen doors just then, laughing and popping each other with wet kitchen towels.

Olivia smiled, shaking her head. "Good Lord, Michael, did you two leave Herschel in there to do the actual work?"

Finn landed a sharp crack on Michael's hip, then held up the towel like a white flag and tossed Michael a Heineken from the cooler behind the bar.

"No, I sent him home to his kids hours ago so he could be sure everyone got in before the storm kicked up a notch."

"That was smart."

"Wait." Michael held up his hand. "What is that? Did you hear it?"

Everyone paused, quiet, but there was nothing but the sound of the wind rattling the windows as it raced past.

Olivia looked over at her brother. "Hear what?"

Just then a lingering sound, almost like a moan but at a higher pitch, came from the direction of the staircase.

Aisling looked down the hall behind the bar that led to the stairs. "Do you think it's the Tribe?"

"No way," Olivia said, joining her in the hall. "You can barely hear whatever this is, and the ladies of the Tribe are not known for being subtle, let's put it like that."

"True story." Michael nodded as he and Finn joined them at the door to the hall.

Another, sharper moan filled the air then, and Olivia started to walk down the hall to the base of the stairs.

Michael put her hand on his sister's shoulder to stop her. "Hell no. I know you're big and bad and all, but you're not going in there first."

He and Finn walked slowly down the hall, stopping suddenly at the supply closet when another moan rose from inside. Finn slowly opened the door to the small room that held backup supplies for the bar. It was dark, but once their eyes adjusted, they saw a small figure on her knees, leaning forward, her hands braced on one of the lower shelves, crowded at every angle with jars of martini olives and crisp packets.

"Alwen!"

CHAPTER SIXTEEN

Alwen turned toward Finn's voice, her face and chest drenched in sweat. A blue vein throbbed in her neck as she grabbed her belly, leaning face-first onto the shelf.

Finn sank to her knees and put her hand on Alwen's shoulder.

"I'm here," she said softly, squeezing her shoulder. "Tell me what's going on."

"I don't know." Alwen's voice was strained and tight, and she was breathing as though she couldn't get enough air into her lungs. "I think I might be having the baby."

Aisling and Olivia stepped around the corner then, and Olivia crouched down beside her. She put her hand on Alwen's belly as Alwen doubled over again in pain. "You're definitely having contractions. Let's get you out of this closet, okay?"

Finn stood and started to reach for her, but Alwen grimaced and shook her head, her chest and neck shimmering with moisture. "No. I can't." She groaned and gripped the shelf tighter, her fingertips white. "It hurts too bad. I can't walk."

"What about standing?" Finn leaned down, her voice low and smooth at Alwen's shoulder. "Can you just stand for me?"

The contraction loosened its grip slightly and Alwen nodded. Finn slipped her hands under Alwen's arms from behind, lifting her gently to her feet.

Michael arched an eyebrow from the door. "Jesus, man, you must work out."

Finn nodded. "Well, I don't much anymore, but I used to do circuit training and—"

Olivia smacked her brother on the arm.

"You've got to be shitting me here." She shook her head and was clearly trying not to laugh. "Alwen's having her baby in the supply closet and you two are trading workout tips?"

Alwen groaned again and leaned forward suddenly, her hands spread across her belly. Finn picked her up and carried her out of the closet, whispering to her as she walked around the bar and into the main area of the pub. Alwen's hands were tight around her neck, her head resting on her Finn's shoulder.

"Shit," Aisling said as she followed them. "I forgot we had everyone take their furniture."

Michael pointed to the snug along the back wall by the fire and pulled over the one chair that remained from across the room, a worn wingback covered in burgundy leather.

"Okay," Finn said, still holding Alwen in her arms, her voice soothing and calm as if they were all on a Sunday walk along the beach. "Michael, can you pull out that table? Then let's put this chair in facing the snug, leaving about three feet between them."

Michael quickly pulled out the table and pushed it to the side while Olivia and Aisling scooted the chair into place. Finn stepped into the space between and set Alwen gently down into the chair. The pain seemed to ease for a moment and Michael left to get Alwen a glass of water.

Finn sat facing Alwen in the snug, Olivia at her side, while Aisling pulled out her phone and stepped away.

"Can you tell us when these contractions started?" Olivia asked, her hand moving gently over Alwen's belly. "When did you first start feeling them?"

"Early this afternoon, before the party." A tear rolled down her face and she looked to Finn. "I know I shouldn't have stayed. I just couldn't have the baby...at home."

Finn put her hand on Alwen's knee and made her look her in the eyes. "Alwen, I'm so glad you're here. You did the right thing, and I promise you, we're going to get this handled."

The next contraction started and Olivia hit the timer on her phone, then looked at Finn for a long second before she spoke.

"Please tell me your girl is getting an ambulance here."

Finn nodded, her voice low. "She's trying, but it feels like she's been on the phone forever. I don't know what's taking so long." Finn glanced at Alwen, whose eyes were shut tight as the contraction moved through her. "Do we even have a hospital in Cwylldbridge?"

Olivia shook her head.

"What about a midwife?" Finn whispered. "Please tell me there's a midwife that lives locally."

Olivia shook her head again. "The nearest hospital is Cardiff. And it takes them a good forty minutes to get here even when the weather's clear. That's why I stayed in Cardiff with my mum for the last two weeks of my pregnancy."

The contraction seemed to ease as Aisling motioned them over to where she was standing. Michael sat down with Alwen to hold her hand while they stepped away. Small pinging sounds made them look toward the windows, where tiny balls of ice were pelting the glass.

The three of them stepped from behind the bar into the hall.

"I can tell by your face that the news isn't good," Olivia said, her hand flat against her forehead as she spoke. "What's going on? Are they on the way?"

"The short answer is no," Aisling said quickly, dropping her voice. "They asked what midwife her GP had assigned her, and I had to tell them she hasn't actually been to the doctor at all yet."

"Holy shit." Finn leaned against the wall and gathered her thoughts as she looked at the ceiling. "You're joking me here, right?"

A loud moan ending in a near scream filled the room as the next contraction hit Alwen. Olivia looked at her phone and stopped the timer. "Fuck me. Her contractions are less than two minutes apart."

"Okay," Finn said, squaring her shoulders. "What's the plan?"

"You two go back in there, and I'm going to get them back on the phone and see if there's someone that can talk us through this at the very least."

Another half moan, half cry filled the room.

"Olivia," Finn said, turning to her as she spoke, her words low and rushed, "unless you have something to tell me about Michael that I don't know, you're the only one of us who's had a baby." She paused. "You're on."

Olivia's eyes filled with tears, and she dropped her face into her hands. "Finn, I can't. I can't handle the sight of blood. I just faint instantly. I couldn't even do it when I had Ella, they had to clean her up before they handed her to me."

Finn stepped back and peered out at Michael, who now had an overwhelmed look of panic on his face. "Jesus. This just gets better and better."

She held up one finger to Michael to let him know they were coming. "Can you stay with Aisling until she gets someone on the phone?"

"Aye. Of course."

Finn headed back into the seating area, which was beginning to feel a lot like stepping into the ring. Michael got up and Finn slid into the snug, smiling at Alwen, who had hunched almost completely down in the leather chair, tightly gripping the armrests.

"Michael." Finn looked up at him standing behind the chair with a worried look on his face. "I have a down jacket under the bar. Can you bring that to me? And just in case, can you also grab a stack of clean kitchen towels? You'll find them in a basket under the prep table."

Finn turned her attention back to Alwen, who seemed to be on the downslope of a contraction. "Hey," she said, locking eyes with Alwen, her voice relaxed and warm. "How are you feeling?"

"I've been better. When is the ambulance going to be here?"

Aisling, her face suddenly pale, stepped around the chair, followed by Olivia. "Lads, this isn't great news, so I'm just going to give it to you straight and we can go from there."

Finn's heart sank and she looked up at Aisling, who gave her a barely perceptible shake of the head before she continued.

"The ambulance can't leave the hospital until it's safe to travel, and right now we have seventy-mile-an-hour winds between here and Cardiff."

"Did they give you an estimate of how long it will be?"

"They say it truly depends on the weather, but when they get to all clear to drive, they'll be here as quickly as they can." She paused, drawing a deep breath. "Which means it could be one hour or five hours, we just don't know."

Finn listened, keeping her face neutral and squeezing Alwen's hand as she started another contraction.

"And there's one more thing you should know."

"What?"

"We just lost cell signal, so I couldn't get through to anyone to coach us through this."

"Finn," Alwen said, panic in her eyes, squeezing her hand so hard Finn struggled not to show pain. "I feel like I need to push."

Olivia stepped back from the chair, mouthing *Holy Mother of God* to Aisling as she tried to compose herself.

"That's natural," Finn said, squeezing her hand then looking up. "Could I ask everyone to step back and give Alwen and me a minute alone?"

All three headed back behind the bar, where Aisling was already rummaging through every drawer looking for the first aid kit.

Finn leaned forward, elbows on her knees, her eyes locked on Alwen. "Hey, did you know that I used to box?"

Alwen shook her head, the last contraction slowly subsiding.

"I boxed in the semipros in my twenties, until I got hurt and couldn't do it anymore."

Alwen smiled for the first time since they'd found her in the closet. "You look like a boxer."

Finn laughed, taking Alwen's hands in hers. "Yeah, I get that a lot." She paused, looking into her eyes. "But because I did that, I learned to tell right away which people were going to be hardest to beat. Which ones were the toughest."

Alwen smiled. "That's me and you, isn't it?"

"Exactly. I've known it since the first day in that shop."

Alwen nodded, eyes still on Finn as she smiled and squeezed her hand.

"So I think delivering this baby might be up to us now. But I'll let you in on a little secret that those three over there don't know yet." Finn paused, her voice dropping to a whisper as she leaned closer to Alwen. "You and I are going to win this fucking fight."

Alwen laughed out loud, prompting swiveled heads and instant confusion from behind the bar.

"We're going to do this thing together," Finn said, smiling. "You tell me what's happening, what you need, and I'm going to do my best to make sure your son or daughter makes it into this world safe."

"I know you will. I trust you." Tears shimmered in Alwen's eyes as she squeezed Finn's hand, then took a deep breath. "Let's do this."

Before the words were out of her mouth, another contraction hit her and she moaned, eyes shut tight in pain, her face red and straining. Michael returned with the jacket and towels and set them in the snug beside Finn, who looked up and nodded toward the bar.

"Can you let the girls know it might be time to do this thing?" She glanced over to Olivia. "But I need you to stay behind the chair and keep Olivia with you, no matter what."

Michael rolled his eyes. "Because she faints flat out at the sight of blood?"

"Exactly." Finn winked at Alwen. "See? That's what I'm saying. She wouldn't last two minutes in the ring."

Alwen half laughed, half moaned, gripping her stomach.

"Just in case, if you feel like you need to push, then it might be time to get these clothes off, okay?"

Alwen nodded, grimacing as she lifted her hips to push down her jeans and underwear. Finn helped her slide them off, then pulled her own shirt over her head, leaving her in just a sports bra, and laid it over Alwen's hips.

"That might give you a little bit of privacy," Finn said, grinning. "But that's all I got, so we gotta get this done."

Alwen braced her feet against the seat of the snug booth on either side of Finn, just as Olivia appeared behind Alwen's head and reached for her hands, smoothing the damp hair away from her forehead and whispering words of encouragement.

Aisling had finally found the first aid kit and ran to the snug, handing the kit to Finn, who set it down beside her.

"Okay, Alwen," Finn said. "Round one. Push as hard as you can with your next contraction and let's see where we are."

It hit a few seconds later and Alwen curled forward as she bore down, her cheeks wet and red, straining until the contraction eased. Tears slipped down the sides of her face.

"Hey, mama, you know what I see already?" Finn said with a smile, eyes locked on hers, one hand flat and warm against her belly. "Your baby's head."

"Really?" Alwen smiled through the tears. "You see it? That's good, right?"

Finn nodded as the next contraction hit. Alwen's shirt was soaked through with sweat and tears, and she gripped Olivia's hands with tense, white fingers as she pushed, the pain draining from her slowly in a low, guttural growl.

Finn looked up just in time to see Michael standing behind Olivia, looking like he might be sick at any moment. She nodded in his direction, and Aisling caught her glance.

"Hey, Michael, do you think you can try the hospital again, just to see if we have a cell signal back?"

Michael nodded and retreated into the hall with lightning speed, phone in hand.

Alwen bore down again, but for the next few contractions the baby's head stayed where it was. Long minutes that felt like forever passed, and more contractions came and went with no progress, until suddenly the energy in the room changed. The pain was starting to get to Alwen, veins pulsing in her forehead and neck, lower lip swollen from biting down on it with every contraction.

Olivia looked at Finn from behind the chair, clearly worried, but careful not to alarm Alwen.

Finn reached quickly for her blue down jacket, sitting forward as much as possible until her knees almost touched Alwen, then spreading the jacket across her thighs.

"Finn, what's wrong?" Alwen said, her breath fast and heavy, panic settling in her voice. "I can tell something's wrong."

Olivia stepped backward from the chair, tears of panic and worry streaming down her face. Aisling gave her a quick hug and took her place. The wind rattled the windows violently and Alwen looked over, watching them shake in the window frames, hail etching the outsides.

"Nothing's wrong, Alwen, I promise." Finn leaned forward and put her hands over Alwen's, cradling her belly. "But this is the final round, and trust me, that's always the hardest. You're beat up, you're exhausted, and all you want is for everything to stop."

Alwen nodded, her breathing slowing slightly. "That's exactly how it feels."

"I'm not going to lie to you, we need to get your little one out so we can make sure he or she is okay." Alwen nodded, her eyes never wavering from Finn's. "And the last round is the one that wins or loses a fight." She paused, squeezing Alwen's hands. "Are we ready for this?"

They nodded together and Finn sat back in the snug.

"With the next contraction, I want you to bear down with everything you have, okay?"

The next contraction collided with Finn's last words, and Alwen bore down, caught her breath, then bore down again, only this time she didn't stop until she saw her baby slide into the arms of Finn, who placed her forearm gently over its body and turned her arms over and down so the baby was supported on a downward slope.

No one moved for the next few seconds, no one even drew a breath, until there was a sudden piercing cry that ricocheted around the walls of the pub. Everyone exhaled at the same time, every one of them laughing and crying simultaneously. Even Michael was wiping tears of relief onto his shirtsleeve from behind the safety of the bar.

Finn wrapped the down jacket snugly around the baby and handed the small bundle to Alwen, who looked up and smiled through her tears.

"It's a girl, isn't it?"

Finn nodded, her hand still resting protectively over the baby in Alwen's arms.

"How did you know?" Aisling asked, wiping the tears from Alwen's ruddy face with a clean towel.

"I don't know. I guess I've always known." Alwen smiled. "Are you sure she's okay?"

The distant wail of a siren cut through the scrape of the wind across the windowpanes, and Finn met Alwen's gaze.

"I'm positive. She's strong and beautiful, just like her mama."

The siren's wail drew closer, and Michael came running back into the room, holding his cell phone aloft like a trophy. "We have cell service. It's back!"

"I'm going to go outside and make sure they know where we are," Olivia said, pulling on her coat as she pushed the door open. "It sounds like they finally decided to grow a pair and get out in the weather. It's about bloody time."

Aisling sat down beside Finn as the baby's cries subsided.

Alwen looked instantly in love as she brushed her thumb against the perfect fist of the baby, who grasped it immediately, bringing it to her tiny face.

"Her name is Finley." Alwen smiled, looking up at Finn and Aisling. "Finley Rose. After you and your grandmother."

That was it. That was all it took for Finn's tears to finally fall, and she leaned over to kiss Finley's tiny cheek just as the paramedics rushed through the door.

CHAPTER SEVENTEEN

It seemed like they'd waited forever for the paramedics to get there, but after they'd checked Alwen and the baby over, they loaded them both up and left for the hospital in less than a minute. Olivia had insisted on riding to the hospital in the ambulance with Alwen, and Michael headed home right away to tell Jack and Marjorie.

The door shut behind them, and after the siren wail faded Aisling finally fell into Finn's arms. Finn held her tight, kissing the top of her head.

"I can't believe how amazing you were tonight, Finn." Aisling relaxed against her chest and wrapped her arms around her waist. "You were an absolute rock for Alwen."

Finn laughed. "Are you kidding? I was scared out of my fucking mind."

"Well, no one would have guessed." She smiled. "Of course, to be fair, you didn't have much competition. Michael was nearly hurling in the hall. Olivia, who's had a baby herself, almost fainted, and I couldn't even find the sodding first aid kit until it was almost over."

"Well, no matter what happened before she got here," Finn said, bringing Aisling's face to hers, "Finley Rose is strong and healthy, and our Alwen rocked that childbirth thing like a boss."

"That's the truth," Aisling said, stepping back and grabbing her scarf that was under the bar. "And how precious is that name? I can't believe she—"

"Nope. Can't talk about it yet." Finn shook her head as she reached for Aisling's jacket and handed it over. "Or I'm going to start bawling again, for fuck's sake."

Aisling laughed and slipped on her jacket, rounding the corner of the bar and turning off the few lamps they had left after everyone had taken the loaned items home. "All I'm saying is that it was pretty sexy how you stepped up and saved them."

Finn leaned into the hearth to check that the fire was out, then looked back at her, already heading for the door. "Oh really? Is this something I can use to my advantage later?"

"Sure." Aisling smiled, waiting for Finn at the door while she turned off the lights behind the bar. "Not that you're going to need any help in that department. Provided you can tell me why Kaitlyn told Olivia you two had 'history' tonight?"

"She did?" Finn shook her head. "Aisling, I promise, you know every single thing that's ever happened..." Her voice trailed off as she watched a sudden smile flash like sunlight across Aisling's face. "You're just torturing me with this now, aren't you?"

"Definitely." Aisling said, bumping her shoulder to Finn's. "She's clearly lying but she just gets under my skin, I guess."

By the time they got back to the cottage, the wind had died down to a gentle reminder of the storm that had passed, and the moonlight glinted off the remaining stalwart icicles still clinging to the eaves of the church. Silence settled around them as they walked past the cottage gate to the edge of the cliff, looking down into the dark, foamy sea. Finn wrapped her arms around Aisling from behind and she leaned back into Finn's chest, the sounds of the waves crashing onto the rocks below replacing words. They stayed there for a few minutes, until their faces were damp with the salt spray tossed up with the wind, then turned and opened the gate to their cottage.

After they'd gotten ready for bed, Aisling turned toward Finn as the fire crackled in the bedroom, her fingers wandering lightly over Finn's abs. The driving wind and hail had been replaced by delicate white snowflakes floating and falling outside the bedroom window.

Aisling dipped her head and whispered into the warmth of Finn's neck. "I don't think I can fall asleep yet."

Finn clicked on her small bedside lamp and turned to her under the duvet, somewhat distracted by the taupe sueded silk slip she'd worn to bed.

"I can't either, but I don't think it's the adrenaline." She brushed Aisling's nipples lightly with her palm, watching them tighten under the gossamer sheer silk. "But I'm pretty sure this insane body lying beside me probably has something to do with it."

Aisling laughed and rolled over to sit across Finn's hips, wild hair falling around her face like a shifting sunset, the delicate strap of her slip falling down one shoulder.

"I have an idea."

Finn smiled and let her continue.

Aisling leaned forward and traced the line of Finn's neck with the tip of her tongue, her body warm across Finn's hips. "Do you trust me enough to let me tie you?"

Finn laughed, hands moving up Aisling's legs, slowly stroking the ivory skin of her inner thighs with her thumbs. "That was definitely not what I thought you were going to say, but sure, I'm up for it."

She slid her hands around to Aisling's ass, gripping it with a strength that Finn knew would make her instantly wet.

"And just how are you planning to do this, Miss Moss?"

Aisling kissed her, brushing Finn's ear as she slid out of bed and retrieved two silk scarves from the closet. She climbed back in bed and settled across Finn's body. Finn's hands spanned Aisling's thighs again, shifting her to bring the slow warmth of Aisling's center closer to her own bare skin.

Aisling picked up one of the scarves and brought Finn's wrist to the head of the bed.

"Baby, I'm all for this, but do you seriously think those little scarves are going to hold me back if I want to touch you?"

Aisling just arched an eyebrow as she twisted a scarf tightly and tied a small knot at each end, then wound it several times around Finn's wrist, tying it so that the back of her wrist was flat and firm against the bedpost.

She looked at Finn as she lifted the other wrist to the bedpost. "Do you seriously think I can't tie a knot that will make you behave?"

Aisling smiled as she picked up the second scarf and wound it around Finn's other wrist, tying it securely to the opposite bedpost.

"All right, I'll play. You've got me now. Or at least you think you do," Finn said, sliding her tongue over her lower lip. "What are you going to do with me?"

Aisling found the hem of her slip and pulled it over her head, leaving just a pair of silk panties tied at both hips.

"It's not really what I'm going to do to *you*, at least not yet."

She leaned forward and put two fingers into Finn's mouth, closing her eyes as Finn stroked them with her tongue. When she finally took them back she circled her nipple with her wet fingertips, her hair falling down her back as closed her eyes, then started on the other.

"Holy God." Finn instinctively tried to touch her but was held back by the knots that surprisingly didn't let her move an inch. "You can't be serious about this."

Aisling smiled, her hand dipping lower into her panties, then back to her mouth where she ran her tongue languidly from her palm to her fingertip. Finn groaned as she watched her hand disappear again under the silk as her thighs tightened around Finn's hips.

"Finn." Aisling's fingers moved under the delicate fabric. "Do you want to touch me?"

"Jesus Christ." Finn's breath deepened and she pulled against the restraints. "I can't believe I'm saying this, but you've got to untie me."

Aisling laughed, her fingertips lazily tracing the hollow at the base of Finn's neck and then, slowly, moving down to her nipple. She bit her lip as she held Finn's nipple between her index and middle finger, stroking the top of it with her thumb before she answered.

"Oh, we are not even close to that point."

She smiled as she slid off the bed again, then slipped Finn's boxer briefs off and tossed them onto a bedside chair.

"I mean, I guess if you really can't take it, you can say a safe word, like maybe *Guinness* for example, and I'll untie you then…" Her voice trailed off as she turned away from Finn and slowly slid her panties down her legs, leaning over to pick them up and brush them across the inside of Finn's thighs. She turned back around and sat across Finn again, her wet center sliding across Finn's lower abs. Finn watched as she slid one finger across her glistening clit and leaned back, bracing the other behind her on Finn's thigh. Finn saw every delicious part of her now, her eyes following every move as Aisling continued to stroke her clit, the bud tensing and shimmering in the firelight as she continued to stroke it with just the tip of her middle finger.

"Aisling, I'm not kidding," Finn whispered, intense and breathless. "I have to touch you."

Aisling dipped her fingers lower, then inside, visibly losing her breath when she started to move them inside her. Finn arched her neck, her head straining against the pillow, turning her wrists to try to slip out of the knots.

"I wouldn't waste your time trying," Aisling said, slipping her fingers out and over her clit again before putting them into Finn's mouth. "And I wasn't kidding about those knots. They get tighter if you struggle."

Finn closed her eyes and sucked the wetness from Aisling's fingertips. Her hips moved in a restless rhythm, every muscle in her arms straining against the scarves.

"Fuck, baby." Her voice was a low scrape. "You're killing me here."

Aisling started stroking her clit again, this time with more pressure, her wet fingers sliding over the tense bud again and again before dipping back inside. Finn groaned, eyes locked on Aisling's.

"Come for me. Let me watch you."

Aisling leaned forward to kiss her, tracing her lips with the tip of her tongue.

"Do you want to see me come?"

"God, yes," Finn said, her voice husky and rough, eyelids dusky and heavy with desire.

Aisling shifted from sitting across Finn's hips to kneeling over her chest, her knees on either side of Finn's shoulders. Her wet clit was swollen and ready, shimmering in the flickering light and just inches from Finn's mouth. Aisling closed her eyes, leaning slightly back as she stroked inside then went back to her clit, her breathing becoming heavier, eyes fluttering closed as she fell into a steady, intense rhythm.

Finn watched as Aisling's breath became a moan and she arched even closer to Finn's mouth. Finn strained toward her but she was just out of reach; all she could do was watch as Aisling fell over the edge, fingers working her clit, shoulders thrown back and thighs trembling as her orgasm moved through her like a sudden gust of wind sweeping the edge of a cliff.

She shivered as she caught her breath, the last tremors still visible as her fingers slowed. She opened her eyes and saw Finn biting her lip, muscles straining against her knots.

"Ready for me to let you go?"

"Yeah," Finn said, smiling as Aisling leaned down to kiss her. "That's the understatement of the year."

Aisling untied the knots quickly, dropping the scarves on the bed, then snuggled down into Finn's arms. Finn lifted her chin and kissed her.

"Ah, you think you're just going to sleep now, do you?"

Aisling eyes fluttered shut. "Aye. Maybe just for a minute…"

Finn shifted, settling Aisling in the duvet with a kiss on her forehead while she got up to throw another log on the fire. A spray of red-gold sparks raced up the chimney when the split log landed on the glowing coals, and Finn kept her eyes on Aisling as she reached into the closet. Aisling's breath was soft and deep, the duvet pulled all the way up to her chin with just one freckled shoulder peeking out, warmed by the golden firelight.

When she got back into bed behind her a few minutes later, Finn pulled Aisling back into her arms, watching her stir then open her eyes and turn over in the semidarkness.

"Finn," she whispered. "Tell me that's for me."

"Only for you, baby." She smiled, sitting up behind Aisling and lifting her easily to her knees, feeling the heat of her thighs on top of her own as she sat back against her, achingly slowly, Finn's hands circling her hips.

"Oh my God…" Her words disappeared into a moan as Finn's strap-on slid slow and deep inside her. When Finn's hips finally met hers, Aisling leaned back, her head resting on Finn's shoulder.

"How do you feel, baby?" Finn said, her hips still as Aisling got used to her being inside. "Is it too much?"

"It's…no, it's perfect." Aisling started to move her hips, reaching up to hold the back of Finn's head. Finn's hands spanned her waist, pulling her back on the shaft, biting her lip when she felt Aisling's hips press back harder, asking for more.

"Do you want this?" Finn whispered the words into her ear, hands sliding up her body to cup her breasts. "Because I want to give it to you."

Aisling didn't answer, just leaned forward slowly until her shoulders touched the pillows. Finn's breath caught as she waited for Aisling to answer.

"I want all of you."

That was more than Finn could take. She leaned into Aisling, sliding all the way inside her, one hand wrapped around her hip, the other at the small of her back, and started to move inside her. The sight of the woman she loved taking her like that, the haze of trust and intensity, brought tears to her eyes. Finn held Aisling's hips in her hands and memorized every move as Aisling reached up, bracing her hands on the headboard.

Finn slowed her pace then, reaching around to Aisling's clit, gliding her fingertips over it in circles while she took her from behind. Aisling moaned into the pillow, pushing hard back against her.

"God, I'm already…" Her words turned to a faint groan as Finn slid her fingers over Aisling's clit with more pressure, enveloping it, feeling it tense and still suddenly under her fingers. Aisling's breath deepened. "I'm already so close."

Finn realized as she felt Aisling's lush ass pressed against her, taking every inch and straining for more, that she was close too. She leaned back and brought Aisling with her, taking a slow breath before she lay down, turning Aisling to face her and pulling her over to sit across her hips. Aisling sat back slowly, her eyes closing as Finn slowly filled her. Finn watched as she lifted her damp hair from her neck with both hands and started to ride her.

Finn didn't recognize the raw scrape of her own voice. "Jesus Christ."

She gripped Aisling's hips, pulling them tight to hers, sliding the smooth leather of the harness against her own swollen clit. Aisling, seeming to realize what Finn needed, slowed the pace, moving her hips back and forth across her as Finn gripped her thighs and a fine mist of sweat glistened across her chest. She opened her eyes to see Aisling's fingertips working her own clit as she rode her, eyes closed, biting her lip as her thighs tensed around Finn.

Aisling caught her eyes and leaned forward until her forehead touched Finn's.

"I love you, Finn." Her words were slow velvet against Finn's lips. "Like I've never loved anyone."

"Good." Finn smiled, stroking her cheek gently with her thumb. "Because you've been the love of my life since the moment I saw you."

Finn held Aisling's face in her hands for a moment until Aisling sat back and started to move against her again. Finn held her hips, guiding her, watching her glistening clit slide across the smooth leather of the harness until she couldn't take it anymore. Aisling leaned back, her hands behind her on Finn's thighs, and moved against her harder, sliding the harness over Finn's swollen clit in a steady, unrelenting rhythm. Finn arched her back and came hard with Aisling, the same shimmering orgasm washing over them with the crashing intensity of the ocean waves breaking in the darkness just below the bedroom window.

❖

When Finn unlocked the pub door the next morning, walking into a wide, empty space with no furniture was a shock. Spotting Greystone behind the bar shaking up a morning martini was not.

"It's about time you two got here, it's nearly half eleven," she said with an eye roll, shaking her martini with one hand, then popping off the cap with her thumb and pouring it expertly into a chilled glass on the bar. "The village will be parched before you get your act together and open the doors."

"How lovely to see you, Ms. Greystone," Aisling said, shrugging off her coat as she came around the corner of the bar. "Would you like a bag of crisps with that?"

"That would be lovely, dear. Prawn cocktail if you have them lying about."

Finn tried not to laugh and sat on a barstool, opening the crisp bag for Greystone after Aisling plunked it down on the bar.

Greystone arched an eyebrow in Aisling's direction.

"I took the liberty of having a little wander around and noticed the kitchen was stocked. Are you planning on serving food eventually?"

Aisling nodded, elbowing Finn when she saw her smile out of the corner of her eye.

"Smart girl. Might as well turn a profit on as many things as possible during opening hours, I always say." She took a sip of her martini, then pulled one of the pimento olives off the swizzle stick and chewed slowly, as if they'd asked her a question and she was mulling it over. They hadn't.

"I've also been keeping an eye on your numbers, which, if you watch your expenses, should give you more than enough income if you plan on keeping the pub after the year is up, so well done."

Finn smiled, reaching over the counter and loading another

swizzle stick with olives, which she wordlessly traded for Greystone's empty one.

"The one thing on my list I gave you that hasn't been attended to is the patio outside."

"It's the next thing we want to tackle, there just hasn't been enough time." Finn glanced at Aisling, who nodded reluctantly, eyeing the crisp crumbs scattered across the bar.

"Well," Greystone said. "When you do, have someone move the statue to the center of the courtyard. It was always meant to be there." She looked from Aisling to Finn, her face softening for just an instant. "You two have done well here. It's nice to know that the pub is in good hands."

She paused, then met Finn's eyes. "And, Finn, what you did to bring little Finley Rose into the world yesterday..." She paused, as if searching for the words. "You did all of us proud."

Finn paused. "How did you—"

A sharp knock at the door startled all three of them, and Greystone knocked back her martini in one long gulp when she spotted the furniture trucks through the window. "I'll just show myself out."

By the time they'd propped open the doors for the delivery, she was gone and the back door to the patio was standing wide open.

That afternoon, when the delivery team had finally finished the setup and Finn and Aisling had just gotten the furniture arranged perfectly, there was another knock at the door.

Aisling twisted her hair into a knot on the way to the doors. "Good Lord, the pub is just as busy closed as it is when it's open."

But it was only Olivia and Alwen with little Finley, wearing a tiny knit hat and wrapped in a fuzzy pink blanket. Aisling hugged them both and Alwen handed the baby to Finn, who instantly started talking to her while she walked around, bouncing Finley softly against her shoulder.

"Marjorie called and told us this morning they were letting you out of the hospital." Aisling paused, a smile lighting up her face. "And that they'd managed to convince you to stay with them for the moment as well."

"Ella's just in love with her already, of course," Olivia said, shaking her head. "Although she's lucky to get to see the baby at all. Mum just flat-out refuses to put her down, kind of like Finn over there." She smiled, shaking her head. "From the looks of it, Marjorie may have some competition."

The three of them watched Finn standing by the hearth cooing to Finley for a moment before Aisling pulled her phone out of her pocket and took a picture of them.

She smiled. "If there wasn't a ButchesandBabies hashtag on Instagram, there is now."

They watched as Finn finally wandered back with Finley and reluctantly handed her back to her mum.

"While you two are here, we were wondering if you'd be interested in helping us out with something eventually?" Finn glanced at Aisling, who nodded and motioned them toward the stairs.

"This is exciting. I've never been upstairs in the pub," Olivia said as she followed the rest, her hand sliding silently over the mahogany banister as they climbed. "I've always wondered what was up here."

When they got to the top of the stairs, Finn stepped aside and let the girls look around. They walked through the kitchen, chatting, then down to the three bedrooms at the end of the hall. In the last bedroom, there was a drift of sawdust on the floor and a small piece of furniture in the middle of the room.

"Is this what I think it is?" Alwen ran her fingers over the edge of the wood, rocking it back and forth.

"Is it a crib?" Olivia asked as she gently took Finley so Alwen could look closer.

"It is," Aisling said, bumping her shoulder to Finn's with a smile. "Finn and Barry made it for you."

"Don't be too impressed. 'Putting it together' might be more accurate," Finn said, pointing to the rockers on the bottom of the crib. "There was an old rocking horse in the kitchen closet up here, and before Alwen even had the baby I thought it might be a project Barry and I could work on. We used the rockers and built a simple crib for the top. All the tools were already here, so it was pretty easy."

Alwen smiled. "So Barry Wright helped build this?"

"He did, and he's excited to know what you think. He's pretty proud of it."

"I'll go over to his house today and let him know I love it." She looked up at Aisling and Finn, tears gathering in her sky-blue eyes. "Thank you both. For everything."

"And since Finn has you buttered up with the crib..." Aisling paused. "We were wondering if you two might be interested in helping us fix up the flat."

Olivia and Alwen lit up with smiles and looked at each other.

"Absolutely," Olivia said. "I love that kind of thing, and it would get me out of the house a little bit. Mum means well, but she's literally driving me a bit more mad every day."

"Honestly," Aisling said, tying back the curtains in the room to let in a bright pool of sunlight that instantly warmed the hardwood floors, "you'd be doing us a favor. We have so much we want to do downstairs." She looked at Finn and playfully rolled her eyes. "Including the outside patio, apparently. It would just sit here empty if you two didn't move in and help us out."

"Wait," Olivia said, excitement creeping into her voice. "You want us to live here, with Finley and Ella, while we help you fix up the flat?"

"As long as you want, actually," Aisling said, smiling at Finn, who had somehow managed to get Finley back in her arms. "It doesn't need anything major, just paint and decorating. And it may make childcare easier on both of you. But if you decide you don't want to do it, we completely understand."

"Yes," Alwen said before the last words were even out of Aisling's mouth. "I would love to do that." She looked at Olivia and they both burst out in excited laughter, running down the hall to look at every room again.

Finn looked down at the sleeping little girl in her arms and smiled, planting a gentle kiss on her forehead. "Well, Finley Rose, welcome to the Tribe."

CHAPTER EIGHTEEN

After a long day of rearranging furniture and getting the pub ready to open for the weekend, it was almost twilight when Aisling and Finn stepped outside to lock up the pub.

Aisling stopped, the key still in the lock. "What is that sound?"

What had been a low rumble quickly turned to a distant, deafening din, so loud it almost seemed to rattle the windows. As they left the pub and started walking toward it, they noticed their neighbors doing the same thing, some coming out of their houses in aprons or with kids in tow, as if they'd just been ready to sit down to dinner. Jack and Marjorie stepped out of the butcher shop as Finn and Aisling were passing the square and hurriedly joined them.

"Where is it coming from?" Aisling turned around to search as she spoke, until Finn put a hand on her shoulder and pointed to something in the field just beyond the village.

"Oh no," Marjorie said. "They weren't supposed to start until tomorrow." She paled, and Jack put his hand on her shoulder and squeezed it.

"Go," he said. "Go find them. I'll do what I can."

Marjorie turned, running back into the shop and locking the door behind her. Aisling saw through the glass that she already had the phone pressed to her ear as she hurried to the back of the shop toward their living quarters.

"What's going on?" Aisling asked, more and more people joining them on either side as what seemed like the entire village hurried toward the field.

"I'll tell you when we get there." Jack was puffing, his face red.

"But we need to get there before they start, or it will be destroyed in less than three minutes. Once they start, it doesn't take long."

"What will be destroyed?" Aisling said, anxiety starting to creep into her voice.

Jack just pointed ahead to dozens of heavy equipment vehicles turning off the main road and rumbling along the bumpy field in the direction of the castle. There were several bulldozers, enormous dump trucks, and a crane that was taller than the layers of gray mist hovering over the raw top edge of the castle. Hanging from the front of the crane was a wrecking ball, secured by steel cord, swinging like a pendulum as it moved into position behind the castle.

"Oh my God." Aisling stopped, the blood draining from her face, panic instantly replacing anxiety. "They're tearing down the castle to build this mine, aren't they?"

Jack put his arm around Aisling's shoulders and squeezed. "I'll explain as we go, love, but we need to get there as soon as we can. From what I understand it's a done deal, so it's coming down, but I want those bastards to have to look us in the eyes when they do it."

"And it seems like the rest of the village feels the same way," Finn said as they hurried through the field, long grasses swiping at their legs as they walked. Dozens of their friends and neighbors were on every side, and more were streaming in from the village to the field every second.

"I can't believe this," Aisling said, picking up the pace. "How is this possible?"

Finn took her hand as they hurried toward the castle. "They buried the fact that the castle would have to be destroyed when they were trying to get the deal to go through because they knew no one would let that happen."

"Can they even do that?" Aisling asked, pulling on her gloves as she walked. "Isn't it on the historical register?"

Finn shook her head as they passed several young women pushing strollers. "That's what I thought until Herschel told me the other day that it used to be privately owned. Until around fifty years ago, I think some of his distant relatives actually owned it. Then right around that time, the castle and the land it's standing on was sold to the township of Cardiff."

Aisling looked up in shock, the wind whipping her hair around her face. "And then Cardiff turned around and sold it to Rockfield Acquisitions, knowing it was going to be torn down?"

"The short answer to that is yes," Jack said as they neared the castle and the crowd gathered thick and dense around them. "But Marjorie said the disclosure of the castle demolition was buried under a mountain of legal mumbo jumbo, so no one really knew it would be affected. The location was described using only the geographical location from the surveyors that they knew no one would bother to look up."

"So all they saw was the money." Aisling watched as several expensive-looking black cars turned off the main road and made their way to the castle behind the equipment.

Jack went on, tall field grass brushing the sides of his apron.

"Aye. Several million pounds tends to have that effect on people. The only ones who really knew were the council members, and I'm not even sure all of them had the full story."

They finally reached the front of the castle, roped off in every direction with blaring yellow caution tape, just as the demolition team was moving into place to the side of the structure. Security guards were patrolling the perimeter, and several men in hard hats carrying clipboards bearing the Rockfield Acquisitions logo exited the castle's main entrance and stood in a circle, speaking in low tones. In the center of the group was Kaitlyn Matthews.

Aisling looked around her at the townspeople that had, at some point she couldn't specifically remember, quietly become family. Some were clearly angry, others crying with shock that the castle was being torn down, but everyone was pulling together to try to save this part of their history. At the very least, it was clear that if Dun Laoghaire castle was going down, she'd go down surrounded by the people that loved her.

A handful of the men, wearing odd combinations of scuffed hardhats and expensive tailored suits, stepped up to the front of the castle, security closing ranks at either side. Smack-dab in the middle was Kaitlyn, and it was a good thing she was standing because her skirt was short enough to become a belt if she dared sit down. Aisling rolled her eyes. *Of course.*

The crowd shifted and jostled for position as one of them lifted the megaphone around his neck and switched it on.

"Hi there, folks. My name is Jason Jansen, and I'm a project manager with Rockfield Acquisitions." A thick Texas accent coated his words so completely he might as well have been reading lines from the set of *Walker, Texas Ranger.* "We all know why the demolition team is here, and although I know you're sentimental about this old building, we hope this step toward progress is just the beginning of a very profitable relationship between Cardiff, Coldbridge, and your friends at Rockfield Acquisitions Inc."

A soft murmur spread through the crowd as he butchered the name of the village; it hadn't escaped their attention that he'd rocked into town to knock down the most beautiful part of the landscape and couldn't even be bothered to get the name right. He passed the megaphone to Kaitlyn, who aimed a sugary smile at the crowd and pitched her voice to the level of college cheerleading championships.

"I know you are all just as excited as we are to start building the future of Coldbridge!" She paused dramatically for the applause that never came. The entire crowd was silent, and the only movement came from Michael's dog Harold, a sweet, portly beagle, who was wandering slowly across the grass in the direction of the castle. Kaitlyn cleared her throat and looked behind her at Jansen. He motioned for her to continue, eyes narrowed, and she turned quickly back to the crowd and brought the megaphone to her mouth, her over-whitened teeth glinting in the sunlight.

"We hope you share our vision of making this village a success and will look at today as just a symbol of setting the past aside to make room for a new—"

Kaitlyn stopped abruptly and followed the gaze of the crowd down as they watched Harold relieving himself on her leg, a look of sheer bliss on his face at the impressive stream running down Kaitlyn's calf and into her shoe. She screamed and dropped the megaphone, and the smattering of hesitant applause from Rockfield staff faded quickly as Kaitlyn and Jansen retreated, surrounded by security and staff.

"Well, those were the most condescending speeches I've ever heard," Finn said, anger burning behind her eyes. "He knows we're 'sentimental about this old building'?"

Jack shook his head and smiled. "On the upside, though, I've never been so proud of our Harold. That was some perfect timing from the old boy."

From the corner of her eye, Aisling saw Kaitlyn approaching, the dagger points of her high heels sinking into the soft loam of the field. Despite Aisling's unwavering gaze, she walked up behind the group and put her hand on Finn's shoulder.

"Finn, could I have a word with you in private?"

"Kaitlyn," Aisling said, turning around to face her. "Anything you have to say to my girlfriend you can say with me here." Kaitlyn looked up at Finn, but Finn was smiling at Aisling. "Or maybe you didn't think she'd tell me that you threw yourself at her the other night when you thought I was out of the pub? Or that you flat-out lied to Alwen and Olivia about having some fictional relationship with Finn?"

Kaitlyn's syrupy smile dropped instantly, and she squared her shoulders. "I may have exaggerated a bit or come on a little strong, but frankly, Ashlee, that's none of your business."

"Actually," Finn said, her jaw tense. "It's completely her business. I'm in love with *Aisling*, which I said to you in no uncertain terms the other night." She paused. "Are we finally clear? Or would you like Aisling to explain it to you this time?"

"Fine," Kaitlyn said, pulling her left heel out of the soft soil and shaking off the clump of grass stuck to it. "Your loss. I was just saying—"

Jack interrupted, smiling. "I'd cut your losses and walk away, lass, if you can manage it. As you can see, Aisling has plenty of backup, and we're all dying to have something to do with our time at the moment. We don't take to liars too well."

Olivia and Alwen, who had been listening as they reached the group, stood on either side of Jack. Alwen handed Finley to Jack and looked at her watch. "I just had a baby yesterday, but I'd be happy to knock a little sense into you if you're having trouble getting the point, love."

Finn smiled as Aisling stifled a laugh with her hand.

Olivia nodded and pushed the sleeves of her cardigan up to her elbows. "Actually, that sounds fun." She tilted her head to the side and looked Kaitlyn up and down. "From the look of her it won't take fifteen seconds."

"Fine!" Kaitlyn jerked her other foot out of the loam, leaving the shoe behind. "I get it." She glared at Aisling. "You can call off your ridiculous posse of savages. I'm leaving."

She yanked on the shoe until it came loose and she tottered off, tilting and sticking into the earth with every step.

"Cheers, girls," Aisling said, smiling. "I think we've seen the back of her now. Thanks to you it looks like she finally got the point."

"Can we get the crowd to back up?" a workman with a megaphone shouted from the steps of the castle, his voice piercing the cold air like thunder. "At least twenty meters from the taped-off area, please. Demolition is set to start in eight minutes' time."

Maggie walked up and joined them, her face lined with worry. She had a basket of muffins wrapped in paper on her arm, the names of each written on the top. Beside them was a stack of napkins.

"Alwen, love, Marjorie sent me to ask if you'd like me to take your little Finley back to the house for you?"

"That would be wonderful, Maggie," Alwen said as Finn took the basket and Alwen carefully placed Finley into Maggie's arms. "I'd have to leave soon if not."

"You stay here, petal," Maggie said. "This is a rare treat for me. I raised five of them, but it's been too long since I had a baby in my arms." Finley wrapped her little fist around Maggie's thumb and sighed. "We'll be just grand, won't we, little one?"

As Maggie walked away cooing at Finley, Olivia pointed at three figures in the distance teetering on what looked like bicycles, shifting and leaning in the grasses but traveling at an impressive clip considering the conditions.

"Continue moving back, folks." The man with the megaphone was back, barking directions at the crowd. "You're welcome to watch the demolition if you must, but only from a safe distance." He glanced down at his watch. "Start time is five minutes from now."

As they got closer, Finn and Aisling recognized Marjorie, accompanied by Herschel and another, slightly more portly, figure.

"Is that Mr. Clydd?" Aisling squinted into the sun. "Rose and Joan's attorney?"

"Judging from that pipe dangling out of his mouth, I'd say it is," Jack said, laughing. "The old boy's got some life in him yet!"

When they finally reached the group, Mr. Clydd was winded, the immaculate silver hair they'd seen previously standing precariously on end. Marjorie's cheeks were bright pink from the wind, and she was holding a fistful of papers.

"What's going on?" Finn said, taking the bicycles and wheeling them to the side where they'd be out of the way. "Please tell me it's good news."

Herschel smiled, leading the others toward the group of suits to the side of the castle. He looked at them over his shoulder as he hurried away.

"We don't know yet, not for certain anyway, but it just might be." He waved as the three of them picked up the pace toward the Rockfield Acquisitions group. "Wish us luck."

"Good luck," Olivia shouted to him and waved back enthusiastically, her gaze lingering until she realized everyone was looking at her with identical raised eyebrows.

"What?" she said, a blush rising in her cheeks. "It's nothing, I just…"

"Something's up, love," Jack said, winking at Finn and Aisling. "I haven't seen you so excited since the shop down the road started carrying those Cadbury Eggs you can't get enough of."

Olivia glanced at Alwen, trying to hide a smile. "Certainly not. I just have—"

"She has a date tonight with Herschel," Alwen said. "He's cooking her dinner."

"It's definitely not a date." Olivia giggled, her face in her hands. She looked up finally, her face flushed with happiness. "Okay. Maybe it is a date. We got to know each other a little bit at the party."

When they looked back to the suits, Marjorie and Mr. Clydd were head-to-head with someone from the Rockfield team, standing off to the side.

"Rockfield looks nervous," Aisling whispered.

Jack squinted, then pulled his glasses out of his pocket and slid them onto his face. "And it looks like whatever Marjorie and Clydd were talking about, now they've pulled Herschel in on it."

Aisling looked over at Jack. "What in the world would Herschel have to do with all this?"

"You've got me there, love. I've no idea."

Finn stared at the group, rubbing her temples with her fingers. "It looks like there is a tiny, tiny chance that this may turn in our direction."

Before Finn had a chance to go on, the gentleman who had been speaking to Marjorie and Herschel a moment before headed for the front of the castle, accompanied by the Rockfield spokesperson they'd heard from earlier.

An expectant silence hung heavy in the air and the crowd was silent for the first time. Aisling noticed that Marjorie had started walking back to their group, leaving Herschel and Mr. Clydd still talking to the suits.

"If I can have everyone's attention, it looks like there may be a change of plans." A cheer went up and the Texan raised his hand for quiet, which it took him a long while to get. "We apologize for any inconvenience, but it seems that there is a legal issue that's been raised that may mean our contract with the city is in question, so the demolition may have to be postponed."

The other gentleman in the suit leaned into him and spoke softly, his mouth hidden behind his hand. The Texan reluctantly raised the megaphone again.

"Well, it looks as if I misspoke."

The crowd was still, a thick silence blanketing the field, as if not one person dared take a breath. Even the forest beyond the castle was still and watchful.

"The entire mining project has been canceled. Indefinitely."

Whatever he said next was lost in the cheers and shouts of the crowd, and the two men walked back to their group, where it was clear they were directing the workmen to leave. One by one the trucks started pulling out and back to the main road, including the gigantic lumbering crane with the wrecking ball dangling precariously from the front.

Herschel caught up to Marjorie as she was headed back to the group, and they walked the rest of the way arm in arm, laughing and chattering. Jack grabbed Marjorie and hugged her when they arrived, holding his forehead to hers.

"Well done, love," he said softly. "I knew you could do it."

"What the hell just happened?" Finn said, holding Aisling in front of her, arms wrapped around her shoulders. "Well, the condensed version, anyway. We're all going back to the pub for a well-deserved drink after this, and you can lay out all the details then."

Herschel smiled, his face lit up by happiness. "Finn, do you remember when you and I had that conversation about the sale of the castle to Cardiff?"

Finn nodded.

"Well, I couldn't stop thinking about it, so last night I looked up that contract. I knew my mum had kept a copy of the agreement somewhere. At one point she and my dad were planning on turning the castle into an event space to boost tourism in the area. I thought I remembered them talking about leasing it from the city, but then she fell ill and it just never materialized."

"There's been nothing here for as long as I can remember, although I always wondered why not." Olivia glanced over at the castle, standing proud against the blue sky and fluffy white clouds behind. "It could be gorgeous."

"That's the truth," Aisling said. "I did wedding planning in London for a decade. A venue like that, so close to the sea, would rent for around twenty thousand pounds for the weekend. At a minimum. If it's located in a smaller community, the local services, like bakeries and florists, earn huge profits, too. It becomes an industry in itself."

Herschel looked at her, shocked. "Really?"

"Absolutely. I used to negotiate those contracts every day."

"Well," he said, shaking his head and smiling, "I climbed up in the attic in the middle of the night to see if I could dig up the bill of sale, and I found it."

Finn bit her lip, her jaw tense. "And what was on it?"

"I was right. It was a lease," Herschel said, putting his arm around Marjorie. "But I noticed one little detail that I thought might make all the difference. So I called Jack and Marjorie first thing this morning."

No one even drew a breath after that.

"It was a lease," he said, his face lighting up with a brilliant smile. "But it was *our* family that leased it to the city."

Finn's jaw dropped. "So it was never actually sold to Cardiff?"

"No, the castle and about thirteen acres around it were never sold to the city, they were leased. And that lease ended in 2012."

Marjorie smiled. "So the sale that the city council voted on is null and void. In fact, they can't legally step foot on Herschel's property without risking trespassing charges, which is what Mr. Clydd is still trying to get across to them now."

Jack laughed, his blue eyes sparkling. "That's why they turned tail and beat it out of here like their tires were on fire."

"Aye," Marjorie said, looking back over her shoulder at the few remaining Rockfield representatives. "Exactly."

Finn jumped into the air and high-fived Herschel, and everyone let out a sigh of excited relief. Even Jack was wiping away tears.

"I think this calls for a celebration," Finn said, pointing straight ahead to the village. "To the pub!"

They all started back to the village then, walking the bicycles that Herschel had borrowed from his sons to get them to the site in time to stop the demolition. Alwen volunteered to stay behind to tell Mr. Clydd where they were headed, and Herschel caught up with Finn and Aisling at the front of the group.

"Before we get to the pub," Herschel said, "I just wanted to see what you two thought about something."

"Anything. How can we help?"

"Well, I know I just started at the pub, and I'm so grateful for the opportunity—"

Aisling cut in, her voice kind. "Don't worry for a minute about the job, Herschel. We can find someone else. If you want to do something to develop the castle, nothing should get in your way."

"That's good to hear," Herschel said, smiling. "Because I was hoping to keep my job with you and have the three of us develop the castle to host events, like the weddings you were talking about." He paused. "Do you think anyone would want to rent it?"

"Are you kidding?" Aisling laughed and spun around, arms stretched out wide enough to take in the blue, foamy sea beyond. "Look at this place, it's gorgeous! Anyone would want to get married here. You'd be booked out for years at a time."

"Would you two consider going into business with me?" Herschel said. "With the three of us, I think we could make it a success. Finn and I can do the food, although we'd definitely have to hire some staff with the pub open as well, and Aisling could do the event planning." He looked from one to the other. "It would bring so much money to the village. I think it would change people's lives. And if that's possible, I can't think of anyone I'd rather do it with."

He smiled as Finn and Aisling looked at each other, then started running to catch up with Olivia. "Just think about it," he called back over his shoulder.

Finn stopped and pulled Aisling into her arms.

"What do you think, Ms. Moss? Think you'd be willing to consider staying in wild Wales with me?"

"I wouldn't want to be anywhere but here," she said, the sunlight sparkling in her eyes, "with anyone but you."

"Then it's official." Finn tipped her chin up and kissed her tenderly. "Wild Wales is home."

"You're my home, Finn Morgan," Aisling said, her hands slipping under Finn's shirt at the waist, looking up at her, the last of the amber sunlight falling across her face.

Tears shimmered in Finn's eyes as she pulled her close, wrapping her arms around Aisling with a whisper. "And you're mine."

❖

Two hours later, most of the village were packed into the pub, holding sloshing pint glasses aloft and endlessly retelling the story of how quickly Rockfield's heavy machinery had kicked it into reverse on their way out of Cwylldbridge.

Aisling opened the cash register with a clatter and dropped a new roll of pound coins into it just as Finn leaned around the corner.

"Can Michael handle the bar for a few minutes?" Finn looked down the bar where Michael was laughing as he handed over a foaming pint of lager to a punter.

Aisling got his attention to let her know she'd be back in a few minutes and followed Finn to the back and out the door. Beyond the alley, light spilled from windows set into the brick buildings, layering the darkness with a sheer wash of warm color. Seagulls called to each other in the distance over the faint sounds of the village laughing inside the pub, and as the door closed behind them, a teenage couple kissing in the doorway of the shop across the street glanced their direction and started walking out to the street.

Finn squeezed Aisling's hand. "Do you remember when Greystone was here the last time?"

"With a martini at her side and crisps crumbled everywhere?" Aisling smiled. "Aye, it's coming back to me now."

Finn laughed and led her over to the statue. "And do you remember right before the furniture trucks pulled up, she asked us to be sure to move the statue into the center of the patio—"

"'Because it was always meant to be there'?" Aisling said, her voice thoughtful. "I do remember that. I was just about to ask her what she meant when the furniture guys knocked on the door."

"Well, look at what I found." Finn crouched down and cleared the leaves off the base of the statue. Just below the foot of one of the women, two initials were etched in deep strokes into the marble.

H.G.

Aisling looked at Finn and whispered, her fingertip still tracing the initials. "Helen Greystone."

Finn looked at Aisling and they wordlessly raced into the pub and up the stairs, rounding the corner of the living room to the attic door and skidding to a stop. Finn opened it and reached back for Aisling's hand. The old mahogany staircase creaked under their feet as they walked carefully up into the darkness to the small landing and opened the door to the study, where the light was already on, the pull chain swinging above their heads.

"Finn, look."

Aisling pointed at the row of photographs above the small wooden desk. The first time they'd seen the pictures there had been two blank frames, one dated 1922 with no photo or name, and the other completely blank.

Aisling and Finn leaned in to look again at the first, which now had a picture of a stocky older woman in a gray wool pantsuit, leaning back on one elbow against the bar, a bottle of Jameson Irish Whiskey at her side. On her feet were a pair of shiny oxblood brogues.

"Helen Greystone," Finn read aloud. "1922."

Aisling smiled and held up her arm to show Finn the sudden goose bumps making the downy hairs stand up. They moved down the row to the last frame as Finn stepped behind her and wrapped her arms around Aisling's shoulders.

In the same frame that hung empty last time, there was now a beautiful black-and-white photo of Finn and Aisling behind the bar, laughing together, Finn's arm around Aisling's waist.

Finn Morgan and Aisling Moss Morgan
2019

They were silent for a moment as they looked back down the row at the dozens of other couples, some together for more than fifty years, who were never given the chance to marry their partners.

Finn smiled. "Look at your name. Do you think they're trying to tell us something?"

Aisling turned in Finn's arms, standing on tiptoe to kiss her.

"Maybe." She smiled, with another long glance at the tribe on the wall behind them. "Or maybe they just believe in us."

EPILOGUE

One year later to the day, Finn and Aisling stood behind the bar in their eerily quiet pub, glancing up at the clock. Again.

"It's Friday night," Aisling said slowly, shaking her head. "And not one person has walked through those doors. This place is usually shoulder to shoulder by this time." She scanned the streets through the front windows opposite the bar. "Where is everyone?"

"I don't know," Finn said, grabbing both their jackets from underneath the counter. "But even Herschel called in sick today, and he's never once done that."

Finn handed Aisling her jacket and hopped over the bar.

"Where are we going?" Aisling asked, slipping her jacket over her shoulders. She peered into the mirror behind the bar at her hair and accepted defeat, letting it fall wild around her shoulders as they left the pub and locked it behind them.

"We're going for a walk," Finn said. "I'm going to lose my mind if I stay in that pub for one more second."

"Look." Aisling pointed across the square at the café, where the windows stood dark and empty, a closed sign hanging sideways by one string on the door. "The café's closed, too." She turned around on the sidewalk, looking down the street in the other direction. "And even Jack has shut up shop. What is going on?"

"The Welsh version of the Twilight Zone, apparently," Finn said, turning as she walked to check out the rest of the square. Night was falling and the only sign of life was a handful of teenagers hanging out outside the shop as they passed, uncapping bottles of Lucozade and laughing.

"Call me crazy," Finn said, her voice low. "But I'm almost glad to see those kids. I was starting to wonder if the entire town had been abducted by aliens."

Aisling looked at her watch and grabbed Finn's hand, pulling her toward the open field in front of the castle. "Do you think we have time to stop by the castle? There's something on the mantel that I've been meaning to show you for ages."

Finn glanced at her own watch, then over her shoulder in the direction of the pub. "The what?"

"The mantel, above the fireplace."

Finn smiled and kissed her hand. "Okay. We can't stay for long, though."

They stepped off the street together and waded through the waist-high grasses, the castle in the distance silhouetted against the darkening sky. The salt air swept in from the sea, mingling with the scent of fresh grass and the soft, earthy scent of dusk. Aisling stopped, closing her eyes and tipping her face up to the sky. She was still for a moment, her hand gliding over the silver points of the grass that brushed her palms, all swaying in the same direction of the wind. When she opened her eyes finally and looked for Finn, she had disappeared.

Except she hadn't. She was on one knee in front of Aisling.

"Aisling Moss," Finn said slowly, her voice strong, yet tender with emotion. "I've loved you since the moment I saw that wild red hair, and I never want to spend another day without you by my side." Finn paused, tears gathering in her eyes. "You're my whole heart, and I promise I'll love you with every breath I have left if you'll marry me."

Aisling covered her mouth with her hands, her eyes wet with tears, sinking to her knees in front of Finn and throwing her arms around her with so much happiness that they both rolled backward and disappeared into the tall grasses, Aisling wrapped tight in Finn's arms.

"Is that a yes?" Finn whispered, holding her face tenderly in her hands. "Will you be my wife?"

Aisling smiled, wiping a tear from her cheek with her fingertips. "Yes."

As Aisling said the word Finn had been waiting to hear, she pulled a black velvet ring box out of her jacket pocket. Inside was a white gold ring set with a deep green emerald, the color of the ocean at twilight, surrounded by a halo of glittering diamonds.

"Finn..." Aisling's voice faltered as Finn slipped the ring on her left hand. It was a perfect fit. "I've never seen anything so beautiful."

"I have," Finn whispered, kissing Aisling tenderly as she met her gaze. "And now I get to look at her for the rest of my life."

Finn smiled, pulled Aisling to her feet in the gathering darkness, and jumped into the air, waving her hands toward the sky. An instant later, the castle lit up in a blaze of golden light, floodlights outside the castle walls clicked on, and the sounds of people cheering and laughing floated on the air, champagne glasses already tinkling in the distance.

"Come on," Finn said, picking up Aisling's hand and kissing it. "We have an engagement party to get to."

They crossed the field in record time. When they finally climbed the castle steps, Finn paused and slipped a hand around the back of Aisling's neck, kissing her softly. She touched Aisling's forehead to hers for just a moment, then took her hand as they walked in.

A cheer went up as they crossed the threshold, classical music swelled in the background, and Herschel handed them each a foaming flute of champagne.

"Congratulations, my friends," he said, giving them both a long hug. "Of all the events we've done together, and will do in the future, I can tell you now that this one will always be my favorite." He picked up a glass of champagne from a passing waiter balancing a silver tray on his hand. "Besides, I have to admit, organizing the seating for this particular party couldn't have been easier. They even delivered."

Finn and Aisling fell into laughter as they realized that the beautifully decorated thirteenth-century castle, strung with what seemed like a thousand twinkling lights, also contained some very familiar items. The pink corduroy papasan chair was unsurprisingly very popular once again, and the Hello Kitty glitter lawn chair by the hearth had been claimed, as usual, by the village priest. An eclectic collection of random kitchen chairs and nightstands, most of which had spent a few days of the previous year in the pub, dotted the room. Even the legendary leg lamp had made an appearance, placed proud and tall on a pedestal by the door.

The crowd parted somewhat as they made their way in, and that's when Aisling saw the two faces she was longing to see through the crush of people. She ran to them and hugged them tight, then looked behind her to Finn, motioning for her to come closer.

"Mum, Dad, this is Finn, my fiancée. And Finn, this is Rhys and Jane Moss, my parents."

Finn stepped up beside Aisling and offered her hand. "Mr. Moss, I apologize for not meeting you at the airport. Things got late and I—"

She stopped short as Aisling's father pulled Finn into a long, tight hug. Finn softened, then hugged him back, and they both had tears in their eyes when they finally let go of each other. Rhys paused for a moment to collect himself, then held Finn's shoulders and looked her in the eyes.

"Finn," he said, his voice trembling. "I need you to know that you've always been my family. You're a part of me, and not a day has gone by since my brother died that I haven't thought of you."

Tears spilled down Finn's face, and she wiped them away with the heel of her hand before she spoke. "I know, sir. And I'm so happy to finally meet you."

"Now then, enough of that 'sir' business," Jane said, pulling Finn into her arms and holding her just as tightly as her husband had. "You're family. You always have been, and now you always will be."

The four of them talked for what seemed like forever, finally parting reluctantly with a promise to meet the following day for dinner. As they walked away, Aisling stopped and reached into Finn's jacket pocket, pulling out her handkerchief. She tenderly wiped away the last of Finn's tears, nudging her toward the fireplace that was ablaze and sparkling with a crackling fire that warmed the night air around it.

"Where are we going?"

"I have something I've wanted to show you for a long time..." Aisling's voice faltered, and Finn squeezed her hand as they reached the fireplace. Aisling nodded toward the rough-hewn edge of the mantelpiece, then reached up and traced the ancient pattern etched into the mantel with her fingertip, watching as Finn recognized it, held her breath, and leaned closer.

"It's my tattoo." Finn shook her head, quiet for a moment as she smoothed her hand across the stone. "But how is that even possible?"

Aisling looked up and started to laugh as Finn shook her head and pulled her closer, smiling as she kissed Aisling's forehead. "Why do I even bother to ask that question anymore?"

Aisling felt a tug on the hem of her skirt, and they both looked down to see little Finley Rose insistently waving her arms to be held. Finn scooped her up, holding her close for a moment, then bouncing her in her arms until she squealed with excitement and hugged Finn's neck.

"Good timing, princess," Finn whispered.

Alwen and Olivia, just steps behind Finley, hugged them both at once, squealing with excitement when Aisling held out her hand to show off her ring. Aisling turned then as she caught a glimpse of Finley Rose, still in Finn's arms, waving excitedly at the sky, her little hands grasping at something that seemed to be just out of her reach.

"What is it, Finley?" Aisling said, smoothing her hand over her back. "What do you see?"

She followed Finn's eyes up to the first few orbs spilling like a golden waterfall over the tops of the castle walls. She turned to Finn, her voice the softest whisper. "Do you see them?"

Finn smiled and pulled her close as they sank lower in the sky, the pale pink orb in front surrounded by a glowing tribe of golden lights hovering behind.

"See what?" Aisling heard Alwen ask Olivia. "What are they looking at?"

"I have no idea." Olivia smiled. "But whatever it is, your little Finley Rose seems to see it too."

They all turned to look at Finley, who was still reaching for the orbs, some of which were dropping lower and lower, just inches from their heads. Finn took Finley's tiny hand and held it open with her thumb, cradling it from below with her own. Finley seemed to understand and held stone-still as the one rose-tinted orb sank slowly onto her palm, glowing with beautiful pink light. When it rose again, it hovered just long enough to touch Finn's forehead, then shot up into the sky, the other orbs surrounding it. They ascended together, playfully dipping and swirling, finally fading into the tiniest pinpoints of light against the black night sky.

And then they were gone.

"What in the world are you three staring at?" Olivia whispered as Finn kissed the baby's cheek. "I've never once seen Finley Rose be still like that." She paused, smiling. "Well, at least when she's awake."

Finn pulled Aisling close just as Alwen asked what little Finley had in her hand. Aisling met Finn's eyes, and they knew even before they looked down together.

It was a perfect, blush-pink rose petal.

About the Author

Patricia Evans is currently writing your new favorite novel in her hand-built tiny house, nestled deep in the forest, where she's surrounded by a bevy of raccoons and a sleepy brown bear named Waddles.

She travels to Ireland and Scotland several times a year in search of the perfect whiskey and cigar combination and spends most of her time trying to ignore the characters from her books that boss her around as she writes by the fire.

Follow her adventures:
www.tomboyinkslinger.com
@tomboyinkslinger on Instagram
patricia@tomboyinkslinger.com

Books Available From Bold Strokes Books

Back to Belfast by Emma L. McGeown. Two colleagues are asked to trade jobs. Claire moves to Vancouver and Stacie moves to Belfast, and though they've never met in person, they can't seem to escape a growing attraction from afar. (978-1-63679-731-1)

The Breakdown by Ronica Black. Vaughn and Natalie have chemistry, but the outside world keeps knocking at the door, threatening more trouble, making the love and the life they want together impossible. (978-1-63679-675-8)

The Curse by Alexandra Riley. Can Diana Dillon and her daughter, Ryder, survive the cursed farm with the help of Deputy Mel Defoe? Or will the land choose them to be the next victims? (978-1-63679-611-6)

Exposure by Nicole Disney & Kimberly Cooper Griffin. For photographer Jax Bailey and delivery driver Trace Logan, keeping it casual is a matter of perspective. (978-1-63679-697-0)

Hunt of Her Own by Elena Abbott. Finding forever won't be easy, but together Danaan's and Ashly's paths lead back to the supernatural sanctuary of Terabend. (978-1-63679-685-7)

Perfect by Kris Bryant. They say opposites attract, but Alix and Marianna have totally different dreams. No Hollywood love story is perfect, right? (978-1-63679-601-7)

Royal Expectations by Jenny Frame. When childhood sweethearts Princess Teddy Buckingham and Summer Fisher reunite, their feelings resurface and so does the public scrutiny that tore them apart. (978-1-63679-591-1)

Shadow Rider by Gina L. Dartt. In the Shadows, one can easily find death, but can Shay and Keagan find love as they fight to save the Five Nations? (978-1-63679-691-8)

Tribute by L.M. Rose. To save her people, Fiona will be the tribute in a treaty marriage to the Tipruii princess, Simaala, and spend the rest of her days on the other side of the wall between their races. (978-1-63679-693-2)

Wild Wales by Patricia Evans. When Finn and Aisling fall in love, they must decide whether to return to the safety of the lives they had, or take a chance on wild love in windswept Wales. (978-1-63679-771-7)

Can't Buy Me Love by Georgia Beers. London and Kayla are perfect for one another, but if London reveals she's in a fake relationship with Kayla's ex, she risks not only the opportunity of her career, but Kayla's trust as well. (978-1-63679-665-9)

Chance Encounter by Renee Roman. Little did Sky Roberts know when she bought the raffle ticket for charity that she would also be taking a chance on love with the egotistical Drew Mitchell. (978-1-63679-619-2)

Comes in Waves by Ana Hartnett. For Tanya Brees, love in small-town Coral Bay comes in waves, but can she make it stay for good this time? (978-1-63679-597-3)

Dancing With Dahlia by Julia Underwood. How is Piper Fernley supposed to survive six weeks with the most controlling, uptight boss on earth? Because sometimes when you stop looking, your heart finds exactly what it needs. (978-1-63679-663-5)

The Heart Wants by Krystina Rivers. Fifteen years after they first meet, Army Major Reagan Jennings realizes she has one last chance to win the heart of the woman she's always loved. If only she can make Sydney see she's worth risking everything for. (978-1-63679-595-9)

Skyscraper by Gun Brooke. Attempting to save the life of an injured boy brings Rayne and Kaelyn together. As they strive for justice against corrupt Celestial authorities, they're unable to foresee how intertwined their fates will become. (978-1-63679-657-4)

Untethered by Shelley Thrasher. Helen Rogers, in her eighties, meets much younger Grace on a lengthy cruise to Bali, and their intense relationship yields surprising insights and unexpected growth. (978-1-63679-636-9)

You Can't Go Home Again by Jeanette Bears. After their military career ends abruptly, Raegan Holcolm is forced back to their hometown to confront their past and discover where the road to recovery will lead them, or if it already led them home. (978-1-636790644-4)

A Wolf in Stone by Jane Fletcher. Though Cassilania is an experienced player in the dirty, dangerous game of imperial Kavillian politics, even she is caught out when a murderer raises the stakes. (978-1-63679-640-6)

The Devil You Know by Ali Vali. As threats come at the Casey family from both the feds and enemies set to destroy them, Cain Casey does whatever is necessary with Emma at her side to bury every single one. (978-1-63679-471-6)

The Meaning of Liberty by Sage Donnell. When TJ and Bailey get caught in the political crossfire of the ultraconservative Crusade of the Redeemer Church, escape is the only plan. On the run and fighting for their lives is not the time to be falling for each other. (978-1-63679-624-6)

One Last Summer by Kristin Keppler. Emerson Fields didn't think anything could keep her from her dream of interning at Bardot Design Studio in Paris, until an unexpected choice at a North Carolina beach has her questioning what it is she really wants. (978-1-63679-638-3)

StreamLine by Lauren Melissa Ellzey. When Lune crosses paths with the legendary girl gamer Nocht, she may have found the key that will boost her to the upper echelon of streamers and unravel all Lune thought she knew about gaming, friendship, and love. (978-1-63679-655-0)

Undercurrent by Patricia Evans. Can Tala and Wilder catch a serial killer in Salem before another body washes up on the shore? (978-1-636790669-7)